NEXT OF
TWIN

NEXT OF TWIN

A NOVEL

JASS AUJLA

SPARKPRESS

Published by SparkPress, a BookSparks imprint,
A division of SparkPoint Studio, LLC
Phoenix, Arizona, USA, 85007
www.gosparkpress.com

Published 2023
Printed in the United States of America
Print ISBN: 978-1-68463-198-8
E-ISBN: 978-1-68463-199-5
Library of Congress Control Number: 2022914546

Interior design by Katherine Lloyd, The DESK

To Sahrina, Sajjan, & Shaun,
my little beans.

GLOSSARY

Āuṇṭīe-ji—the respectful form of address given to a woman from the previous generation.

Chacha-ji—the term used for one's father's younger brother.

Dādā—the term used for one's paternal grandfather (i.e. Father's father).

Dādī—the term used for one's paternal grandmother (i.e. Father's mother).

Ganda—means "dirty."

Jalēbī—a sweet snack made by deep-frying flour batter in pretzel or circular shapes, which are then soaked in sugar syrup.

Jauṛē—means "twin".

Nānā—the term used for one's maternal grandfather (i.e. Mother's father).

Nānī—the term used for one's maternal grandmother (i.e. Mother's mother).

Rōṭī—a round flatbread made from stoneground whole-meal flour.

Rupees—the basic monetary unit of India.

Sāṛī—an elegant outfit consisting of several yards of light-weight material that is draped around the body.

Salwar-kameez—a casual outfit consisting of loose-fitting pants and shirt worn by men and women.

Yaar—means "friend" and is primarily used as a term of endearment.

ONE

Monday, September 12th—Late Morning

Riah Arora snips out the *San Francisco Magazine* article, meticulous and careful, gliding the scissors along the line she's drawn with a pencil. Once the paper is free from the magazine binding, she folds it in half, cautious not to damage it. Riah stares at the woman's glossy image in the editorial before taping the picture to the bathroom mirror. She aligns the photograph with her reflection.

With curiosity, she reads the article's byline: *Anjali Murphy left the corporate world to pursue her passion for the arts and celebrates the second anniversary of the opening of her successful venture, The Artists' Café.*

Riah studies Anjali's photo, her espresso-brown eyes darting back and forth from Anjali's image to her own. She compares the structure of their identical smooth caramel-colored faces, observing that their eyes' size and coloring are alike, except for a fascinating shine in Anjali's eyes—perhaps a trick of the camera? Or a true reflection of a certain kind of happiness, foreign to Riah. She can't find any differences in the perfect angles of their noses. Riah peers closer at the snapshot, squinting at Anjali's mouth. Straightening her posture, Riah tilts her head and poses in the same position as Anjali. Riah smiles in the mirror, trying to show the same number of teeth. *Something's not right.*

She reaches for her makeup bag, which sits within arm's length on the counter, and rummages around in it. She pulls out a thin nude-pink pencil. Riah draws a subtle line above her upper lip and colors in the difference. She proceeds to do the same below the bottom one as well. After completing the reshaping, she taps a small amount of gloss on her bottom lip, pressing and rolling them together to even out the coconut-flavored lip gloss. She grins in the mirror again. This time Riah is satisfied with the flawless semblance of their smiles.

Lastly, their hair—the color and texture appear the same, with the only difference resting in their hairstyles. Anjali is sporting a short and sleek bob, whereas Riah's coiffure is shoulder-length, which she often ties in a semi-loose bun because she can't be bothered to style it. This distinction in their appearance will come in handy if Riah needs to be inconspicuous in public. She has brought a couple of wigs along for equal measure.

Riah's phone vibrates on the countertop, dragging her gaze away from the mirror. She answers it with urgency.

"Hey, B—," she says. "Your intel was correct."

"*Ciao*, Ri-Ri," says Brandon in his natural Italian flair. "So, I take it you found her?"

"Yes, I did." She attempts to keep her voice steady. "But I haven't approached her yet."

"Well, little reason in delaying the inevitable. Or are you scoping *her* out for additional opportunities?"

Would Brandon ever stop his plotting and scheming? Why did everything have to turn into a scam with him? "No, B—I don't want to scare her off. Call me cautious, but—"

"*Va bene*, you know best. How about the other gig?"

"It's all set. After the pick-up, I'll drop it off at the same place as before."

"Okay, and my guy will take it from there."

"And my share of the money?"

"You'll get your cut. Have I *ever* disappointed before?" asks Brandon, switching to an American accent. How he seamlessly toggled between accents to suit the context was beyond her.

"No, you haven't. Okay, I must go. I was in the middle of something."

"Alright, chat later! And stay safe, Ri!"

"Yup, will do," she says, ending the call. Eventually, she'll have to tell Brandon this is the last job she can do with him.

Riah and her mother had escaped from Riah's grandparents' home in Delhi when Riah was sixteen. They survived as domestic servants in Mumbai's affluent households for almost nine years before migrating from India to Italy. When she met Brandon five years ago, she was peddling stolen goods to unsuspecting tourists in the streets of Florence. She was a pro at it—it's what attracted Brandon to her.

Brandon had introduced her to the game—*the game of the con*—and an altogether new life. She'd become good at running the game. But now, it was time to retire from the game—before the *game* ran her. Indeed, it was time to go legit—and live an honest life.

The scams she and Brandon pulled off have made more money than she'd ever expected, allowing Riah to move her mother from their cramped one-bedroom apartment in Florence to a spacious villa in Tuscany. Her mother had turned half of the estate into a rental property, allowing couples and families to rent out rooms during the summer months. Her mother loved playing the role of host. She wholeheartedly enjoyed catering to people who were appreciative of her hospitality. But six months ago, Riah's mother was diagnosed with stage four stomach cancer. And it was also when her mother told Riah she had a *jaurē*—a twin—a term as foreign to Riah as she was to Italy. Her mother's dying wish was to meet her other daughter and explain why she'd given her away for adoption. Her mother said her soul would never be at peace until she knew the daughters who'd shared her womb were reunited in this life. Riah owed her mother, at least this much, to fulfill her final wish. Now, Riah *just* had to persuade Anjali to visit Italy and meet their mother—*or* what was left of her.

She closes her eyes and lets an unfamiliar feeling wash over her. Riah allows herself to bask in joy. At last, she has found her—Anjali Murphy, her flesh and blood. Brandon was right—little reason to delay the inevitable. She must meet Anjali. It's remarkable to see Anjali's photograph and marvel over their uncanny similarities. Yet, it will be a whole other reality to stand in front of her and confirm she is her sister—and indeed, her *jauṛē*.

She leaves the small bathroom and heads over to the night-stand. Scooping her wallet, sunglasses, and key card, she tosses them into her messenger bag. Riah smooths out the white linen comforter, scans the periphery of the bed to ensure she hasn't left anything behind, and departs her hotel room.

—

As Riah stands in front of the door of *The Artists' Café* on Valencia Street, reproach for her rash plan creeps through her head. What had she been thinking? Riah had begun searching for her sister once she learned of her existence. Often, she thought of nothing else—but now, they're nearly face-to-face, and she hasn't thought this far in advance. Should she introduce herself to her sister? What will she say to her? And how will Anjali react? Yes, these are questions Riah didn't fully consider before.

Standing on the deserted street, looking in at her sister, Riah's sudden consciousness of her appearance looms over her. In her dark blue jeans, burgundy hoodie with black leather sleeves, and fake Doc Martens, she's nothing compared to Anjali, who appears like she stepped out of a Chanel magazine ad in her sleek black dress and matching high-heel pumps. As Anjali climbs the winding oak staircase leading to the second floor of the café, Riah catches a glimpse of the bottom of her stilettos—*red!* Riah recalls seeing those shoes in the windows of expensive and intimidating European stores she had never dared to enter.

The Artists' Café itself is impressive as well, with its open-concept design. The piece on Anjali boasted about how she pursued a visionary idea and brought it into existence. The café, from what Riah read in the article, caters to artist types looking for a quiet space to write, draw, or connect with other emerging artists in the local area.

Riah lingers in a moment of contemplation, but as Anjali returns, descending the stairs, Riah steps back from the door, bumping into a young man entering the café.

"Oops, excuse me," he says. "You gonna go in?"

"Uhm, no, I was just passing by." She stuffs her hands into her hoodie's pocket and walks away as if she's fleeing a crime scene.

TWO

Monday, September 12th—Mid Afternoon

Anjali Murphy opens the front door of the café and peers across the street. She swears she'd seen a young woman standing outside, staring through the window at Anjali. She shakes her head, dismissing her paranoia. The stranger could've been an artist scoping out a new workspace or a curious passerby. Anjali closes the door and turns her view to the room.

She can't help but beam in awe. The place is buzzing with mid-afternoon customers, some socializing and others working away on laptops in the corners of *her* café. The article in September's issue of *San Francisco Magazine* gave her place newfound publicity. This idea was her dream ages ago, and now she's living it. She gathers a couple of used coffee cups and saucers from an empty table, straightens the chair, and places the dishes near the dishwasher. She starts wiping the serving area countertop when the backdoor leading to the dumpster area scrapes open.

"Babe, I semi-fixed the broken stair railing. It should hold temporarily," says Michael, stepping into the café.

"Thank you, my darling handyman husband!" She pecks Michael on the cheek as he reaches past her to grab his to-go coffee cup.

"Anj, where's Laine? I thought the point of you hiring an assistant was so she could take care of the counter stuff here?"

She hears the annoyance in his questions. "She needed the afternoon off. For a medical appointment."

Michael frowns. "Okay, I want to ensure you're getting value out of your assistant—so *you* can concentrate on your art during the day. And perhaps I can have my beautiful wife back to myself for the evenings," he says.

"Of course, darling, I know I've been spending a lot more time here—"

"Anj! I'm teasing! I get it—you want everything to be perfect."

Anjali comes out from behind the counter, "Yes, but I miss my adoring husband—"

Michael stops her mid-sentence, kisses her on her lips, and says, "Your husband, who is going to be late for his special partners' meeting and dinner."

"Oh, I forgot it's tonight."

"Yeah, so don't wait for me, babe," he says as he plants another kiss on her lips.

Anjali passes his oatmeal-colored Burberry trench coat to him. "Off you go," she says.

He grabs the coat from her hands and leaves through the front door. Anjali watches him go, her anxiety melting away as he disappears from her view.

Anjali resumes wiping the counter with a damp paper towel, mentally planning for her evening. It'll be nice being alone. Nestling in bed with a refreshing glass of white wine and starting a new suspense-thriller audiobook is promising. The ringing of the café telephone interrupts her thoughts. She tosses the dirty paper towel in the garbage bin and grabs the red receiver off the hook. Striving for an eclectic look, she had been purposeful when she opted to get a wall phone for the café.

"Hello?" she says.

"Anjali—is that any way to answer the phone for your business?"

It's her mom—her adoptive mother—the only mom she's ever known. "Mom, sorry I was cleaning and was distracted—"

"Well, my dear, you need to put your head in the game."

"Mom! I'm sure you didn't call me to critique my phone etiquette." She takes a deep breath and prays her mom hasn't heard the irritation in her tone.

"No, of course, I did not call because of that."

"Then what?"

"*She* is in San Francisco."

"Who?" asks Anjali, but already knowing the answer to her question. *Riah.*

"She came into town last week," says her mom.

Anjali rubs her collar bone. How should she respond? She's known for nearly a year she has a twin sister but has been hesitant to meet her.

"Anjali?"

"I'm here, Mom. I'm processing."

"This is a *good* development, Anjali. We can move ahead with—"

"Mom!" she says in a hush. "We shouldn't talk about this on the phone."

"Conveniently, I am in town."

"Then come by my place this evening. Michael will be out."

THREE

Monday, September 12th—Late Afternoon

Riah wakes with a start. She lies still, trying to remember where she is, hoping to disperse the fragments of the nightmare clinging to her mind. The rays from the descending sun stream through the hotel suite's window and gleam off the leather couch. The half-open silky drapes sway in the ceiling fan's draft. Riah's partially eaten kale salad from lunch sits abandoned on the oval-shaped coffee table by the window.

There was a time when the nightmares had left her alone. But since her mother's diagnosis, they have resurfaced with a vengeance, dredging up the most haunting moment of her life. Although fifteen years have passed, it's as if her soul is hell-bent on ensuring she never forgets the horrible *thing* she did—and the reason she and her mother fled from Delhi, forced to live in hiding. Her mind travels back to that dreadful night.

She is sixteen again and lying on her cot in her paternal grandparents' house. The evening sounds fill the tiny room where she and her mother used to sleep. Years prior, her mother had painted the walls a bright shade of ocean blue to make their space feel less confined. Her mother often tried to make things appear better than they were. Riah heard her *Dādī* yelling at one of the servant boys, bellowing about opening the front gate to let the dogs back in. Then

Dādī directed her verbal thrashing on someone else—most likely her mother—complaining the *roti* wasn't round. *Dādī* was *always* screaming—she appeared frail, but her voice carried like a rabid dog's bark.

The hinges of the veranda door screeched open, and *Dādī's* stomping echoed through the long hallway toward Riah's room. Riah rolled off the cot in a single swift movement, opened the side panel of the oversized storage chest in the corner of the room, and ducked into the hiding spot she'd discovered as a child. In seconds *Dādī* would burst into her space on another rampage. She held her breath.

Riah's bedroom door crashed open against the wall with intentional force. *Dādī* yelled in Punjabi, "Riah, get your ass out of your room and help your wretched mother with dinner!"

Silence.

The old woman grumbled some more. "Where's that useless child?"

Then the bedroom door slammed shut.

Riah remained motionless in the thick, airless trunk, assessing the quiet for a bit longer. When she was confident *Dādī* had retreated, she came out. She stretched her limbs. The hiding spot had been the perfect size for her ten-year-old body, but was a tight fit at sixteen.

Riah snatched her Sidney Sheldon novel from the floor; she must have dropped it in her haste. Relieved *Dādī* hadn't found the book, she tucked it under her pillow. *Dādī* barely knew how to read English, but somehow, she infallibly sensed the difference between Riah's schoolbooks and the American thrillers she devoured. *Ganda* is what *Dādī* would say—those books are *dirty*. *Dādī* would lecture her mother about Riah's reading choices—as if her mother could *or* would have any control over what Riah read. And her *cha-cha-ji* would leer at her, suggesting that he'd take pleasure in Riah reading *ganda* books to him.

Dādī didn't like the books Riah read in her spare time. *Dādī* considered fictional novels impious propaganda meant to put wild thoughts in young girls' minds, causing them to veer away from being virtuous and obedient. Although *Dādī* never expressed it in so many words, she was terrified Riah would read these books and believe this life wasn't enough, and that women could indeed be anything and everything they wanted to be. She'd say books caused a rebellion in girls; it was why girls ran away from home and brought shame to the families left behind. This thought simply scared *Dādī*.

Riah contemplated what to do next. She could leave her room and help with dinner, or she could sneak to the rooftop terrace and use the ladder to escape into the city. *Dādī* probably thought she was roaming outside anyway and was undoubtedly berating her mother about it already. Riah decided on the latter. She had done it a dozen times in the past and didn't see the harm in getting some fresh city air. Before she felt guilty and reconsidered, Riah changed from her *salwar-kameez* to a pair of jeans and a t-shirt, threw on her denim jacket, and tucked some spare *rupees* into the inside pocket. She opened her bedroom door, hoping it wouldn't scrape on the cement floor, and held still for a moment, ensuring the veranda was empty. She emerged from her room and crept across the hallway to the stairs, leaving the bedroom door ajar.

Riah admired how this house had been designed with multiple entrances and exits, making it easier for one to sneak in and out without being noticed. She was confident that her *Dādā* had clear intentions when he created their home. Although never knowing her *Dādā*, she was certain he had designed this house with the additional functions of hiding and escaping his shrew of a wife.

Riah's mother, who was barely twenty years old when she was married off to a stranger far from her birth village, had come to live with her in-laws. She had Riah within her first year of marriage and became a widow by the second year. When Riah was eight, she had asked *Dādī* why she didn't have a father like all the other children in grade school. *Dādī* told her that her father was killed in a motor vehicle accident—a cow, her father's motorcycle, and a truck had collided; the cow and the truck driver survived, but her father did not. Much to *Dādī's* dismay, Riah burst out laughing after hearing the story. It seemed like a ridiculous way to die.

In the same year, her *chacha-ji*—her father's younger brother and *Dādī's* only remaining offspring—decided to move in with them as well. When she was little, she adored her *chacha-ji*, but now that Riah was older, she felt increasingly uneasy around him. In addition to incessantly following her with his eyes, the parental pats from her childhood had morphed into unwanted caresses when no one else was around. She wondered whether her *chacha-ji* would have treated her this way if her father had been alive. Would her father have loved her enough to stop his brother? The thought that she would never know the answer to this question haunted her.

Riah reached the rooftop a minute later. She crouched low on the first step and scanned the area. The terrace was empty except for a few clothes hanging on a makeshift clothesline, billowing in the evening breeze. Multiple lounging cots were scattered haphazardly; it looked like the housemaids had spent a few minutes soaking in the sun earlier and had to disperse at a moment's notice. She was sure *Dādī* would have something to say about that—yet another opportunity to scold the servants.

Riah crossed the rooftop and peered over the ledge to assure the ladder was in place. Once she reached the ground, she let out the breath of suffocating air trapped in her chest. She jogged through the back alley, crossed over to the other side of the road, and arrived at one of Delhi's busiest shopping streets a few blocks later.

She loved living near the heart of the city and particularly enjoyed the hectic, buzzing atmosphere at dusk. Somehow it made her feel less like a local. It allowed her to blend in with the tourists and practice her English. Her English must have been good because the local shop owners, who didn't know her, would overcharge her for anything she wanted to buy.

The city's streetlights sporadically flickered on. Before Riah headed to her intended destination, she stopped in front of her favorite sweets shop and watched an old man making *jalēbīs*. He sat on a small stool in front of a pot of boiling oil. He squeezed thick, pale-yellow batter from a bottle into the pan with small circular motions. As the mixture hit the surface, the oil sizzled and bubbled. Using a perforated ladle, he dunked each freshly formed *jalēbī* deeper into the oil, and as it rose to the surface, it flipped over. He continued to do this to the others in the pot, cooking them until they turned golden. The man scooped the *jalēbīs* from the pan, letting the excess oil drip out, and dunked them into a large bowl of sugary water. He laid a dry cloth over the dish, leaving the *jalēbīs* steeping in the syrup until they were sweet and sticky.

Riah was mesmerized watching him make the delicious dessert. He glanced at her and signaled to a bowl of cooled *jalēbīs*. Riah nodded, not hiding her yearning for the sticky pastry. The man smiled, wrapped a *jalēbī* in wax paper, and handed it to Riah. She attempted to give him a few *rupees*, but he waved his hand, turning his back to her. This routine had been their regular exchange for the past six years. When Riah was younger, her mother would be with her, but she learned to sneak out and navigate the city alone as she got older. Her first habitual stop was to visit the kind old man with the best *jalēbīs* in town.

Riah walked away from the sweets shop and headed through the narrow, paved road to where she expected to find her friend, Parshana. Parshana's parents owned several luxury textiles shops in Delhi and often left Parshana in charge of the smaller one on Riah's side of the city. Riah entered *Thakur Fabrics* and mulled around the front until Parshana caught a glimpse of her. Parshana was helping a pair of older women but winked at Riah from across the shop. Riah gazed at the rolls and rolls of vibrant turquoise fabric against the wall as she ran her hands along the silky, magenta-pink wedding *sārī* the mannequin was wearing.

"Yes, yes, don't worry, the outfit will be ready by the end of the week," said Parshana in Punjabi to her customers—no doubt shopping for lavish wedding attire. Parshana showed the women out of the shop. "Thank you, *Āuṇṭie-ji*, I'll see you soon!"

Parshana turned to Riah. "*Yaar*, I didn't know you were going to visit me today!" Parshana had a heavy accent when she spoke English, but she liked practicing anyway. Parshana had wanted out of India ever since they were kids and was obsessed with the idea that they would both marry *cool* American guys and leave the dusty, crowded streets of Delhi behind. Riah teased Parshana about the likelihood of that *actually* happening. But Parshana didn't care; she dreamed of a brilliant, exotic life—anything to get her away from tending her parents' shop for the rest of her life.

"Let's go to the back—I've got some new smokes," said Parshana. She flashed a mischievous smile as she changed the door sign from *Open* to *Closed*.

Riah stumbled through the ill-lit passageway back to her house. She cursed herself for her reckless disregard of the clock, but time seemed to melt away whenever she hung out with Parshana—especially when *P* had smokes and moonshine to share. Parshana often passed out on the couch in the small storage room after a long day of keeping *Thakur Fabrics* open; her parents seldom missed her since they knew where she was. Riah didn't have the luxury of not going home. Her goal was to get to her house unscathed and sneak into her room unnoticed. Her mother would be there, but she never scolded Riah for being out with her one friend. She suspected her mother felt guilty about not affording Riah a better life and permitted tiny bursts of happiness in stolen moments. Riah concluded an outing with Parshana where they smoked and drank was harmless—after all, men did it all the time—but somehow, it was scandalous when women behaved like men.

Riah reached the back entrance of the house and felt along the wall for the wooden ladder. She often found climbing was more challenging than descending the ladder. She hated that she couldn't simply leave or enter her home through the front entrance like an ordinary person; she loathed her life for the lack of fundamental freedoms. Although, as she contemplated these thoughts, she knew the answer—this way was better—much better than having to deal with *Dādī.*

Riah climbed over the ledge and planted her feet firmly on the concrete. She scanned the area. It looked as though someone else had been on the roof since she left earlier in the evening, but it was difficult to tell for sure in the dark. Riah turned to face the sleeping city below and sighed. She wasn't even back for a minute, and she already longed to be gone again, longed to be free. She loved the city at this moment—quiet and serene, oblivious to the traumas of the day.

There was a rustle behind her. Riah spun around to find herself face to face with her uncle. He tried to say something, but his words came out in a garbled slur. He was drunk again. He raised his hand and touched Riah's face in what appeared to be affection.

"Nisha. Nisha, help me to bed," he mumbled in Punjabi. Nisha was her mother.

Riah stepped to the side. He followed her and advanced to embrace her.

"Nisha, you never come to me," he said.

"*Chacha-ji*, it's me—Riah!"

"Nisha, I love you, but you keep me—"

"*Chacha-ji*! *Chacha*! Wake up!" said Riah. "Wake up!"

He was too drunk to know who she was. She guided him to a nearby cot and eased him into a lying position, hoping he would pass out there until the morning. Riah turned to leave.

Unexpectedly he grabbed her leg, and she froze.

He let go of her leg and rose with a sly maneuver. "Where are you going?" he asked. The drunken slur—gone.

"*Chacha-ji*, it's me, Riah," she said.

"I know who you are!" He spat the words as he shoved her.

"*Chacha-ji*—"

"Don't call me that! You're no blood of mine!"

As he continued, a heaviness in Riah's stomach weighed her down.

"You're not even a child anymore, are you? You pretend to be innocent, to get attention, but I'm wise to you. You're evil. And immoral."

"*Chacha-ji*, you are dreaming!" Riah inched away from him.

He lunged forward, grabbing her by the wrist. He flung her onto the cot. She scrambled to rise, but he was on top of her before she could escape—he had her pinned. His thumbs dug into her shoulders. His sour, stale breath made her stomach revolt. The emptiness in his eyes sent chills swimming through her—she had to get away from him. As he straddled her, he yanked at her jeans, pulling and tugging them from her skin. Tears burned her eyes—a mixture of anger and disbelief pummeling all her senses. With an eruption of rage, a strength unknown to her, she pushed him off her.

He hit the cement pavement with a dull thud. Riah glared at him, holding her breath—waiting for him to rise. He lay there on the ground, in the eerie stillness of the dark.

With a start, Riah registered her mother's presence by her side. She didn't know when her mother had arrived or what she had witnessed. Her mother stood there motionless, wide-eyed and mute.

Riah tugged at her mother's *salwar*. Riah's mother inched forward and crouched over her *chacha-ji*, shaking him slightly. Nothing.

Her mother stepped back as a pool of blood formed around her *chacha-ji's* head. She retreated away from the body and turned to Riah. "He's dead." After a frozen moment, "No one will believe this was an accident."

FOUR

Monday, September 12th—Evening

Anjali craves a glass of wine—or something—to ease her nerves, but decides to wait for her mom to arrive. Besides, her mom has a particular taste for wine, a new skill she discovered when she traveled to Italy last summer with a couple of her other widowed friends. The three women had treated themselves to several wine tours during their grand Tuscany excursion. From the daily pictures her mom posted on social media, it appeared the women had the time of their lives. In addition to her mom returning from the trip as a self-proclaimed wine expert, she seemed spiritually altered. At first, Anjali hadn't understood why the trip had a profound effect on her mom—even more than her dad's passing.

Her parents, Sangeeta and Sanjay Patel, had adopted Anjali as a newborn from an orphanage in India over thirty years ago. Her dad had spent much of his career as a government dignitary, which granted them the opportunity to live in foreign locations during Anjali's formative years. Her parents were inseparable; they were like best friends whose sole purpose was to please each other. She couldn't recall ever witnessing her parents argue, or even speak to each other in a tone other than pure affection. When Anjali was in her teenage years, some of her friends' parents divorced. Her friends often told Anjali that she didn't know how good she had it—but she did know. And she was thankful. She had two loving parents who were there for her and each other. She never felt the need to advertise her *perfect* life; it was as if publicizing her happiness would jinx it.

When her dad passed away five years ago, her mom was beyond devasted—they both were. Her mom had no one—no other family to help her through mourning the loss of the *love of her life*. But Anjali had Michael to help her through the loss.

Gradually, her mom chose new hobbies and made new friends—crafty diversions from her grief. Her mom carried on despite the undertone of sadness. However, the Italian trip seemed to stir something else in Anjali's mom. Her mom became fixated on Anjali, obsessively calling at least five times a day. Even Michael scrutinized her mom's sudden compulsion. After a few months of tolerating her mom's possessiveness, confronting her was no longer optional.

"Have I been a good mother to you, Anjali?" her mom asked.

It was late October, and they were having dinner at their favorite restaurant by the pier, *Greens*, when her mom sprung the question on her.

"Mom, why would you ask such a question?"

"As your mother, I've been wondering if I've done right by you."

"Oh, Mom, I know you already know the answer to your question—you've been the best mother I could've ever imagined."

"But I'm the only mother you've ever known, Anj. What if you knew your birth mother? Would you still need me?"

"What are you saying? Why are you asking ridiculous questions?"

During her adoption, the orphanage told Sanjay and Sangeeta that Anjali's birth mother was a homeless teenager who had died giving birth. There was no reason to question why she'd been adopted or search for her birth mother. Tears were pooling in her mom's eyes. Anjali reached for her mom's hand. "Mom, what is it? Tell me—you can tell me anything."

"I've been doing a lot of thinking, Anj, and I want to—no, I *need* to tell you the truth."

"The truth? The truth about what?"

"I never meant to keep this from you, but I've been struggling with how to tell you."

"Tell me—we'll handle it together."

Her mom cleared her throat, took a gulp from her glass of Chianti, and recounted her European vacation. "In July, when I went to Italy with Vibha and Rashmi, we stayed for a few days at a villa in the Tuscany region. Vibha had been responsible for booking all of our hotels and Airbnb stays and chose this particular villa because she'd heard it was owned by a woman originally from India. Vibha and Rashmi thought it was unusual for someone from our birth country to have made a life in Italy. And they were curious."

Gossipy busybodies! Vibha and Rashmi were a few years older than her mom, and they seemed to know everything about everyone and anyone. And if they didn't know, they made it their business to find out.

Her mom continued. "The owner—her name was Nisha Arora—was a pleasant, meek Punjabi woman. She mostly kept to herself, but she always ensured we had everything for a lovely stay. But Vibha and Rashmi were their usual nosey selves and peppered the poor woman with questions about where she was from and how she came to live and own property in Italy. But she elegantly dodged their mini interrogations. One night after the three of us retired, I had gone to the kitchen to get water. The woman—Nisha—was sitting at the dinner table. She looked sad and deep in thought. She hadn't seen me standing in the doorway and was startled—and a bit embarrassed—when I stepped into the kitchen. I filled my water jug and was about to return to my room when she asked me a question."

"What was the question?" Anjali took a sip from her martini glass.

"She asked me if I have any children—to which I told her I had one daughter who's the true love of my life. To my surprise, she broke out crying. I wasn't sure what to do, so I sat with her. She said the three of us staying with her brought back memories of when she and her daughter lived in India. I'm sure Vibha and Rashmi's pestering inquiries did not help. She told me how she and her daughter migrated from Mumbai to Italy, and even though they had struggled to make a life in Italy, they were happy. Then she told me she missed her daughter."

"Where was she?"

"I asked her as well. Nisha told me her daughter was away—she traveled for work and often needed to be away a few weeks at a time. She said she understood but also missed her when she was away. I noticed Nisha was clinging to a picture of her and her daughter. I asked to see it. When Nisha showed me the snapshot of her daughter—I was speechless."

"Mom, why?"

"Because Nisha's daughter was the spitting image of you." Her mom squeezed her hand. "I don't think there is an easy way to say this, my love. Anjali, I think Nisha Arora is your birth mother. And you have a sister—an identical twin sister—from what I could tell."

Anjali studied her mom's body language and the emotion on her face. Her words, *twin sister*, were lingering in the atmosphere with invisible ink, waiting for a reaction.

"Is this *why* you've been acting overly protective lately, Mom?"

"Honey, please don't get me wrong. I didn't mean to keep this from you for so long."

"You don't need to explain."

"I want you to know your birth mother and your sister—"

"We don't know if that's the truth, though, do we? Besides, you're all the family I need." And it was true. Anjali didn't need a new family in her life. Her life was already so complicated with

Michael that she couldn't risk exposing any potential blood relatives to her world—she had to protect them.

The intercom of her penthouse apartment buzzes, thrusting Anjali back to her present reality. Her mom would be in her doorway in a minute. And they would flesh out the idea they had concocted a few months ago. Now that Riah was voluntarily in the city, the plan might be easier to put in motion.

It has to work. The words swim inside Anjali's head as she opens the apartment door to let her mom in.

FIVE

Tuesday, September 13th—Early Morning

Riah waits for the elevator in the silent hallway. She catches a glimpse of herself in the vanity mirror, noticing the dark circles under her eyes. After waking from the nightmares last evening, she stayed in bed. She wanted to go out and grab dinner but didn't have the energy; instead, she remained isolated in her hotel room, tossing and turning for the rest of the night. She's as empty as her grumbling stomach.

The hotel is a sizeable historical building but only has a dozen rooms on each floor. Generally, the place is buzzing with people—either coming and going or laughing and chatting in their rooms—but this morning, other than the faint hum of the electricity, no sounds come from the other suites sharing the same hallway. The elevator dings as it arrives on her floor. She steps into the empty lift and presses the button for the lobby.

The elevator chimes its arrival on the ground floor, and the doors open to reveal the lively foyer of the Edwardian Hotel. The luxurious boutique hotel has a life here, from the guests at the lobby desk to the early risers eating a hearty breakfast at the chic café.

Riah leaves the hotel and turns left on Market Street. Although it's barely seven o'clock, the sun is already out, and the streets bustle with traffic. Riah heads toward the tea shop she discovered a week

25

ago. She orders a half-sweet cappuccino and two plain bagels with extra cream cheese. Riah typically isn't a breakfast eater, but today she's ravenous and could inhale her food.

Sitting on a park bench with her coffee in hand and bagels on her lap, Riah faces the hotel, watching strangers drift by. Observing people, cataloging minute details, and becoming familiar with their habits is part of her routine. And it's how she chooses her *mark*. Today, her prey is a woman named Margaret Oxley.

Margaret is also staying at the Edwardian and, from the moment of her arrival, has made her presence known. Riah noticed Margaret when she checked in—she was hard to miss. Last Thursday, she arrived mid-afternoon when Riah returned to the hotel from an afternoon run. Riah stopped in the lobby for a cup of lemon-cranberry-infused water from an elegant crystal dispenser. Margaret was at the check-in desk with several designer weekender bags lying on the floor near her feet. Her voice was loud and agitated. Two bellboys were waiting with her suitcases, ready for instructions on where to take her luggage. The man at the desk contained his annoyance and diligently tried to switch her room. Riah couldn't help but linger in the lobby, becoming an invisible part of the scenery. As she hung about drinking her water, browsing the tourist pamphlets, she absorbed the details from a distance. Margaret was brimming with potential and casually dropped tidbits of information like she was feeding pigeons. All of which would be beneficial to Riah in due course.

On Sunday, Riah had seen Margaret return to the hotel toting many designer stores' bags. One in particular—with the classic *Tiffany & Co.*'s blue color—had caught her attention. The spectacularly oversized *Tiffany & Co.* carrier bag made Riah suspect Margaret had bought something exquisite and expensive from the luxury shop. And later the same evening, Riah had overheard Margaret making an appointment to get her hair styled before her noon flight. Margaret didn't want to take her luggage but indicated she would be packed and ready to go. Her luggage would be in her room for one of the bellboys to retrieve when she returned from her appointment.

At first, Riah was going to pass over the opportunity to steal from Margaret. After all, she is in San Francisco to find her sister. She almost reached out to Brandon for guidance—but who was she kidding—Riah is just as opportunistic as Brandon, and she'd never walk away from an occasion to score extra coin. The plan, simple enough, promises to be lucrative.

Finally, Margaret emerges from the Edwardian and gets into the waiting Lincoln town car. As the sleek black ride pulls away from the curb, Riah notes the time and estimates she has under fifteen minutes to make a clean steal.

Riah glides back into the hotel, avoiding the lobby cameras. She has learned the location of each of the cameras, which aren't many compared to other five-star hotels. In the elevator, she presses the number for her floor. Once there, she walks past her room and continues toward a stairwell exclusively for employees. She swipes the card she lifted off one of the housekeeping staff a couple of days ago.

Riah treks two flights and enters the twelfth-floor hallway, where there are no cameras near the stairwell entrance—devilishly convenient for her. She finds Margaret's suite and knocks on the door—a light tap, but loud enough for someone to hear if they were inside the room. She pauses, listens for a couple of seconds, and swipes the access card against the entry pad. Riah enters Margaret's quarters. This room is much larger than Riah's suite and is spotless; it even appears that Margaret didn't sleep in her bed last night. Her luggage is organized in a neat line by the desk near the window.

By good fortune, Margaret hasn't locked her suitcases. Riah studies the bags' positioning for a few seconds, then opens the first one. She rummages through the clothing. Riah picks out a few items, checks the designer labels, and stuffs them into her messenger bag. She closes the first suitcase and starts on the second one. This one proves much more beneficial, as Riah finds what she is looking for.

Riah's heart quickens as she holds the large square box. She unties the white ribbon, revealing a black satin case. Without delay, Riah opens the package and nearly drops it. She had been expecting something expensive, but this—this was over the top! A new sense of respect for Margaret bubbles within her. Riah has witnessed Margaret's brief interactions with the hotel staff—she has an air of superiority, richness, and royalty, an expectation that people should bend over backward to please her. And now, Riah knows why— Margaret is filthy rich!

Riah hesitates, doubt nagging her—should she do this? This isn't why she's here in San Francisco. She imagines what Brandon would say if he were here—his voice crisp in her ear—*take it, Ri-Ri, she won't miss it!* She unhooks the necklace, and removing it from the box, she bundles it in a scarf from Margaret's suitcase before placing it in her own bag's interior pocket. Riah replaces the jewelry case in the blue box and ties the ribbon back on. She shoves the empty box into the suitcase among a few other *Tiffany & Co.* packages. Riah doesn't need to wonder what's in them—she had listened to Margaret tell one of the hotel staff that in addition to treating herself to a priceless gift, she had splurged on her husband's nieces. She bought all five girls matching *Return to Tiffany* gold beaded bracelets.

Riah closes the last suitcase and ensures Margaret's luggage is precisely how she left it this morning. She backs out of the room, taking one last look to ensure she hasn't left any evidence. She exits as discreetly as she had entered.

Riah heads back downstairs, taking the same route as she had earlier. The lobby is busier than before. It's Tuesday morning, and most people are checking out after a weekend in the city. Riah reminds herself that she will have to check out tomorrow or pay for another week for her room. The hotel wouldn't mind in all probability, but Riah doesn't want to get used to being in one place for too long.

Once she is outside again, Riah heads toward the subway station. Misty raindrops pepper her skin. As she yanks out her umbrella and opens it, she observes a man taking a cigarette drag. He turns away before she can catch his eyes. *Has he been watching me?*

SIX

Wednesday, September 14th—Mid-Morning

Anjali studies the photograph of her sister. Riah is sitting on a park bench, sipping from a paper coffee cup. Riah appears to be rooted in thought. What's going through Riah's mind? Is it a coincidence she's in San Francisco? Or is she here looking for Anjali?

"So, she did nothing yesterday?" she asks.

"Nothing of great importance," says Leo, a private investigator her mom had hired. "I tailed her all day. She grabbed a coffee in the morning, sat in the park for a while, went into the hotel for a few minutes, and headed to the train station when she came back out. She sat in the terminal for an hour. I thought she was waiting for someone, but she watched the reader board for a long time and then hopped on one of those red city-tour buses. She returned to her hotel suite quite late in the evening and remained there for the rest of the night."

"Alright, Leo, you've been most helpful, but I'll take it from here."

"Please let me know if you need further assistance in this matter, Ms. Murphy."

Leo leaves Anjali's office, closing the door behind him. Anjali gathers the photographs and stuffs them into a padded brown envelope. She walks across the room and tugs a painting off the wall, revealing a fireproof safe behind it—something her insurance company had advised her to purchase. She punches several numbers into the keypad. The door opens, and she places the envelope in the safe. She's about to close it but hesitates.

She reaches for another envelope. Opening it, she pulls out a frail, crinkled sheet of paper. Anjali gazes at the foreign language, studying the beauty of the letters' curves and curls, imagining she can read it. This is her original birth certificate. At least, it's what the orphanage had given her parents at the time of her adoption.

Anjali slides her birth certificate into the envelope and places it back within the titanium box's protection. Returning to her desk, she swivels in her leather office chair, contemplating what to do next. Since Monday, when her mom revealed that Riah was in San Francisco, she hasn't been able to concentrate on anything else.

Last year, based on her discovery during her Italian trip, her mom hired Leo to investigate and obtain more information on Nisha and Riah Arora. Leo learned that Riah had lived in Italy for most of her life. Before Italy, there was little evidence to indicate where Riah and Nisha had come from. Anjali wonders what their story was. Was Nisha, in fact, Riah's birth mother? Or had Riah also been adopted like Anjali? Had they been separated intentionally?

Anjali has tried not to feel bitter. But over the past year, she has questioned why she was given away for adoption, and why the orphanage told her adoptive parents that she had no family. Anjali is grateful for her life, but how would her life have been different if she hadn't been placed in an orphanage—if she hadn't been split from her twin? Anjali is used to not having birth ties, but learning she potentially has a next of kin, her actual flesh and blood, has changed her. Anjali doesn't know how to explain it, but knowing she has a sister—one with whom she shared a womb—Anjali is suddenly incomplete. Her mother is right; it's time to approach Riah. *But how?*

Anjali paces the floor, weighing her options. She could go to Riah's hotel. But how would she explain how she knew where Riah was staying? She could tell Riah the truth; it wouldn't be uncommon for one to hire an investigator to find a long-lost sibling. She has to meet Riah somewhere private. Meeting her out in the open is too risky, especially if she wants to continue to keep Riah a secret from Michael. She hasn't told Michael about her—nor does she plan to. He knows Anjali was adopted as an infant and has no known blood relatives, which was the truth until last year. Her marriage hasn't been in a stable place for the past few years. And she doesn't know what the future holds for her and Michael.

Anjali sits on the window ledge and stares out at the street. This morning, Valencia Street is bustling with tourists as a prime stop on the city's tour-bus route. It's a nice break from the regular artistic breed her café attracts. She once had grand ideas for this place, but her mind has been diverted to a new plan—a plan made possible with Riah being in San Francisco. Anjali, deep in thought, almost misses seeing the woman standing on the street across the café. Anjali springs forward and stares at her long and hard. *What's she doing here?*

Without thinking, Anjali races out of her office, her Gucci sneakers pounding the stairs. Her assistant, Laine, is hunched over her laptop at a small round table near the stairs. She drags her gaze from the screen, casting a curious glance at Anjali as she rushes out the front door.

Anjali stands on the street, staring at the spot where Riah had been standing. She scans left and right, but Riah is nowhere in sight. Could Riah have seen her from the window and gotten frightened? She has to find Riah—immediately! Anjali goes back into the café to grab her raincoat.

"Anjali, can you sign these checks?" asks Laine.

"Not now, Laine, I have an errand to run—I'll be right back!" says Anjali. She shrugs on her coat and leaves the café, ignoring the baffled look on Laine's face.

As Anjali scurries along Valencia Street, she has a hunch about where to find Riah.

SEVEN

Wednesday, September 14th—Late Morning

Riah observes Anjali. She needs to play it cool. Her heartbeat began to race a few seconds ago when she spotted Anjali standing twenty or so feet away from where she was sitting. Did Anjali follow her here? Did Anjali already know of her existence? She can't tell if Anjali is shocked to see her. This is not how she imagined meeting her sister. Taking in a deep breath, Riah gives Anjali a small wave. Anjali seems to relax and flashes her a disarming smile. Riah gestures to the empty seat beside her. Anjali scans the terminal as if she's looking both ways before crossing a traffic-jammed street. She approaches Riah and takes a seat. They stare at each other.

"Hi, Anjali," she says, breaking the silence.

"Hi, Riah."

"I guess you know I'm your sister if you know my name."

Anjali turns away and faces forward. What is going through Anjali's mind? They sit side-by-side in the subway station's passenger waiting area, watching the reader board. The low rumble of trains passing through fills the thick atmosphere between them. Anjali doesn't appear to have a purse with her—as though she had grabbed her coat and ran to follow Riah here. Strangers hurry past to reach their destinations, but it's as if time is standing still for them. Minutes pass.

Anjali interrupts the silence. "We should go somewhere else."

"To talk?"

"Yes."

"Where did you have in mind?"

"How about my place, in Pacific Heights," says Anjali. "I'll give you my home address."

"Here, add it to my phone."

Anjali takes her phone. Her fingers move with graceful urgency over the keys as if she may change her mind at any moment. She passes it back. "I also entered in the buzzer code, so you can just use the private elevator. I need to go back to my café to grab my purse, so I'll meet you there."

Riah stands to leave first. "I'll be there in an hour," she says.

••

Riah scans the water, hypnotized by the hues of the blue waves. She could get used to this. Anjali's condo is in one of the wealthiest areas of San Francisco, and although Riah already knew this, she's stunned by the view.

"Do you want anything to drink?" asks Anjali. She's standing by the bar on the other side of the room.

"Some water, please?"

"Do you drink?"

"Not particularly, at least not this early in the day," she responds.

"I'm going to have one if you don't mind," says Anjali. She pulls a bottle of vodka from the freezer and reaches for a martini glass.

"Sure, I guess it *is* almost noon. And it's not every day you meet your twin," says Riah, tearing herself away from the window overlooking the massive balcony. Was Anjali as nervous as she was?

"No, it's *not*." Anjali fills a glass from a sparkling bottle of spring water.

34

Riah takes a seat on the white leather couch. She reaches for the picture frame on the end table. Tracing the structure with her index finger, she's mesmerized by Anjali and Michael's perfect smiles. From everything Riah's recon uncovered on the carefree couple, this picture was an example of their quintessential life.

Anjali hands Riah the glass and sits across from her. "I love that picture—it was taken in Hawaii on our honeymoon."

"You both look happy and content."

"I was—I mean, we are. Are you married?" asks Anjali.

"No, and I don't think I ever will be."

"Oh? How come?" Anjali appears eager for details.

"I haven't quite met *the one* yet, I guess. You have a beautiful home," she says, changing the topic. They are feeling each other out, exhausting the small talk before getting to the heavy stuff.

The apartment is spotless with its pristine white walls and dark hardwood floors. Tasteful art in ornate frames pops from the walls, contrasting against the color of the bar cabinets, end tables, and the floor—the all-white furniture adding to the elegant theme. When Riah and her mother were decorating their new villa, they had read in an interior decorating magazine that white made a place look more spacious—not like this place needed to look any more prominent. With its open-concept layout, high ceilings, and panoramic view, this was one more thing in Anjali's life that could've been a page straight out of those magazines.

"It's a place to live," shrugs Anjali. "So, Riah, tell me, what brings you to San Fran?"

"You. Anjali, I came looking for you."

"Why?"

Riah creases her brow at Anjali's brittle one-word question. This isn't the same person who had followed her to the train station. Controlling her reaction, she responds. "Anjali, I only discovered a few months ago that I had a twin—I mean, that we are twins. As soon as Mum told me, I started looking for you. You weren't easy to find."

Anjali leans over and asks, "Why did you bother looking for me? What do you want?" Anjali glares into Riah's face as if she is searching for the answers there.

"Because we're sisters. I want to know you." Is Anjali looking for a different reason? What other reason could there be? "I've always felt a piece of myself missing, but I never knew why. At least not until Mum told me the secret she'd been carrying for thirty years. She told me because she wanted me to find you before she—" Riah's voice catches in her throat, and she pauses to take a sip of water. This isn't going to be as easy as she thought.

"Before she?" prompts Anjali.

"Anjali, Mum is very sick. She told me about you because she doesn't want me to be alone in this world. She was also hoping to meet you."

Anjali shifts in her chair and then gazes into her martini glass. The silence stretches between them. Anjali is fixated on the clear liquid as if it may disappear without warning. "Riah, were you adopted?"

"No! What makes you think that?"

"Because I was. And I'm wondering why I was put up for adoption, and you weren't."

Anjali has asked a valid question—Riah didn't expect her to ask it so soon. "That's what Mum wants to explain. But to answer your question—no, I wasn't adopted. Mum is our birth mother."

Anjali leans back into the couch and looks like she's reflecting on Riah's words. This is not going well, although Riah has no prior baseline for this kind of conversation. She has to alleviate the tension—and the growing distance—between them.

"Tell me about yourself, Anjali," she says. "I know nothing about you other than the fact we look alike."

Anjali scowls at her. "But you do know a lot about me, Riah. You've been in San Francisco for over a week! You've been stalking me."

"Stalking you? Is that what you think?" How could Anjali accuse her of being a stalker?

"Isn't it the truth?"

"Anjali, I wasn't sure how to approach you. Hell, I didn't even know if you knew you were adopted, let alone you had a twin! But you clearly knew."

"I only recently learned I had a twin sister from my mother—from my adoptive mother, I mean. My mother hired someone to find you, Riah. And to my surprise, I find out you are here, hanging out in San Francisco! You could have reached out."

A jolt of empathy hits Riah. Perhaps Anjali is more like her than she expected—broken, not quite whole. Riah leans back on the couch, feeling defeated. "You're right. I should have contacted you sooner. I honestly didn't know how to deal with the situation."

"I appreciate your honesty," says Anjali.

A moment of silence lingers in the air.

"Well, you are here now," says Anjali and flashes her a sincere smile. She stands, makes her way to the bar again, and pours herself another drink. "Do you want to see the rest of the place?"

"Yes, if you don't mind," says Riah, relieved they have gotten past the general awkwardness of the situation. Anjali seems to have an uncanny ability to effortlessly move from anger to forgiveness.

Anjali leads the way. As they climb the stairs, she tells Riah how one of Michael's architect friends, Jordan Weekes, designed the penthouse suite for them as a wedding gift.

"How long have you been living here?"

"Just over six years. Michael and I lived in my old apartment on the other side of town until this place was ready. By the time we moved here, we were eager to start a family."

"I didn't know you had children!" Riah hasn't seen any evidence of kids around the apartment.

"We don't. I guess it wasn't meant to be."

"Oh, I'm sorry—must be a difficult situation to deal with—perhaps there's still time?"

"It's okay. I think we've had time to accept that I can't get pregnant."

"Things could change—you can never be sure of the future," she says. At the top of the stairs, Riah gasps. "Wow, this is spectacular! Is this entire floor your bedroom?"

The apartment's second floor is also an open concept, much like the main floor; however, this level is decorated in white and gold. The skylight situated above the king-sized bed bathes the room in natural light. The décor of Anjali's bedroom reminds Riah of something one would expect to see in a palace or a high-end luxury hotel.

"Yes," says Anjali, appearing to be delighted by Riah's awe-struck reaction. "There's a small en-suite room we would've used as the nursery. But instead, Michael uses it as his office—away from the office. And here's the walk-in closet—Jordan built it for me." Anjali leads Riah to the other side of the floor and opens a set of white double doors.

"It's gorgeous," says Riah, not even attempting to conceal how dazzled she is.

"It's over the top, isn't it?" asks Anjali. Is she probing for Riah's true feelings?

"Not at all, Anjali, it meshes with the décor, and I love that there's a skylight here."

Anjali smiles, "Yes, I love skylights. They're pretty at night too."

Riah sits on a round cushioned seat in the closet. She runs her hand across the smooth marble countertop and gazes into the vanity mirror. The two other mirrors, on the left and right of the large one, make the room appear even grander than it already is. Riah catches Anjali's eyes in the mirror's reflection. She's flawless and elegant—even in a simple outfit like a pale blue turtleneck and fitted black tailored pants with posh sneakers. It's difficult for Riah to wrap her head around the fact they're identical twins. Although they look the same, they are different. From opposite sides of the world in more than one sense. Did Anjali even *want* Riah in her world?

Anjali breaks the silence between them, "Riah, I'm sorry, I don't know how to do this."

"Do what?" she asks, turning to face Anjali.

"This—this small talk."

"Yeah, me neither. I was following your lead—you are the older sister after all," she says.

"Am I? I'd like to hear more—why don't I make us some lunch?"

"I could go for a snack or something," says Riah, remembering she hasn't eaten since this morning.

Anjali guides them back downstairs and through a set of dark mahogany doors leading to the kitchen. As Riah enters, she abruptly comes to a halt.

"Wow, how fuckin' big is this apartment, Anjali?"

Anjali laughs, "Come on, Riah, it's not *that* big!"

Anjali moves further into the kitchen and shifts a baseball bat and duffle bag off the massive marble island, dropping them less than gently on the floor.

"Michael's?"

"Yeah. He plays softball on Tuesday nights with his lawyer friends." Was that a surge of annoyance twisting on Anjali's face? Before Riah can draw any meaning from her expression, Anjali turns away and pulls open the fridge, grabbing a few items from the top shelf. "I hope you like deli sandwiches?"

"Sure, fine with me." Riah pulls out a stool on the other side of the island. "Do you want some help?"

"Oh, I can manage in the kitchen, but Michael is the real gourmet cook. This kitchen was Michael's idea."

The kitchen is a contrast to the rest of the apartment. The walls are a pale cappuccino color, and the marble island is also a mixture of various shades of brown, which gives the room an air of warmth and comfort.

"Mum would love this kitchen—even if it doesn't have a skylight," says Riah with a giggle.

"Yes—exactly what this kitchen is missing! Although it would be kind of weird because I'd have a hole in the floor of my walk-in closet!"

"Yeah, it would be weird—but at least you could see when dinner is ready!"

"Yes, I suppose you are right," says Anjali, placing a plate of sandwiches in the middle of the island. Grabbing a couple of placemats and large dinner plates from the cupboard, Anjali asks her what kind of water she wants.

"I'll take sparkling," she says.

Anjali grabs a bottle of sparkling water from the fridge and takes a seat next to Riah. "This kitchen *is* massive," says Anjali. "I sometimes forget because I'm so used to it—in fact, all the cupboard space underneath this island is still empty. I could *literally* hide a few bodies in there," she laughs.

"Oh, sounds scary and tempting," Riah says, not knowing what to make of the comment. She's relieved when Anjali changes the topic.

"Riah, tell me. What is our mother like?" Anjali asks, taking a bite of her sandwich.

"She's everything you'd hope for in a mother. She's a strong woman, given everything she had to deal with in her life. Our father died when I was less than a year old, and Mum and I lived with our *Dādī* until I was sixteen."

"Our father was alive when we were born?"

"Of course, why? What were you told, Anjali?"

"My parents—my adoptive parents adopted me from an orphanage in India when I was a newborn. They were told my birth mother was a homeless teenager who had died giving birth to me." Anjali sets down the rest of her sandwich and pushes her plate away. Tears pool in her eyes.

"Oh, Anjali, I'm so sorry you were told those lies." She places a hand on her sister's shoulder.

"I feel like my life is one big fat lie!" Anjali sobs.

"Don't say that, Anjali. We're together now, and you'll meet Mum soon too." She gives Anjali an awkward side hug.

"I'm not sure if I can, Riah." She pauses and lets out a heavy breath. "I haven't told Michael I'm adopted."

"Well, I see how it could be a problem—but it doesn't have to be," says Riah.

EIGHT

Wednesday, September 14th—Late Afternoon

Riah cautiously enters her hotel room as she pauses and scans the suite. She had extended her stay by a week this morning. The concierge indicated they were pleased that she was considering staying longer but couldn't confirm whether they'd move her to another suite. Riah was at Anjali's place most of the day, and she hadn't left her mobile number with the hotel. They wouldn't have switched her room and moved her stuff without notifying her—would they have? The room appears to have been wiped clean and the carpet recently vacuumed, and even the bed sports a fresh comforter and new sheets. Riah opens the closet, and as she eyes her unworn clothes on the hangers—just as she left them this morning—her trepidation melts away.

She grabs the white terry cotton bathrobe from the top shelf in the closet, unravels it, and lets it fall. She strips her t-shirt and jeans from her sweaty skin and kicks them into the closet, adding to the heap of worn clothes on the floor. She pulls on the bathrobe and heads to the bathroom.

Riah turns on the bathtub tap and throws in a pale-pink bath bomb. The oval spa tub fills with warm water; as the bath bomb melts, giving way to shimmering bubbles, the room fills with the scent of a fresh bouquet of jasmine and lilies. Removing her bathrobe, she slips into the effervescent heaven. The foam bounces around as Riah shifts into a comfortable position. She lays her head on the plastic air pillow and closes her eyes.

Riah replays the entire day in her mind. If she had altered even one of her actions, odds are that she wouldn't have met Anjali today. It was evident that Anjali knew who Riah was. Otherwise, she wouldn't have trailed her to the train station. Meeting Anjali was straightforward; now, getting to know her and earning her trust will be more challenging.

There is a faint knock at Riah's hotel room door. Riah sinks deeper into the tub, losing herself in a multitude of thoughts. What is Anjali doing and thinking right now? Riah left Anjali's high-rise at four in the afternoon. After they ate lunch, they spent the rest of the time talking about their early years. Anjali seems like a decent person. Lying to her was hard, but really did Riah have a choice? Anjali would understand once Riah got her to Italy. Riah can't help feeling Anjali lucked out in life—she entered this world first, was whisked away, and was given a better life than Riah could have ever imagined. Anjali indeed had luck on her side. What would have happened if Riah had been born first? What if—

"A penny for your thoughts?"

Riah's eyes flash open as she starts and nearly capsizes into the water. "Brandon! What the fuck are you doing here!?" she asks, emerging from the confusion.

Brandon lets out a slight chuckle. "I did knock, Ri-Ri," he says as he grabs one of the large bath towels. "You must not have heard me." He stands with his back to her, with one arm outstretched, the bathrobe hanging from his hand like a coat rack.

"The old light knock trick, eh?" Riah rises from the tub and grabs the robe from Brandon. "You could've warned me you were coming." She steps out of the tub, wraps the terry cloth around herself, and strolls out of the bathroom.

"Ah, Ri! You would have told me not to come," says Brandon, trailing behind her.

"You are *absolutely* right," she says, flopping onto the bed. "I want to do this on my own. I don't need your help."

"You don't want to share, do you?"

"I don't know even how much there is to share," she says, grabbing the room service menu from the nightstand. "Do you want to order something to eat?"

He takes the menu from her hand and flops on the bed next to her. "Let's go all out! Why don't we order steaks and a bottle of their best champagne?"

"What are we celebrating?" she asks, raising her eyebrow.

"What aren't we celebrating?"

"Did you fence the *Tiffany* necklace?" She's wary of his generous mood.

"You know the answer to your question—and before you ask where your cut is, you should check your safe," he says with a sly smile.

Riah turns to him, smiling like an evil Cheshire cat. She throws her pillow at him and rises to check the safe. "You better not be lying, Brandon Russo!" She crosses the room, opens the black oak cabinet door, and punches in the code. The safe beeps in a harsh tone and displays "Invalid" in red on the tiny LCD screen. She enters her password another time, and it beeps again to signal she'd put in the wrong numbers.

"When's my birthday?" asks Brandon in a singsong tone.

"You jerk!" she yells back as she punches in the numbers, one—one—two—four. This time, the safe beeps a peppy double tone, and the door opens ploddingly. A beige envelope, thick and full, sits on top of her passport and her *Anjali Research* folder. She tears it open and fans out the stack of hundred-dollar bills. "Woooo!" She turns to Brandon, still lying on the bed, with legs crossed and arms folded behind his head. "Is this my cut or the whole profit?"

Brandon chuckles. "See, I knew you'd be happy to see me in person."

She runs across the room and jumps on the bed, "Yay! Room service on Riah! Room service on Riah," she sings as she bounces on the mattress.

NINE

Wednesday, September 14th—Late Afternoon

Anjali closes the penthouse door after Riah leaves. She leans back against it and shuts her eyes, letting the day wash over her, allowing the eeriness of meeting her twin to sink into her being. Anjali had made assumptions about Riah based on her mother and the private investigator's information. Had Riah shown her true self today? She seemed sincere and rational. After they had passed the initial awkwardness of the situation, their conversation felt easy. Though Riah didn't show any discomfort around Anjali, she tensed up when the conversation turned to how they were separated as babies. It was as though Riah was on the edge of telling her some deep-six secret but then pulled back. What is Riah hiding?

The antique clock above the bar chimes half-past four o'clock. Anjali's eyes flash open. Michael will be home soon. She needs to erase any signs of Riah. Smoothing out the couch cushions, Anjali spots a long dark strand of hair on the seat where Riah sat. She picks at the strand, raising it to the light. The lock is the same texture and color as Anjali's hair, but is visibly longer and clearly not hers. Anjali winds the hair around her index finger and slips it off to keep the loop intact. She opens the silver locket pendant hanging around her neck and stuffs the ringlet in, closing it with a snap.

In the kitchen, Anjali gathers the used plates and glasses and sets them in the sink. She wipes the marble island countertop and puts the placemats away. As she washes and dries the dishes, her thoughts wander. She should call her mom and tell her that she's met her sister. She pushes the idea out of her head, refocusing on the task at hand. Before heading upstairs, she ensures she's caught anything Michael might find out of place.

As Anjali climbs the stairs, she keeps an eye out for more of Riah's hair but doesn't find any. She grabs her coat and purse from the designer chair at the top of the stairs and heads toward the walk-in closet. She reaches into the side pocket of her handbag and pulls out her phone.

"Shit!" she says aloud. She has three missed calls from Michael and a recent one from Laine.

Anjali presses the redial button. "Hi Laine, you called?" She changes into a pair of silk pajamas as Laine talks.

"Yes, Anjali, I had to tell you, Michael dropped by. He was surprised you weren't here. To be honest, he seemed a little mad, so I told him you had gone home earlier because you were sick and possibly had the flu," says Laine.

"Okay, thanks for informing me. I'm home—don't worry about me. Do you mind closing the café tonight?" she asks.

"Sure, not a problem—"

"Laine, and if it's dead tonight, feel free to close early."

"Uhmm—I'm hosting our *Word Slam* event tonight at the café."

"Oh shoot! That's tonight?"

"Yes," says Laine, sounding disappointed that Anjali has forgotten. "I think I did a pretty good job at marketing it. If it gets hectic, do you mind if I ask one of my friends to help? For a small price?"

"Of course! What time does it start? I'll try to drop in—if I can."

"It's at nine," says Laine.

"I'll let you go, but good luck with the event. I'm sure it will be fabulous!" Anjali presses the end call button. She views the call history and deletes the call to Laine. She grabs the clothes she had taken off and hurls them into the laundry hamper—no time to be neat and tidy. She heads into the ensuite bathroom and turns on the hot tap water until it's scalding hot. She runs a hand towel under the tap and then wrings it, squeezing the excess water away. She takes it with her and slides into bed.

After putting her phone in silent mode, she places it face down on the nightstand. She covers her eyes and forehead with the damp cloth. She lies motionless, listening. First comes the whirring of an elevator, then the faint ding as it arrives on her floor. Then the apartment door opening. Finally, the muffled padding of Michael's footsteps on the hardwood floor. Moving closer.

"Anj! Hey Anj, are you home?" he calls. His footfalls are heavy on the stairs.

Anjali lies perfectly still.

"Anj, you're home! Is everything okay?"

She stirs and peels the towel away from her eyes, letting it rest above her eyebrows. "Michael. What time is it?"

"It's after five, babe—how long have you been sleeping?"

"Oh gosh! I think I passed out for the entire afternoon."

Michael removes the towel and touches her forehead. "Aww, Anj! You're all cold and clammy. Can I get you something?"

Anjali struggles to sit upright, and Michael assists her. "I feel extremely achy." She catches the hint of an unfamiliar scent on him as if he'd been hugging a bouquet of white lilies. "I left the café early after this horrible headache came on."

"You poor girl, I think you've been running yourself ragged these past few weeks—you've got to take your foot off the pedal, babe. Slow down."

"You are right. I guess my body is trying to tell me something," she says.

"Would you like me to get you some soup?" he asks.

"I would love your homemade chicken noodle soup—it might kick this bug."

"Oh, babe, I can't." Is Michael crestfallen? Or is it just another show for her? "I have to pack before getting back to the office to finish some paperwork. I'm heading out to the airport—my red-eye to New York is tonight." He grabs her phone, gives her a wink, and heads toward the walk-in closet. "Let me order you something from *Uber Eats*." He doesn't wait for her to answer.

Anjali releases a breath at the thought of Michael leaving tonight. A rush of elation rises in her. He'll be out of town for the next couple of days—maybe she'll have more time to get to know Riah—in peace. Thank God she had the good sense to delete the call history details with Laine earlier. Michael rummages around in the closet for his suitcase and fancy suits—but she knows better.

"Anj, I ordered you a gourmet soup and salad meal—it should be here in twenty minutes." He calls out from the closet.

"Thanks, honey," she answers back.

"Hey babe," he calls out again, this time sticking his head out of the closet. "What were you doing at the train station today?"

And there it is. Anjali takes a sharp breath and holds it inside of her, bracing herself for what is about to come next.

TEN

Wednesday, September 14th—Evening

Riah pops the champagne cork, which ricochets off the wall and lands in the folds of the hotel drapery. She catches the overflowing alcohol in a champagne flute, letting it settle before pouring more.

"You're so bad at that!" Brandon chuckles as he grabs another champagne glass and holds it out to Riah.

"At least I didn't break anything," says Riah. She fills his glass.

"Hey! A guy breaks one window with a cork, and the world won't let him forget it!" He grabs a strawberry from the room service tray sitting on the bed.

Riah holds out her glass, and Brandon drops the strawberry into it. The champagne fizzes around the fruit as it descends to the bottom. "Cheers!" she says.

"Cheers, my friend—to money!"

"To money!" She clinks Brandon's glass.

Brandon takes a long sip. "Ah, this is perfection! Excellent selection."

Riah pulls out one of the armchairs by the window and takes a seat. She stretches her legs on the oval-shaped coffee table and stares out into the city.

Brandon comes over, stands behind her, and places a hand on her shoulder. "It's a beautiful city," he says.

"It is." She basks under the heat of his skin, enjoying the quiet for a moment. "I met *her* today," she finally adds in a measured tone.

They lock eyes in the window's reflection. Brandon's eyes are bright and comforting as he waits for her to say more.

"I'm not quite sure what to make of her yet. I mean, she seems nice and all, but something is off."

"In what way?" asks Brandon. He slides into the seat across from Riah.

"I don't know. Perhaps I'm paranoid—but my intuition is telling me to be careful." She takes another swig of champagne and holds out the flute, so Brandon can pour her more. The bubbles flow right to the rim like lava bursting from a volcano. Riah sips the foam before it has a chance to spill over.

"You need time to get to know her—for God's sake, you met her for the first time today."

"Conceivably."

"Was it intense?" he asks.

"Yeah, mostly because I wasn't sure how much she knew or what her reaction would be to anything I told her. It felt as if I was walking on eggshells the entire time I was at her place."

"Her place? You went to her place?" He leans forward, eager to hear more.

"She invited me."

"Ri, I thought you were trying to be cautious. Wasn't your plan to draw your sister to you? She was supposed to find you—"

"She did come to find me! She followed me to the train station, and she wanted to meet somewhere else. She suggested her place, and I went along with her suggestion."

"You veered away from your plan—"

"I improvised!"

"Riahhhh—"

"Stop—this conversation is getting boring." She rises from the armchair and walks over to the bed. She pops a strawberry in her mouth and mumbles, "These are fresh." She changes the topic. "Let's go out. I haven't been out much since I've been here."

"You haven't made any friends?"

"No, I was trying to keep a low profile as *you* told me to!" She sticks out her tongue.

He pulls out a bright magenta flyer from his back pocket. "Do you want to go to a *Word Slam?*" he asks, passing her the crumpled paper. He flashes her a look she knows all too well.

ELEVEN

Wednesday, September 14th—Late Evening

Laine puts the finishing touches on the temporary stage she has created for the *Word Slam*. Stepping back, she admires her creation—*this will be fantastic!* Working at the café is her first real job out of UC Berkeley, and Laine wants nothing more than success. Her parents were disappointed that she dropped out of pre-med and opted to major in Literature and Medieval Studies. "What will you do with those degrees?" her mother had asked. Her parents said they were concerned she was throwing away a prosperous career, but she knew they were more concerned about how Laine would stack up against their other Asian friends' children. But she pursued her degree anyway, and she is happy with her choice. Her parents will come around in due course, especially when she takes the leap and introduces her girlfriend, Hana, to them—her educational decisions will be the furthest disappointment from their minds. They will flip! She smirks at the thought.

There's an urgent tapping on the café window. Laine turns to see who it is and hurries to open the door. "Hey, you found the place," she says, shaking hands with a lanky blonde guy. "Thanks again for coming on short notice."

"No problem, I'm Ian," he says. "Can we set up on the stage?"

"Sure!" She steps aside as two other guys start bringing in numerous black cases. "How much time do you need?"

"Uh, at least a half-hour—what time does this gig start?"

"Not until nine," she says, glancing at her watch. "I need to grab something to eat—I'll be five minutes."

"Yeah, sure," says Ian. He pulls an array of instruments and musical gear from their cases.

Laine locks the front entrance of the café and heads toward the Italian bistro on the south end of the street. She decides she is in the mood for gnocchi. As she opens the bistro's door, a couple pours out, stumbling and convulsing with laughter. The woman's vibrant red hair is a stark contrast to her white mink coat. Although her face is hidden behind dark blue sunglasses, the sway of her open overcoat reveals a shimmering black dress accentuating her slim build. She is carrying a pink-foiled bottle of champagne. The couple is either going to a party or coming back from one. Where has she seen this woman before? They're oblivious to Laine's presence.

❧

Laine checks her watch in anticipation, her nerves fluttering with excitement and nervousness. She is confident the event will be successful, but with five minutes to nine, self-doubt slithers through her brain. Laine's phone pings, illuminating a text message from Hana: *Good luck tonight, boo! Wish I was there with you—Miss you lots XOXO!*

Laine reads it and smiles; her apprehension disappears. Ian starts playing his guitar, and the other two boys gradually add the drums and piano to the beat. Laine dims the lights to create a warm ambiance, in contrast to the bright lights they have used the other times the café was open late. She makes a mental note to ask Anjali about getting a liquor license for special events. She should have thought of it earlier; alcohol helps shy people come out of their shells—sometimes music and ambiance aren't enough. But tonight, it will have to be.

A pair of girls, walking by, pause at the café window—they giggle when Ian gives them a wink. Then, out of curiosity, they enter the shop. They sit near the front, whispering and ogling the band as they practice. Within minutes the café is crowded. *Showtime!*

"Hello, everyone! My name is Laine, and on behalf of Anjali Murphy and the rest of us at *The Artists' Café*, I wanted to thank you and welcome you to our first-ever *Word Slam* being held here tonight! For those who haven't been to an event like this before, don't let the word *slam* scare you; we're all friends here." There is laughter from the audience. She continues, "We want to hear your words out loud, whether it's something you have been working on for years or something you created on the spot—we want you to get on stage and slam it!"

The clapping from the audience inspires her to take a risk.

"How about I kick us off?"

More clapping.

"This piece is called *The End*." She pauses for effect and begins with deliberate purpose.

"No closure,
I will be forever open
To the idea of us,
In a parallel existence,
Living the rest of our days
In blissful peace."

Laine holds her breath and exhales as the audience claps. Instantaneously, a few other hands skyrocket in the electric atmosphere of the café. Laine points to a petite girl sitting in the first row. The girl pushes her cat-eye horn-rimmed glasses closer to her face and smooths out her wavy brunette hair. As she rushes forward, she excitedly snatches the microphone from Laine.

Midway through the event, Laine spots Anjali standing near the stairs leading to the second level of the café. Finally, her boss made it! She didn't think Anjali would show, given her husband's reaction earlier when he discovered she wasn't here. She didn't know the dynamic between Anjali and Michael, but something didn't feel right. How long had she been watching?

"Anjali!" Laine says. "When did you get here? What do you think?"

"This is a fabulous turnout," says Anjali, ignoring her first question. "Thank you for organizing this event, and all on your own too!"

"I'm so glad you like it!"

"Like it? I love it! This is truly great. Events like this help build awareness of this place, but next time we'll need a bar."

"I had the same idea! I'll look into it tomorrow," she says, turning her attention to the stage—a cacophony of laughter, cheers, and clapping.

"I'll let you get back to the event. I'll be upstairs catching up on work," says Anjali.

"Okay, I left some checks for you to sign," she says before rushing back to the stage.

❧

Anjali enters her office and flicks on the lights. Her office is tidier than this morning. She'd have to give Laine a bonus on her next paycheck. Laine was a godsend and outstanding at managing the finer details of running the café.

Anjali turns on the small screen on her desk. Her insurance company made it mandatory for Anjali to get security cameras on the first floor. They suggested she should be monitoring the floor when she was working in her office. She didn't like it at first. She felt like she was spying on her patrons, mainly because all three cameras were hidden in the artwork on the walls. But at this moment, when she doesn't want to be around people—it's ideal.

Anjali opens a green folder on her desk and takes out the checks Laine organized by due dates. Anjali begins to sign the forms when she observes a couple entering the café. They are disruptive as they stumble into her establishment. A few people in the audience turn to look at them, and they apologetically take seats at the back of the café. There's a shiny vibrancy to the woman's red wavy hair. Why is she wearing sunglasses indoors—is she someone famous? She dismisses the couple and returns her attention to the checks.

Forty-five minutes or so later, Anjali is done signing the checks and logging the details in her accounting record book. She puts the leather-bound portfolio in the drawer of her desk. As she locks the cabinet and reaches across the table to shut off the monitor, she surveys the mysterious couple, who are still sitting at the back. She catches the man lean over and discreetly withdraw a wallet from a woman's purse slung on the chair in front of them. He passes it to his female companion. She extracts cash and a card from the wallet and hands it back to the man, who returns it to the woman's bag in under three seconds.

Anjali rises from her chair in disbelief—the theft happened so fast she doubts her eyes. She contemplates for a moment, her skin prickling with outrage. Forcing her bewilderment aside, Anjali turns the monitor off and leaves her office. When she's halfway to the bottom of the stairs, she spots the redhead leaving her chair.

Laine is back on the stage, speaking to the audience. "This is your last chance to get on stage. Who wants to close this night off?"

The red-haired woman walks onto the stage and takes the microphone from Laine's hand. Laine beams as if she knows the woman. As Laine steps off the stage, the lady whispers something into the guitarist's ear. He begins to strum his guitar steadily. She stares into the audience and then casts a lingering glance at Anjali. Then, straightening her posture, she speaks.

"I'm new to town, but I love this place—it's so busy and lively, nothing like where I'm from. Let me tell you more about it."

As Anjali listens, it dawns on her—*it's Riah!* Her legs tingle with weakness as the blood drains from her face. She holds onto the railing to keep herself steady. As she scans the café, she suddenly becomes conscious that Riah is mesmerizing the audience.

"Venice,
Life slows down here,
If you stand on a bridge and close your eyes,
You will hear:
Laughter and singing,
The chatter of a multitude of languages,
Boats and oars lapping against the water,
The word amoré,
And the gentle click of love.
You will feel:
The warmth of a sunset on your skin,
The taste of old wine on the tip of your tongue,
And the rustling of your heart,
Longing to be free."

Riah pauses and bows her head—the audience breaks out in applause. Riah places the microphone on the stool and steps off the stage. Riah attempts to head back to her chair. But Anjali intercepts her, firmly grabbing her by the elbow, leads Riah toward the back door.

Laine plucks the microphone from its resting place. "Wow! What an amazing poem to close off the night." Laine provides details of upcoming events, thanking the audience for coming out tonight. The patrons chatter among themselves as they shuffle and rise from their seats.

Anjali pushes the door open and shoves Riah out into the dark dumpster area.

"What the hell, Anjali!" Riah shouts, rubbing her arm and turning to face her sister.

"I could ask you the same, Riah! I saw what you did back there."

"What? You mean reciting my poem?"

"No! I saw you and *that* guy take money out of a woman's wallet!"

"Oh." Riah's smile disappears.

"What do you have to say for yourself?"

"Anjali, listen, it's not what it looks like."

"I think *it is* what it looks like—Riah!" She steps forward, closer now to Riah's face.

Riah steps back, but Anjali continues to move forward, edging her toward the wooden balcony railing. Riah appears as though she is strategizing a plausible story Anjali will believe. Will her sister deny it?

"I can't believe you did that! And at my café! Actually, I *can* believe it. I know nothing about you," she says, forcing Riah's back against the railing.

Without warning, the palisade cracks, giving to the pressure of Riah's weight. Fuck!—Michael said he had fixed it!

Riah stumbles backward—almost over the ledge. Riah grasps her shawl, and at the same time, Anjali takes hold of her hand. Anjali yanks Riah forward, and her cloak falls to her feet in the commotion. A horrified expression freezes on Riah's face. Shit— Riah must've seen the fresh bruises on her left shoulder and upper arm. Was that a flash of concern shading Riah's face?

"What happened?" asks Riah. "You look like you've been in a fight—"

"Stop trying to change the subject!" Anjali swipes her shawl from the ground and wraps it around her shoulders, hiding her arms.

Riah's companion comes out of the back door. "Hey, is everything okay out here?" he asks, stepping to Riah's side.

"Who is this?" Anjali glares at him in anger.

"This is Brandon. He's my friend—"

"You mean your accomplice?" she snaps.

"Anjali—"

"Riah, you need to give me back what you stole. It's not right." She senses Laine coming up behind them. "Now!" She demands with one hand stretched out.

Riah reaches into her purse, grabs the money and the bank card, and shoves it into Anjali's hands.

"Come on, let's get out of here," Riah says to Brandon. They scurry down the stairs and disappear through the back alley. Anjali turns to go inside.

As she steps back inside the café, Laine gives her a questioning look. "What was that about?"

"Oh, don't even ask," she says, handing Laine the money and the card. "Please return this to who it belongs to."

Laine glances at the items in her hands, appearing confused. "Sure, I'll try."

"Thanks, Laine. I'm exhausted—I'm going home." She heads out the front door to hail herself a cab.

"Goodnight!" Laine locks the door and gives Anjali a tentative wave through the window.

TWELVE

Thursday, September 15th—Early Morning

Riah raps on Anjali's penthouse apartment door. She had remembered the code Anjali gave her yesterday afternoon, and held her breath as she slipped by the unattended front desk and entered the private elevator. Now, standing in the elegant foyer, her heart beats as hard as if she had taken the stairs and ran the whole way up. She was so stupid! Why had she let Brandon egg her on? She should've known last night that she wasn't at the top of her game with all the alcohol in her system. And usually, Riah would have done thorough recon, including a proper scan for security cameras. She had to explain to Anjali—or offer her a reasonable explanation for stealing. Hopefully, Anjali can find it in her heart to forgive her. Riah scoffs at her racing thoughts.

She knocks again, this time much louder. She checks her watch—it's a few minutes after seven o'clock. Could Anjali have already left for work? This is a bad idea. Maybe she should just leave Anjali an apology note. She turns to leave and presses the button for the elevator. As it dings, there's a hollow click from Anjali's apartment door. Riah halts, swiveling her head with hope.

Anjali stands in the doorway, silent. She draws her robe closer to her body, hiding her two-piece silk pajama set. Her dark hair is pushed back with a milky beige headband. Riah suppresses her awe of Anjali's elegance. She knows they are identical twins, but it doesn't stop her from questioning whether she has ever looked this attractive in the morning.

"Hi," says Riah.

Anjali stands there, staring back at Riah.

"Look, I'm sorry. I know you are mad at me. Can I have a minute to explain?"

"Is that the best you've got?" says Anjali.

"Anjali, I'm sorry." Riah casts her gaze to the ground, turning in the direction of the elevator.

"Wait. You can come in for a few minutes, but I have to get ready for work."

Riah opens her mouth to say something, but Anjali cuts her off.

"You need to explain yourself." Anjali opens the door wider and moves aside to let Riah in.

"I can," says Riah. She steps in and surveys the apartment. "Your husband?"

"He's not here," says Anjali. "He's out of town for work for a couple of days."

"Oh good," sighs Riah in relief.

"What if he *had* been here?" asks Anjali. "Riah, you don't seem to realize how careless you are being—it's like you have total disregard for my life."

"I'm sorry, Anjali! I came here to apologize for last night. I wasn't thinking—"

"You sure weren't—what were you even trying to prove?" asks Anjali.

"Nothing. I wasn't trying to prove anything," she says. "Can I sit down? I'm still a bit dizzy."

"Sure." Anjali points to one of the bar chairs. "I need to make some coffee."

"Brandon's visit last night was unexpected. He saw how happy

I was since I'd finally found you, so he decided to order champagne to celebrate. I usually don't drink, but I had way too much last night."

"Which is all fine and dandy, Riah, but what were you doing at my café?" Anjali flicks the coffee machine on.

"We decided to go out. I had no idea we'd end up at your café."

"And the *costume* you were wearing last night?" asks Anjali. She grabs two mugs from the top shelf.

"I like to doll myself up sometimes—"

"In a red wig, really? The real ones aren't cheap or easy to get—you've clearly done *that* before."

"Done what?"

"Steal, pickpocket, whatever you want to call it." Anjali places a mug of steaming java in front of Riah and slides into one of the bar chairs. Anjali nurses her cup, hugging it close to her chest, tentatively taking a sip. "I'm waiting for an answer."

"Anjali, I could lie to you, and in fact, I *had* intended to lie to you. I was going to tell you I had dared Brandon to swipe the lady's wallet, but I'll be honest."

"*Please* be honest—I don't need any more reasons *not* to trust you."

"Yes, I've stolen before," she admits.

Anjali takes another sip of her coffee and waits for her to say more.

"I'm not proud of it, and I don't do it for fun," she says. "Anjali, my life—Mum's life—it hasn't been easy. I had to do what I could to survive. Some girls sold themselves—I sold stolen *things*. But believe me, Anjali, if I could have done something decent with my life, I would have." She looks away, angry tears stinging her eyes.

"We *always* have a choice, Riah," says Anjali. "You can't blame your circumstances." She sets her cup on the bar island with a slight clunk.

"Well, easy for you to say—you probably haven't had a hard day in your life. You don't even look like you know what the word *struggle* means."

"Why?" asks Anjali.

Was this irritation gleaning from Anjali's question? She baits her further. "Look around you, Anjali. Do you see where you live? This place doesn't exactly scream *struggle*!"

"Stop deflecting." Anjali rises from her seat to put her mug in the bar sink. "Riah, I'm sure you didn't come here to continue last night's argument." Leaning against the counter, a surge of pity pales her face. "If you needed money—you could have asked me. But I get it—you are new in town—you're probably running low on cash."

"Anjali, we *literally* met yesterday. How would that have looked?"

"Well, it would have looked even worse if you had gotten yourself arrested, and for what?"

"I suppose you're right."

"You know I'm right—after all, I *am* the oldest," says Anjali.

"Only by a few minutes," Riah scoffs.

"Still counts," says Anjali. "Look, I need to get dressed and open the café—I gave my assistant the morning off."

"I should get going too—I promised Brandon we'd go sightseeing today."

"What are you going to see?"

"He wants to visit Alcatraz Island, the prison, I guess?"

Anjali rolls her eyes.

Riah laughs. "I promise not to steal anything."

"Gosh, I certainly hope not! But, listen, do you want to come over for dinner tonight? I'd like to spend more time getting to know each other—just the two of us," Anjali adds.

"I'd love that," says Riah as they walk toward the entrance. Perhaps she could broach the topic of their birth mother again and convince Anjali that she needs to visit Italy. It's probably none of her business, but seeing the eggplant-purple thumb marks on Anjali's shoulders last night frightened her. Did Michael put them on her sister? Hopefully not.

Anjali opens the door. Riah pauses in the doorway and stares into her sister's eyes. Then she reaches over for a hug, and Anjali awkwardly embraces her back.

THIRTEEN

Thursday, September 15th—Morning

Riah grabs her change and receipt from the ticket attendant and puts them in her back pocket. As she waits for Brandon by the pier, she rubs her hands together, the fingerless gloves not helping to bring much-needed warmth. The weather has been colder in the last few weeks. She misses Italy. The days would still be hot and the nights comfortably warm. The days here were gloomy at best.

She longs to return to the villa in Italy and bask in the sun by the water. There was no other place in the world that was more serene. One could find peace in the sparkling blue water of the pool, against the lush green landscape and the white-capped mountains in the far distance. She had meant what she recited in her poem last night. Life *was* slower in Italy. Life *was* good in Italy.

What was she doing here? Hadn't Anjali asked her the same question? Riah thought she had been clear about her intentions in coming here, but she is no longer sure what she wants beyond the immediate urgency. Once she convinces Anjali to go to Italy, then what? When Anjali learns the truth, would she still want a relationship with Riah? Although Anjali seemed to easily forgive Riah for last night's transgressions, would she be as forgiving once she knew the full story?

"I see you got the tickets," says Brandon as he waves the tickets in Riah's face.

Riah gives out a small yelp and grasps at her back pocket.

"What did I tell you about putting things in your pocket?" asks Brandon.

"It's an ideal spot for a pickpocket, like yourself, to steal from," she says, looking sullen.

"And you should never be an oblivious traveler," says Brandon.

"Yes, wise old teacher," says Riah. "I shall be more careful in my ways."

Brandon smiles. "I'm glad I've taught you well—young apprentice!" He pulls out his phone from the inside of his jacket, pressing a button to make the screen come alive. "What time is the ferry supposed to come?"

"I think it's already here—we have to board from the right pier number." Riah points at a couple of ferries docked a few piers over. "The number should be on the tickets," she adds.

"Board your full-day excursion to Alcatraz Island on Pier Five from ten a.m. to ten-fifteen a.m.," he reads from the ticket. "Let's go, Ri-Ri! I want to get the good seats at the top." They head toward their ferry.

Riah glowers at her friend. "You were the one who was late— you were supposed to buy the tickets and be waiting for me."

"I'm sorry it took me longer than I expected to get ready."

"Really?" she asks, raising her eyebrows.

"Yeah, you got me, I'm lying—I had to see a guy about a *thing*," he says. His tone is suspiciously jovial.

"You should've stuck with your first explanation."

Brandon smiles. "You are too bright for me, Ri." He walks a few steps ahead of Riah. He turns around and yanks her black baseball cap over her eyes. She swats his hand away and lifts it back up— Brandon is already a few steps ahead of her. She runs and jumps on his back. He holds her legs and spins them around.

"Wooo, I love this life!" he exclaims. The ferry blows its whistle like a prolonged mournful exhale. Riah jumps off Brandon's back and jogs toward the ferry gate, with Brandon trailing closely behind her. They leap off the pier, narrowly landing on the vessel as the metal bridge retracts from the dock. The gate attendant frowns at them and shakes his head.

Riah and Brandon catch each other's eyes and burst out laughing. They make their way to the top deck as the boat moves away from the pier.

"I meant what I said back there," says Brandon. He clings to the railing and gazes out at the water. His cheerful mood is replaced by a sudden air of seriousness.

"What? About loving life?"

"Yeah," he says, smiling. He takes a deep breath in, filling his lungs with the salty ocean air. He holds it for a second, and then—in classic theatrical Brandon style—he exhales. "What's not to love, right, Ri?" he asks, looking over at her.

"You are in a bright mood," she says, moving closer to him.

He pulls her closer and puts his arms around her. She's content in this saccharine moment and in the warmth of his arms. She closes her eyes and imagines they are still together—and happy. She ignores the scent of another woman's perfume on him—*Parisienne by Yves Saint Laurent*—it once used to be hers. But she had no more claim to the fragrance than she did to him. Perhaps if she told him right now that she was ready to retire from the con business, he'd understand. Maybe he'd even support it.

"They say Alcatraz is haunted," says Brandon, interrupting her introspection. He pulls out his phone and *googles* Alcatraz Island and reads aloud: "The prison was built in 1934 and was open until 1963. The prison was closed due to its harsh punishments for inmates. Many inmates died there and still haunt the corridors and cells of the prison."

"You're lying—it doesn't say that!" She tries to catch a glance at Brandon's phone.

"It does so," he says as he clicks his phone off and puts it back in his jacket. "We should have done the night tour. I hear they have an escape room—wouldn't it be cool, though?"

"Cool? Being stuck in a haunted prison is *not* my idea of fun."

Brandon laughs. "I'm sure we'd have no problem escaping. Do you want to try it tonight?"

"Tonight?" she asks. "No. Anjali invited me over for dinner this evening."

Brandon gapes at her, wide-eyed. "Really? When were you going to tell me?"

"I'm telling you now," she says.

"It's great news!" he says. "After last night, I thought we blew it."

"*We?* You were doing your thing and in Anjali's café with no recon. Some things should be off-limits, Brandon."

"I know, Ri, but we were drinking."

"We are *not* on the ball when we are drinking. I went to her apartment this morning to apologize."

"I'm glad to hear," he says. "So, is the plan to get Anjali to Italy back on track?"

"Yes, at least I'm trying to make some progress. I think it's better if Anjali believes I'm a mess— she'll lift her guard, and perhaps she will let me in."

"I agree—you are so smart! Such a mastermind you are," he says, pulling her closer.

The ferry's speed slows moderately, and several passengers snap pictures of the island in the distance. They stare ahead in silence as they near Alcatraz. The sun peeks out through the heavy clouds, casting an ominous shadow on the prison.

FOURTEEN

Thursday, September 15th—Evening

Anjali yanks the door open, her face lighting up with a warm smile. "Finally, you're here!" she says, pulling Riah into the apartment. "I have something to show you."

She leads Riah onto the balcony, where she'd already set the rectangular table for dinner. Plates of appetizers are laid out on the small glass coffee table, and her half-empty martini glass sits on the edge of the balcony railing. The bold orange-pink sunset and the sparkling blue ocean serve as the perfect backdrop to this picturesque view.

"You wanted to show me you could make dinner?" asks Riah.

"No, silly, I wanted to show you this." She glides over to the couch in the sitting area of the balcony and pulls out a mid-sized square painting from behind it. It's loosely covered with bubble wrap. She pulls the frameless painting free from the wrapping and places it on one of the armchairs. Anjali steps back so they can view it from the same point of view. "Isn't it gorgeous?"

"What is it supposed to be?" asks Riah, tilting her head to the left.

"Keep staring at it. The images will become clear." They stand in silence, staring at the picture.

"I'm not sure what I'm supposed to see. Is this one of those paintings to test your IQ?"

Anjali sighs. "No, Riah—I didn't think you would be so cynical."

"I'm just not into art, Anjali." Riah steps away from the painting and leans toward the platter of appetizers. Plucking a baby carrot from the tray, Riah swirls it in the vegetable dip and pops it in her mouth. "What do you see?" Riah asks in between her chomping.

"This painting is by a local artist—I was at an art exhibit a year ago. As soon as I saw this one, I fell in love with it and—"

"Is there a woman in the picture?" asks Riah, tilting her head to the right this time.

Anjali smiles and continues. "I fell in love with it and knew I had to have it." She turns to Riah and asks, "Do you only see one woman?"

Riah tilts her head to the left and then cautiously leans in closer. Riah stares intently at the picture for a few more seconds. "Ah! You're right!" says Riah, stepping closer. "I see it! Is this a mind-trick painting?"

Anjali laughs. "No, it's a particular genre of art." Anjali grabs her martini glass. "Right after I bought the painting, the artist told me the picture was called *Sisters*." She takes a sip from her drink and holds the glass by the stem, laying it flat on her other hand. "As if the universe was foreshadowing my future because shortly later, I learned I had a sister."

"I always knew. Anjali, even before Mum told me, I felt a missing piece of me out there. I initially believed I was missing my soul mate and was looking for the person in men. I thought my soul mate would be my partner, but now I realize—it's *you*, Anjali—you are my soul mate!"

"The perfect other half of you," Anjali says as tears sting her eyes. "I feel the same."

A nasty gust of wind blows through the outdoor patio. The sudden gale catches the bubble wrap and blows it upward, causing it to disappear off the balcony. The stack of napkins on the coffee table near the appetizers also flutters, threatening to take flight. Riah shudders, although she hasn't taken off her jacket.

"Oh, dear," she says. "It feels like it's going to rain. We should take everything inside."

"I think we should," says Riah, collecting the tray of appetizers. "It's a shame—you went to all the trouble of setting up outside."

"Wishful thinking on my end," Anjali says, following Riah inside.

"The thought was nice, though—where should I put this?"

"Just there on the bar," responds Anjali as she puts the picture by the door. "Do you want a drink?"

"Okay, but not the hard stuff you drink," says Riah.

Anjali gives out a half-suppressed laugh. "I've got a nice bottle of a rosé Moscato. Shall I open it?"

"Sure. So, where are you going to hang the *Sisters*?" asks Riah, pointing to the door.

"I had it taken out of storage."

"Oh? Why was it in storage?" asks Riah, raising an eyebrow.

"Michael didn't think it went with the décor here, so I made a compromise. I guess it was the right *thing* to do?"

"I suppose. I honestly wouldn't know. I've never been involved with anyone seriously, let alone married."

"Oh, what about Brandon?" asks Anjali. This was a question she had meant to ask Riah since she saw them together last night.

"Brandon and I are friends," Riah says, seemingly confident with her statement.

"Ever since you met?" she asks, pulling the bottle of wine from the rack.

"Well, no. I had feelings for Brandon when we first met, but I quickly realized it was best to keep it professional—it's better this way. Besides, he has serious commitment issues, and I think he bores easily with the same woman."

"You seem to know him well. How long have you two been working together?" Anjali asks. She releases the cork from the bottle.

"A couple of years," Riah says with an air of vagueness.

Riah seems uncomfortable and guarded about giving details. Sensing Riah's hesitation in answering questions about Brandon, she changes the topic. "So, tell me, what's it like living in Italy? Is it truly like how you described it in your poem last night?"

꧁

Riah watches as Anjali stacks their dinner dishes in the dishwasher. With Anjali's back toward her, Riah peeks at her phone. "Riah, do you want coffee or some dessert liqueur?" Anjali asks, cutting in on her distraction.

"I don't think I could put another ounce of anything in me," she says, clutching her stomach dramatically.

"How about some light herbal tea, then?" Anjali fills the stainless-steel kettle, puts it on the burner, and flicks the switch on.

"Okay, just a little."

"Riah, is everything okay? I only ask because your phone has constantly been buzzing for the last hour. If you must go, I'll understand."

She's surprised Anjali even noticed; her sister spent most of the evening talking about herself, as if she intended to fill up the space with idle nervous chatter. "I'm sorry, Anjali. It's the nurse that is taking care of Mum."

Anjali straightens up. "I've meant to ask."

"She's getting worse. She hasn't been well for days," says Riah.

"Will you be going back soon?" asks Anjali.

"*We* have to go see her—I haven't told her that I've found you yet."

Anjali puts some loose tea leaves in a teapot and pours in the boiling hot water from the kettle. "How do you think she will react?"

"I think she will be ecstatic! Anjali, Mum didn't want me to be alone in my life, and it's why she finally told me about you. But she never gave up hope you two would meet one day. She remembers giving birth to us—"

"I still don't understand how we ended up being separated." Anjali pours the tea through a strainer into two teacups.

"Unfortunately, we were born in a time and a country where baby girls were not desired. And imagine our mum having twin girls! Mum will tell you the whole story. I think you need to hear it from her."

Anjali dabs her eyes with the sleeve of her dress. "I can't imagine what our mother must have gone through. I wonder how different my life—our lives—would've been had we not been separated."

"Anjali, don't dwell on it too much—it happened for a reason—everything happens for a reason. So how soon do you want to go to Italy?"

"Riah, I don't think I can go." Anjali cradles her cup of tea close to her chest, appearing pensive about choosing her next words.

"Why not?"

"There are so many reasons—"

"None of them are a good enough reason *not* to go," Riah says, cutting off Anjali.

"You have to let me explain," says Anjali. She appears to delay her response by placing her cup on the kitchen island.

Riah is silent, waiting for Anjali to speak.

"Michael doesn't know I'm adopted. Or that I have any siblings. I don't know how to tell him or *if* I want to tell him."

"Is everything okay? I mean with Michael. Last night, I thought I saw some bruises on your shoulder and—"

"Yes, of course, everything is fine. Back to our mother—I could go when he is away for work, on a longer trip."

Riah takes the cue from her sister that she doesn't want to talk about Michael. Who was she to pry anyway? "Great, when will that be?" she asks.

"Next Tuesday, he is going to Beijing in the morning," responds Anjali.

"So, then we'll catch a direct flight to Italy the same afternoon."

"There's one other issue," Anjali adds. "I don't have a passport."

"Jeez, Anjali, why not?"

"Mine expired a while ago. And I never renewed it."

"Okay," Riah says, pausing to think. "How long does it take to make a new one?"

"A while. And Michael isn't due to go on another long work trip for months, probably next spring."

Riah reflects on Anjali's dilemma.

"Riah, what if I used your passport to travel to meet our mother?" Anjali asks.

Riah continues to be silent for a moment. "What about me? What will I do?" she finally asks.

"I'll go alone and be back before Michael gets back. You can stay here while I'm gone. Maybe then, nobody will notice that I'm *actually* gone."

"I'm not sure how I feel about this idea, Anjali."

After a long pause, Anjali says, "Oh Riah, I know it sounds crazy! Forget about it—it will never work." Anjali sounds sad and disappointed.

Riah responds steadily, "No, Anjali, perhaps we *can* make this work."

"Oh, Riah!" exclaims Anjali, clasping her hands together. Tears are welling up in her eyes. Anjali steps around the kitchen island and grabs hold of Riah, giving her a tight hug. "Riah, I can't even begin to explain what this means to me," Anjali says, stepping back with tears streaming down her face.

"I think I can imagine how you are feeling, Anjali. And Mum

will be beyond happy," Riah says, trying to contain her excitement. "But are you serious about me staying here?"

"Of course, Riah, it's the least I can do for you—that way, you can save some money rather than paying another week for your hotel room."

"That's kind of you, Anjali." Riah smiles.

"And I know how you like to *doll yourself up*," Anjali says with air quotes. "So, feel free to wear any of my clothes from my closet."

"Hmm, I think I'll need to buy a new wig," jokes Riah.

"Or you could cut your hair," suggests Anjali with a dead seriousness in her tone. Was her sister for real?

"I don't know if I can pull off short hair like you," she says.

"Sure, you can," says Anjali, touching Riah's long hair. "It'll make taking my place more convincing."

"Oh well, I wouldn't leave the apartment while you are gone."

"Don't be silly, Riah, you'll have to show our face around the café."

"Anjali—"

"Don't worry, Riah, you'll be fine—I'll give you a list of anyone you may run into," she says. "You should be glad my adoptive mother doesn't live nearby—you would have a hard time fooling her."

"Lucky me," Riah says apprehensively.

Anjali laughs. "Do you want to stay over tonight and practice for next week?" asks Anjali but doesn't wait for the answer. "Come on, let's go upstairs."

Riah follows her in silence, distracted with thoughts of what she will need to do over the next couple of days to be ready to take Anjali's place.

FIFTEEN

Friday, September 16th—Early Morning

Riah tosses and turns in her sleep. She's lost in a peculiar dream, wandering in a hotel, familiar but foreign at the same time. She glides through one door and exits another; all the rooms look alike, an endless maze of walls and corners. Riah is looking for something, but she's not clear on what it is. Coming across a stranger, she squints, trying to see him better. The stranger's features morph a few times before it settles. Riah recognizes the face—it's her *chacha-ji*!

Her *chacha-ji* is angry; the space between his eyebrows creases, and there's rage in his eyes. Grabbing Riah by the wrist, he drags her through the hotel room doors. They burst through the entrance of their home in India, and her *chacha-ji* flings her onto the hard concrete. Without saying a word, he points at Riah's hands—they are covered in blood. Riah wipes her hands on her jeans, but the blood will not come off. The odor of burning rubber stings her nostrils, and the velvety red stain on her hands becomes thicker, darker— it mutates into tar. Her *chacha-ji* is clutching a rough wood plank. Raising it above his head, it lingers in the air for a moment before plummeting toward her. A scream builds up in Riah's lungs as the board crashes against her head. Her protests are caught in her throat, and the crack of the wood—like lightning—jolts her awake.

Anjali's concerned face looms over her. "Riah—wake up—you're having a nightmare," Anjali says, her voice urgent and hushed.

Riah lies there with her eyes wide open.

"Are you okay?" asks Anjali. She turns on the nightstand light.

Riah props herself on her elbows. "What happened?" she asks.

"You were screaming. I think you had a bad dream. What was it?—Do you remember?"

"No, I don't." Guilt for lying to Anjali niggles at her, but her instincts tell her it's better if she does not share too much with her sister. "What time is it?"

"It's half-past three. I'll get you some water."

Riah rests her head back on her pillow and listens to Anjali's footsteps pad down the stairs. She shoves the memory of her uncle down like he had once shoved her. Darkness engulfs her, and she dozes off before Anjali returns.

—

Anjali stands over Riah, observing her while she sleeps. Last night when she'd returned with water for Riah, she'd whispered her name, but Riah didn't respond. Anjali had placed the glass of water on the nightstand before returning to her side of the bed and flicking off the lamp. She has never heard anyone ever scream like that. It had sounded like a tortured animal gasping its last breaths of life. What is haunting Riah? What deep secrets does her sister harbor?

"Good morning," she says as Riah stirs awake. She blows over the mug she's holding and takes a measured sip. She is dressed and ready to start her day. Anjali has opted to wear a long-sleeved black turtleneck sweater, leggings, and olive-green suede booties. She has selected a similar outfit for Riah.

Riah pulls the covers over her head. "It's not even morning yet," she mumbles.

Anjali chuckles and tugs at the duvet. "Come on. We have lots to do today."

Riah groans. "What time is it even? You promised I could sleep in."

"Yes, and you have slept in. It's after seven, Riah."

"*Clearly*, you don't know the meaning of sleeping in," says Riah. She shifts to a sitting position. "Can I at least take a shower?"

"Of course, but let's cut your hair first. I've already set up in the kitchen."

"Have you done this before?" asks Riah.

"Yes—it's how I put myself through college."

"Hmm, interesting," says Riah as she follows Anjali. "I didn't know you were multi-talented."

She glances back at Riah and shrugs. There's a lot Riah still didn't know about her—where would she even start?

Anjali couldn't sleep after Riah had awoken from her nightmare. She had lain in bed for an hour, building a list in her head of all the things she needed to take care of before she left. Her first preference was to write it down, but in the end, she decided against it—she had to execute the list from memory. When she couldn't think anymore, she decided to get out of bed and do something more productive. She had crept downstairs while Riah was still asleep. In the kitchen, she had emptied the dishwasher of the dinnerware from the night before. She marveled in the fact that she hadn't tidied the kitchen right after dinner like she habitually would have—like Michael would have expected her to do. She likes the new person she felt herself becoming—free. Soon she will be unencumbered for good.

"Wow!" says Riah. "You weren't kidding—you've gone all out!"

In the middle of the kitchen, Anjali has laid a plastic sheet on the floor and positioned one of the tall bar stools on the transparent, protective layer. She has arranged an assortment of scissors, combs, and hair clips on the kitchen island—all placed in a flaw-less, impeccable straight line. Next to these, an electric razor, a spray bottle with water, and her gold-plated hair straightener were well within her reach.

"Have a seat," says Anjali, walking over to the sink and setting down her coffee cup on the counter. "Do you want some hot java before we get started?"

"No, I'll get some after my shower—let's do this before I change my mind." Riah takes a seat on the barstool.

Anjali takes a black cape off a wall hook and drapes it over Riah's shoulders. Anjali combs through Riah's thick hair, parting and pinning it in sections. She works in silence for twenty minutes and then exclaims, "Alright, I'm done!"

"How does it look? Can I see it?"

"It looks amazing! The short hair suits you!" Anjali hands Riah a mirror. "Take a look for yourself."

Riah makes a face as she views her reflection in the mirror. She touches her hair, casting her eye downward. "I didn't think I had *that* much hair."

Anjali laughs. "It was quite thick, so I texturized it a bit. It'll be easier to dry and style—do you like it?" asks Anjali. She catches Riah's eyes in the mirror and marvels at her sister's transformation.

"I think I have to get used to it. It's a big change, though."

"I know, Riah. But trust me, you look fabulous—you should go take a shower." Anjali unbuttons the cape and removes it from Riah's shoulders.

As Riah rises from the stool, she gazes at the pile of hair on the plastic sheet and seems to be overcome by sadness. Should Anjali say something to console Riah? But before she can speak, Riah turns to leave the kitchen.

"I left one of my outfits in the dressing area for you to wear. I will come upstairs and style your hair," Anjali calls out behind her sister.

Riah lets the hot, steamy water warm her skin. She stands still, watching the water roll off her body and swirl into the drain. This shower is triple the size of the one in her hotel room. Riah isn't surprised that the ensuite bathroom is massive, given the size of the dressing area and the walk-in closet alone. Riah is already getting used to the apartment, but she has to remind herself that she'll only be here for a few days next week. She washes the shampoo suds from her hair and then rubs in the conditioner. As she waits for it to hydrate to her roots, she pictures the next few days. Anjali said that Michael will be home tonight, which means Riah will need to return to her hotel room for three days. Michael will leave on Tuesday morning for Beijing, allowing Riah to return to the apartment. Riah will book Anjali's flight to Italy for next Tuesday as well. Once Anjali leaves for Italy, the *real* work will start—she'll take advantage of the opportunity lingering before her, like Margaret's necklace heist, low-hanging fruit she'll reap before she leaves San Francisco.

Anjali calls out Riah's name, bringing her back from her propitious preparations. She turns off the shower tap and wraps herself with a towel. As she steps out of the shower, Anjali enters the bathroom.

"Oh, sorry—I thought you were done." Anjali turns around and leaves the bathroom.

Riah pats herself dry and pulls on the underwear and bathrobe Anjali had left for her. As she walks out of the room, Anjali is holding another black dress. "I can wear my clothes from last night," says Riah. Why is Anjali so intent on dressing her up? Isn't the haircut enough?

"Don't be silly, Riah! You got your pick of the best outfits here—besides, I already packed your clothes in a garbage bag!"

"You wouldn't dare," says Riah. She grabs the dress from Anjali's hands and walks behind the silkscreen divider for privacy.

"Sure, I would!"

Riah is mute while she slips into Anjali's selection. For now, she'll have to be Anjali's dress-up Barbie.

"Oh! It fits perfectly," says Anjali, clasping her hands together as Riah comes out. "Come on, let me do your make-up and flat iron your hair." Anjali ushers her to sit in front of the vanity. "Then I'm sending you out on an errand." Anjali turns on the hairdryer, ignoring Riah's questioning glance.

Through the mirror, Riah studies her sister as she combs through Riah's short hair. Anjali takes a section of her hair and runs a round boar-bristle brush through it with the hairdryer diffuser. Anjali appears to be lost in thought—as if she is dancing with a dilemma. Anjali catches Riah staring and holds her gaze for a second before flashing her a disarming smile. There is something false about Anjali's smile that Riah can't quite put her finger on. Turning off the dryer, Anjali shoves it back in the drawer. Anjali reaches for a small green bottle and pumps a generous amount of serum into her palm.

"What kind of errand are you sending me on?" Riah asks as Anjali smooths the product into her hair.

"Are you nervous?" asks Anjali, bending over to stare into the reflection of Riah's eyes.

"Not at all. Just curious."

"It's fairly simple," says Anjali with a smile. "But why don't I make you a coffee first."

❧

This is so silly. Why isn't Anjali more concerned about meeting their birth mother next week? Instead, Anjali is fixated on how Riah will do in her place. The elevator dings, and the doors open to the main floor. Riah takes a deep breath, relaxes her shoulders, and strolls out of the elevator.

Riah spots the building security desk and strolls straight toward it. She pushes the pang of nervousness away. *Get out of your head,* she tells herself. She spots the man Anjali had described upstairs—a short and round man with a shiny, bald head, named Louis.

As she approaches, Louis flashes a larger-than-life smile. "Anjali, I haven't seen you in days!" he exclaims. "Sweetie, how have you been keeping yourself?" he asks, rising from the security desk with his arms open wide. Anjali had advised Riah that Louis was a *hugger,* and he would be offended if she didn't hug him back. Riah opens her arms, and he embraces her in a tight bear hug. His breath is redolent of stale tuna. Ugh, she could kill Anjali! He steps back and straightens his navy-blue security blazer. "To what do I owe the pleasure?" he asks, still smiling.

Riah flashes a smile back. "Louis, I seem to have misplaced my access card to get in and out of the garage and the private elevator."

"Oh really," he says, scratching his head. "Sure, let me order you a new one," he says as he steps behind his desk and types on the keyboard. "I will cancel the other one."

"Oh, you don't have to cancel it," says Riah. "I think Michael took both cards by accident, but he'll be back tonight." She flashes him a smile. "I was headed out and thought it might be easier to get a new one," she explains.

He stares at her for a long moment. Uh-oh, did she overstep?

He smiles, then lowers his head and resumes typing on the keyboard. "Alright, done! I'll run over to the office in the second tower and gather the new card. Wait right here," he tells her.

"Sure, thanks, Louis." Riah waits in the lobby—she prays Louis will be back soon. She walks over to the far side of the room and admires the waterfall on the wall. Watching the water trickle against the dark brick wall and swirl to the bottom of the fountain, she begins to relax and feel calmed by the sound.

"Anjali," someone calls out.

Riah turns around, coming face-to-face with a tall blonde woman. She is wearing a tight-fitting black dress with matching patent-leather six-inch heels. She carries an oversized Louis Vuitton bag on her left arm. Did everyone around here look like they've come out of a fashion magazine? Riah is about to say hello when a tiny white Chihuahua pops its head from the bag looking at her with curious, bright eyes. And then, overcome by excitement, the pup starts yelping non-stop.

"Aww, looks like Buster wants to say hello to you," she says. As Louis heads back from the other tower, she nudges Buster's head back into the bag. "Gotta go—you didn't see us," she says, giving her a quick wink. The hot blonde exits through the front doors of the building, leaving behind the waft of a pricey perfume.

"Alright, here's your new card," says Louis as he approaches. "Please don't lose this one, all right? I could get in trouble if—"

Riah puts her hand on his arm and says, "Louis, don't worry about it." She flashes her best imitation-Anjali smile.

Louis wipes his brow and hands Riah a small brown envelope with *Penthouse 2B* scribbled on it. Riah gives Louis a quick thank-you hug and heads back toward the elevator.

"Oh, Anjali!—I saw Sienna and that dog she claims to be *fur-babysitting*," he says using air quotes. "She should know our condo rules."

Riah shrugs her shoulders at his frowning face. "I'll remind her," she says, gliding into the elevator labeled Private. As the doors close, she glimpses Louis walking back toward the security desk. Riah presses the button marked P2B. Her brain registers the other three apartment labels for the first time—P1A, P1B, and P2A. Who else lives in the building—particularly in the other penthouses? If Anjali lives in an extravagant dwelling with things worth stealing, so would the other apartments. The elevator door opens, yanking her out of her tantalizing thoughts.

Anjali is standing in the doorway of her apartment. "You're brilliant!" Anjali pulls her in for a hug.

"Wh-what?" Riah stammers. "How did you see it?"

Anjali pushes a button by the doorway. A wooden panel on the wall glides upwards to reveal several twelve-inch screens. Each displays the critical areas in the building. Riah can see Louis at the security desk, busy typing away on the keyboard. He pauses, squints at the computer monitor as though he needs reading glasses, then resumes typing. One of the other units displays what appears to be an underground parking garage, and another is the private elevator. The last screen is turned off, piquing her curiosity.

"Wow! How stealth of you," she says.

Anjali laughs. "I didn't want you to be nervous, knowing I'd be watching."

"Yeah, it's a bit creepy, but I suppose someone is always watching us, right?"

Anjali does not respond. "I thought Sienna was going to bust you!"

"Who is she?" she asks.

Anjali rolls her eyes. "Only the most annoying neighbor in the world!"

"Oh. So, she lives in Penthouse 2A?"

"Yes, and she has a *thing* for Michael," says Anjali, pouring herself a glass of water from the bar sink. "What did she even say to you?"

"Nothing really. She had a dog in her purse and took off when she saw Louis coming back."

"Yes, I saw!" says Anjali. "You should have given her up!"

"Uhm, I wasn't sure who she was. But knowing she isn't a friend—chihuahua is gone!"

Anjali chuckles. "An enemy of mine is an enemy of yours?"

"Absolutely!" she says. "So, you mentioned another errand?"

"Yes, but I'm not so sure if you're up to it."

Riah exaggerates a shocked look on her face. "Do you doubt my abilities?"

❧

Riah walks into the First Republic Bank branch. It is quiet, with at best a handful of clients in the building. Riah had nearly leapt with excitement when Anjali asked her to go to the bank and make a deposit to her café's business account. Anjali was making this way too simple; in a way, her obliviousness was worse than Margaret's. Riah hid her eagerness by telling Anjali it wouldn't work—*it's too risky*, she said. Anjali said she was foolish and handed Riah the bank card and deposit bag.

Riah waits in line for one of the three bank tellers with open wickets serving customers. All of them are older middle-aged women. What are their lives like? Is their existence mundane, spent on their feet, working nine-to-five? In the background, several other bank employees sitting behind large desks with clients in front are probably the personal account managers. Riah is curious to know what it would be like to work a decent, straightforward job. She watches a clerk stamp a series of papers. She seems very efficient in her occupation. Riah couldn't do it, she decides—it would bore her straight out of her mind.

"Next! May I help you?" A cashier yells at the end of the row of wickets.

The woman's voice yanks Riah out of her meandering thoughts with a start. She hurriedly rushes to her wicket.

"Hi, Mrs. Murphy! How are you doing today?" asks the woman.

Riah glances at her nametag before looking the woman in the eyes. "I'm fine, Debbie. How are you?"

"Oh, you know, so-so. It's been a crazy week. I had to hospitalize my dad again because his Alzheimer's is getting worse, and Antonio is still out of work—so he's no help at all."

This woman must know Anjali well to be carrying on. She tells Riah about the kids and what they are studying in school. Riah cuts in on her story: "Debbie, I'm sorry, I'm in a bit of a rush today."

"Oh! I'm sorry! Here I am carrying on and on about my life—your bank card?"

"Oh, yes," says Riah. She hands her Anjali's bank card.

"So, withdrawal or deposit?" asks Debbie.

"Deposit," she says, pulling the black vinyl bag from the purse Anjali had insisted she take.

Debbie opens the bag and removes the contents. As Debbie counts the cash, Riah intercepts her surprise about how much money Anjali is depositing by putting on her best poker face.

"It was quite busy this week at the café," says Riah, feeling the strong desire to over-explain.

"It's wonderful that business has picked up. That's seven thousand, five hundred to be exact! So, this is going into the business account?" asks Debbie as she scans the deposit slip Anjali had pre-filled.

"Uh-huh," says Riah.

Debbie taps into the computer keyboard for a moment. "Okay, I'll be just a minute," Debbie says, turning away.

As Debbie walks to the back of the service area, Riah squints at Debbie's computer screen and studies the list of Anjali's accounts, taking mental note of the high balances. As Debbie returns, Riah rummages through her purse, trying to look distracted.

"Alright, all done! Was there anything else, Mrs. Murphy?"

"Yes, Debbie. Is it possible to get a list of all of my accounts with the balances?"

"Sure, I can do that for you." As Debbie types into the computer, a printout appears on the printer. "Did you know you could get this through online banking?" she asks, handing Riah the piece of paper.

"Oh, really?" asks Riah.

"Yes, I notice you're not signed up for it. It'll take a quick minute, and I'll show you how to log in."

"Sure, that would be great," says Riah.

"I also noticed your bank card does not have the latest tap-to-pay feature—I could order you a new card, and you could pick it up next week."

"Oh, and what would happen to this card?" asks Riah.

"It will be automatically deactivated once the new one arrives, and we activate it."

Riah likes this woman—she is unwittingly accommodating all Riah's needs.

~

Anjali flings her apartment door open and asks, "What took you so long?"

"Oh, have I been gone that long? It didn't feel like a long time, but I think the bank teller was on the verge of telling me her life story."

"Oh, you mean Debbie?"

"Yes! How did you know?"

Anjali laughs. "Because only one person fits the TMI description—Debbie! She always takes twice as long as all the other bank tellers."

"Yeah, I'll say. She talked my ear off!" Riah hands Anjali her purse. "The empty deposit bag and bankcard are in there. Did I pass the test?"

"Test?" she asks.

"Yeah, isn't that why you sent me on the errand?"

Anjali laughs. "Not a test—I just needed to make that deposit."

Riah rolls her eyes. "So, what do we do from here?"

"Well, Riah, this is where we say goodbye—but only for a few days. Michael will be home in a couple of hours, and I need to do a few things at the café before he returns home. Laine's been kind enough to agree to open and close the café today, but I want to give her a break for the weekend."

"Oh sure," says Riah. "I have some things to do as well."

"Thanks for agreeing to take my place while I go and meet our mother."

Riah fixates her eyes on the ground. "I hope I don't mess up your life," Riah says.

"Oh, Riah! Is that what you are worried about? You'll be fine. You're a natural actress." She opens her arms and invites Riah for a hug.

She embraces her sister, and a wave of guilt overcomes her as she releases Riah. "Should I buy your plane ticket for you?" asks Riah. "Since it will be under my name, I'll need to include my passport number," she adds.

"Oh yes, that'd be great—and don't worry, I'll give you the money for the ticket on Tuesday. And you can give me your passport."

"Sounds like a plan," says Riah.

"I packed your stuff while you were gone and put it in one of my bags." Anjali reaches into the closet and pulls out a black nylon Prada bag. She retrieves a hat and a pair of sunglasses from the side pocket and hands them to Riah. "You may want to wear this. Also, you will need this next week," says Anjali, as she passes the security card Louis had given Riah earlier.

They hug once more before Riah departs. Anjali closes the door behind her.

SIXTEEN

Monday, September 19th—Late Evening

Anjali washes their dinner dishes, letting her skin soak in the effervescent suds. Michael is upstairs packing for his trip. Tomorrow. Tomorrow, her life will finally be hers. She'll leave for Italy—and start her new life. The thought of beginning afresh makes her skin tingle. She closes her eyes and imagines that she's a bird. The wind lifts her higher and higher until it releases her into the boundless blue sky. She coasts on the wings of brilliant new beginnings. Flying free. Her breath catches on hope. *Don't get ahead of yourself,* she reprimands herself abruptly; *the plan still needs to be executed.*

She isn't one for dreaming, but she knows her life will be different once she gets on the plane. Once she leaves this place—and Michael—behind. Her new life will be perfect! A few months ago, the concept of a new identity and escaping Michael was a microscopic seed that she buried in the soil of their marriage. To her surprise, the pit grew roots and then unexpectedly flourished into a way forward. All made possible with Riah's voluntary search for her. It is still hard to believe it all came together in under a week. She and her mom had planned all the essential details, and all Anjali has to do is to be a different person—she will become Riah Arora. She practices saying her new name repeatedly in her head. She dares not speak it out loud. The fear that he may hear haunts her like an incessant demon. But all of this will change tomorrow. In a way, she wishes she could be here to see his face when he learns she's gone—gone from *him*. She wants to be here to see him breathe his last breath—

"Babe! Aren't you done yet?" asks Michael, coming through the swinging kitchen door.

She cringes. "Just about," she says over her shoulder, forcing an inflection of warmth into her voice.

Tonight, the atmosphere is thick with his impulsive desire. He's lingering, taxing her patience. Creeping behind her, he wraps his arms around her waist. He nestles his nose between her neck and shoulder blade. Without hurrying, he kisses her skin.

Her flesh crawls. She loathes his possessiveness as if, with every touch, he was telling her she was owned solely by him. His trapped little bird.

"Michael, please let me finish." She recoils and attempts to wiggle free from his embrace.

He doesn't say anything for a moment. He releases Anjali and takes a step back.

She holds her breath. The moment stretches like an eternity, dropping her into a bottomless black hole.

He grabs her by her left shoulder and spins her around. Their eyes are in a dead-lock tango of challenge. She searches his face for the remnants of the man she had fallen in love with eons ago. At this moment, she'd settle for just a sliver—a glimmer of that man. He narrows his eyes, holding her gaze for a nanosecond before his hand goes to the back of her neck. At first, his touch is gentle, caressing her skin. With his thumb, he makes circular motions around the hollow space of her throat, once a sign of tenderness between them. Then, a subtle shift in the energy as a shadow passes over his face. His grip gets tighter—his eyes still holding hers—commanding her into his dark. She refuses to show her fear. This is just another test—he's determining whether she will object or be a good girl and assent to his whims.

A surge of electricity pulsates between them. She needs to push through—through to the other side of tonight. She must diminish her resolve, just for a few minutes. She again pictures the vast ocean-blue sky waiting for her, waiting for her to fly.

"Why don't we take this upstairs?" she says.

He loosens his grip and smiles. "Let's do that."

He relaxes and strolls out of the kitchen.

She follows him like the obedient, docile wife he is fond of.

SEVENTEEN

Tuesday, September 20th—Morning

Riah unlocks the front door of *The Artists' Café* and flips the sign to open. Hopefully, Laine will arrive soon and relieve her of any responsibility for dealing with actual customers. Michael left for the airport at dawn, and Anjali texted her as soon as his flight to Beijing departed. *Get over here as soon as you can*, Anjali's text had read. Riah had bolted out of bed in excitement. Today was the day her plan would be set into motion. She liked planning a con but executing on the scheme—this is where she thrived. The execution phase meant getting closer to the end of the game—and winning the prize.

Yesterday, Brandon advised Riah to stick to the plan at all costs. He knew her tendency to deviate from the course if it meant a more sizeable payout. He made her memorize the scheme and repeat it out loud several times.

> *1) Michael will leave on Tuesday for the San Francisco International Airport around three a.m. His flight for Beijing will leave at five-thirty a.m.*

> *2) Riah will go to Anjali's apartment; Anjali will give Riah the access codes and keys to the penthouse and the café. And in*

exchange Riah will hand over a plane ticket to Italy and her passport.

3) Anjali will leave for Italy at noon; Riah will stay in Anjali's apartment and open and close the café with Laine until Saturday evening.

4) Anjali will be back on Sunday morning. Michael will be back the following Tuesday.

Anjali had concocted the plan, and it was halfway to complete. Riah and Brandon added a few additional steps with one goal—strike it rich!

5) Riah will wait for Anjali to leave on her flight and then head back to the apartment. She will pass by the First Republic Bank branch and see Debbie for her new bank card.

6) Riah will clean out Anjali's apartment and the accounts on Wednesday morning.

7) Riah will leave town on Wednesday afternoon in a rented car and head south to Los Angeles, where she will meet Brandon.

They also decided Brandon should watch Anjali, ensuring she got on her flight. Afterward, he would get a head start to Los Angeles to meet Riah the following evening. It was the perfect plan, nice and easy, not exceedingly complicated.

Riah decides she needs a coffee from the café bar. She isn't familiar with the café's layout, as she hadn't been here since the *Word Slam*. Anjali had gone over some of the basics Riah may need to know, but she missed the how-to-make-coffee lesson. Riah stares at the machine, fixated on the intricate set of knobs, dials, and levers. The jingle of the bell above the café door makes her glance over her shoulder.

Laine scrambles through the threshold, carrying a couple of boxes. "Good morning, Anjali—I'm so sorry I'm late," Laine says.

What would Anjali say? Anjali seemed like an easygoing boss. "Well, I'll forgive you—if you make me a cappuccino."

Laine smirks. "Yes, I know how much you hate this tricky coffee machine."

Riah releases a breath of relief, letting go of the tension in her shoulders. "Thanks! Extra hot, please."

"Of course—extra hot, half-sweet, light on the foam—I remember how you like it," says Laine.

Riah lingers as Laine makes the cappuccino.

"Did you do something different with your hair?" asks Laine.

"Oh, not really—I didn't have enough time this morning to blow dry it thoroughly," she says, self-consciously touching her hair. Laine is already pointing out the differences between her and Anjali.

"I like it! It's got extra volume," says Laine, passing her the cappuccino cup on a saucer.

"Thanks for the compliment and for the cappuccino, Laine!"

"I know—what would you do without me, right?"

"Without question," she says. Balancing the cup and saucer, she climbs the stairs to Anjali's office.

"Oh, by the way, Anjali," says Laine. "Hana is coming by today to say hello. I'm hoping you'll be around to meet her?"

"Uhm, sure! Sounds good." Riah hesitates on the stairs.

"My girlfriend, remember? She couldn't make it to the *Word Slam* last week, but I still want you to meet her." Laine's voice carries a hint of trepidation. Something in her words tells her this is important to Anjali's employee.

"Oh, yes! Now I remember! Sorry I momentarily forgot," she says and continues climbing the stairs.

"Awesome! Thanks, Anjali!"

"No problem! I'll be in my office all morning."

"Yup, I'll let you know if I need you here—but likely not," says Laine.

"Thank God," mutters Riah to herself. She wouldn't even know what to do. Anjali's office door is ajar, and Riah pushes the door open with her foot. The office is neat—almost to a fault, which Riah has been half-expecting based on the immaculate state of Anjali's penthouse apartment. The office is humble in size but has plenty of light. A massive mahogany desk sits in the middle of the room with an executive chair. A cappuccino-colored leather couch fills the right corner of the office, and on the left side is a series of lush green houseplants in grey stone planters. Behind the desk, a wide window spans the entire back wall. On the wooden windowsill, several pictures of Anjali and Michael, Anjali and her parents, and Anjali in her childhood days showcase Anjali's perfect life. Riah closes the door behind her. She isn't sure how she will kill the morning, but at least she has Anjali's office all to herself.

Riah takes a seat and tests the buttery leather chair for a moment before swinging her feet onto the desk. She holds the cappuccino between her hands like she has seen Anjali do several times before. "I'm the boss," she says out loud. She likes the sound of those words. She takes a sip of the cappuccino; the hot liquid trickles down her throat, warming and awakening her being. It reminds her of her childhood days when she would sit on her mother's lap, and her mother would allow her to take sips of her spicy chai tea. She aches for her mother.

What will Anjali do when she arrives in Italy and discovers their mother is no longer alive? Her mother had succumbed to her illness months earlier. Riah had been lost in a maelstrom of grief over her mother's death for the first month. It was like being lost in a fog, a sad and lonely haze that intermingled with the smoke from her mother's cremated body and dissolved her heart into ash. When she was clearing out her mother's belongings, she found her mother's letters for her and her twin. Riah had been half-expecting a letter, as she'd witnessed her mother scribbling on flowered gossamer-like stationery during her final days. But the letter for Anjali she had not predicted.

Riah knew she had failed her mother. She hadn't found her sister—her mother's other daughter and the other half of her mother's heart—in time to reunite them. In Riah's letter, her mother explained she wanted her ashes scattered by both of her daughters. This is the only reason why Riah needs Anjali to go to Italy, so that Anjali can read the letter that her mother left for her. Riah couldn't bear to tell Anjali that their mother had already passed. Anjali will understand once she found the package that Riah has left for her.

The odds of Anjali not hating her once she learns the truth are not in Riah's favor. Perhaps, in time, her sister will forgive her? Unlikely, but at least Riah will have the money.

Riah leans her head back and closes her eyes. She imagines what it will be like to sit on a beach in California. She supposes Malibu or Santa Monica will be beautiful this time of the year. She can stretch out on the sand and let the sun soak through her skin. She isn't one for water, but she does love the sun. She'll have to think of a new name and backstory to match her future sun-kissed persona. Brandon will need to get them new identities, and perhaps he'll accept her plans to retire from the game for good.

The low buzz of her phone nudges her out of her daydream. She reaches into the pocket of her cardigan, retrieves her phone, and reads the text message from Brandon: *All on track. Anj has left for the airport.* Riah smiles. She slides the phone back into her pocket and takes her feet off the desk. She decides she should start her investigation of Anjali's office. She turns on the computer screen, and it comes alive with high-quality images of the café. Interesting. It seems Anjali likes to watch her establishment unnoticed. This is how Anjali must've seen her and Brandon steal the cash and bank card last week. She was here the whole time watching them—watching Riah. "Okay, let's see who you are, Anjali Murphy," Riah says out loud as she yanks on the desk's drawers. They are locked. Other than the computer screen and the large leather placemat, the surface of Anjali's desk is bare.

It's evident Anjali is a minimalist and likes a clean and neat environment—but a locked desk drawer means she also has secrets to hide. The drawer might contain regular business effects, but Riah has to be sure. She has to make sure she is taking full advantage of Anjali's absence. *Get as much as you can—and get it fast*, Brandon had said to her last night as they finalized their plans. In truth, Riah has time—Anjali isn't due to arrive in Italy until tomorrow afternoon. Riah had booked the flight and had made sure to choose a long layover in Paris. Riah had told Anjali that their mother loves the idea of Paris, and that it would warm her heart if Anjali got her a few things from there.

Riah runs her hand along the leather placemat, feeling a slight bump in the middle of the mat. She lifts the cloth and finds a key taped to the bottom side. She frees the key, examines it for a moment, and then rises from the chair. She crouches so she is eye-level with the keyhole of the desk drawer and inserts the key into the lock. The key sticks when she turns it left. She jiggles it and rotates it to the right. The key turns without resistance this time and opens the lock. Riah yanks the drawer open to reveal a row of folders. The row starts with a few green files, followed by yellow and red ones. It reminds Riah of traffic signals.

Riah sifts through the folders, only finding materials related to the operations of the café. She finds papers stating that the café is owned by Sangeeta Patel—Anjali's adopted mother. Interesting, how well-to-do are Anjali's adopted parents? Riah might have to do some further recon. When Anjali had mentioned Sangeeta's name, it sounded vaguely familiar. The rest of the files must be relevant to

Anjali, and Riah dismisses them from holding any valuable secrets. She diverts her attention to the left side of the desk and tries the same key. This drawer is empty, except for some tea boxes and biscuits. Riah is about to close the drawer when something catches her eye. It is a small, round box, painted a dark burgundy color with a glossy laminated picture. The image is a classic depiction of two cherubs painted by Michelangelo. She recognizes this box—it's a trinket often sold on the streets of Florence. Many museums in Florence have small gift shops that sell these types of souvenirs. Riah has often stolen and resold these same items to unsuspecting tourists for double the price.

Riah shakes the box, and something rattles inside. She twists the top of the box to find a tiny key. Taking the key out of the box, she studies it for a long, drawn-out moment. It's like the key for the desk drawers. Both appear to be made for the same desk. This is strange—she has already opened the two drawers with the other key. But upon further examination of the desk, Riah pinpoints a compact panel in the middle. She yanks at it, and it opens upwards. She lowers to her knees and peers underneath the board. There's a small handle for what appears to be another drawer. To the right of the handle is a tiny keyhole. She inserts the key from the trinket box and turns it to the right. She tugs the handle, and the drawer slides open. Realizing the drawer is empty except for a five-by-seven-inch envelope, she snatches the envelope and shoves the drawer shut.

Riah turns the envelope around in her hands. The pouch is sealed. She places it on the placemat with the sealed side facing upwards. Out of habit, she returns all the other items, precisely how she found them.

She leans back in the leather chair and swivels from side to side, thinking. Clearly, the envelope is vital, as Anjali has taken such care to hide it. If Riah were to open it, she couldn't reseal it without Anjali knowing someone had opened it. Could she seal the contents in a new envelope and place it back? Anjali would be none the wiser.

She takes her phone out from her pocket and texts Brandon: *Found envelope in a secret compartment of A's desk—should I open it?* She places her phone on the desktop surface beside the envelope and waits for Brandon's response. She continues to rotate in the chair when her gaze lands on the computer screen. A few customers sit at tables downstairs, working away on their laptops. This reminds her that she has to log into Anjali's online banking account and move money around. There is much work to do over the next couple of hours. Her attention diverts back to the security monitor. A woman strolls into the café and smiles when Laine approaches her. The two women embrace and peck each other on the lips. This has to be Laine's girlfriend. There's something familiar about her, but it's hard to tell from the security camera. Riah's phone vibrates to signal an incoming text from Brandon: *Leave it. Probably not important.*

Riah frowns. She briskly texts back, *K, fine,* and places the phone in her pocket. She pauses for a second to reflect. She swivels around in the chair to face the window. On the windowsill is a round penholder, painted the same burgundy as the trinket box. A shiny silver letter opener catches Riah's eye; she plucks it from its resting place. She inserts the letter opener into a small opening at the top of the envelope and glides it along the crease, splitting it open with ease.

Riah pulls a thick stack of glossy pictures from the envelope. She peers at the first photo—it's an image of a woman and a man sitting together in a restaurant. The photo was taken from outside the restaurant without the couple knowing. Riah flips through a series of photographs of the couple taken from different angles. She then comes upon a shot of the couple coming out of the restaurant, where the woman is latched onto the man's arm. Riah looks closer at the photograph and recognizes the pair—Anjali's husband, Michael, and their dog-carrying neighbor, Sienna!

Riah swivels her chair to face the window and holds the picture in her hand against the one on the ledge. Although Riah has not met Michael in person, it's plain as day that it's the same person in both pictures. She zones in on Sienna. The woman is wearing a red dress and matching red heels. Sienna has a leopard-print wrap hanging off her shoulders, and on her left arm, she carries the same oversized Louis Vuitton purse she had with her last week—minus the puppy. Sienna dripped money and dirty sex appeal. So Anjali wasn't exaggerating when she said Sienna had a thing for Michael. Riah flips to the following picture—it's one of Michael and Sienna embracing in a full-on mouth-to-mouth kiss. *Oh! It appears the feelings are mutual.*

She flips through the rest of the snapshots. Michael and Sienna went from an innocent lunch to making out on the street to a steamy rendezvous in bed. She peers closer at the images of the naked couple in bed. It doesn't look like Anjali's apartment; perhaps they are in Sienna's penthouse apartment. How very convenient for Michael!

Riah places the evidence in her lap, closes her eyes, and takes a deep breath. She imagines how Anjali might have reacted to these photos. Did she cry? Did she get angry? Did she know Michael was cheating on her before seeing these pictures, or was it a shock? Perhaps she had suspicions Michael was seeing someone else and had hired a professional to follow him. And then all her doubts about Michael were validated with these indecent revelations. Poor Anjali! She hid this proof in her office because she couldn't dare say anything to him. Or she was planning on confronting him, but was waiting for the right moment. What would Riah do if she were in Anjali's place? If Riah were married to a lying cheat, would she confront him, forgive him, or leave him? It's one of those dilemmas Riah has never thought about before. She has never had to worry because she has never let anyone, not even Brandon, get close enough to hurt her. It must have been devastating for Anjali. She must have been crushed; she must have felt her whole world shatter. What an asshole Michael is! Someone should pay—for Anjali's sake.

Riah's thoughts are interrupted by a light knock on the office door. Riah swivels in her chair as Laine opens the door. Riah haphazardly gathers the photographs and tosses them into Anjali's tote bag on the floor.

"Hi, Anjali. I wanted to introduce you to Hana."

"Of course," Riah says. She leaps from her chair and glides around the desk. "Hi, it's so nice to meet you."

Hana's hand is extended, but she drops it as soon as she spots Riah. "Riah?" Hana asks with bewilderment. Stepping forward, she pulls Riah into a bear hug. "*Yaar*, I thought you were dead!"

Riah squirms from Hana's embrace and steps backward. Shit! This has to be more than a coincidence—what the hell is her childhood best friend doing here? Parshana Thakur—after all these years.

Laine is also confused. Riah is thankful when Laine steps forward and puts her hand on Hana's arm. "Honey, this is Anjali, my boss. The one I told you about?" Laine says in a stern, mother-like voice.

Hana steps back; her cheeks are flushed from embarrassment. "Oh, I'm s-sorry," Hana stammers. "You look like an old friend of mine from India."

"Oh, I think I have a common-looking Indian face," Riah says, composing herself. "So, you used to live in India?" she asks, changing the topic.

"Yes," says Hana. "I came to the States on a student visa many years ago."

"Yes, and it's where we met—at UC Berkeley," says Laine. She steps closer and links her arm around Hana's waist. "Hana fast-tracked through law school and passed the bar last year. She's been hired by one of the top criminal defense law firms in San Francisco!" Laine's voice is full of pride.

"That's very impressive," Riah says. "Were you always interested in the law?" Riah wants to hear Parshana speak more, as she can't detect the heavy accent Parshana used to have when they were teenagers—she must have worked extremely hard to get rid of it.

"Not really," laughs Hana. "I wanted out of India. My parents were killed in a car accident seven years ago. And I didn't have any other reason to stay in Delhi. I sold all the shops they had—they owned over ten textile stores. I knew two things at that point. One, I wanted to come to America. And two, I wanted to put their money to good use. And so I took a bunch of exams, applied to the top schools, and got into one in New York and another one in California. I ended up choosing Berkeley because I wanted to be close to the sun, beach, and water."

Laine laughs. "Well, I'm glad you chose Berkeley—otherwise, I would never have met you."

"Aww, ditto, boo!" Hana pecks Laine on the lips.

Riah is proud of her old friend, Parshana. She has evolved and is light-years away from the person she used to be when they were younger. She remembers how Parshana would steal moonshine and smokes any chance she could get. They would waste hours drinking, smoking, and talking. She has missed her friend. When Riah was in Mumbai, she often thought about reaching out to Parshana and telling her what had happened. But she always hesitated. She had needed to distance herself from the trauma and move on with her life. Back then, she couldn't risk Parshana revealing where or why Riah and her mother had disappeared. But now, everything was different; they were meeting under other circumstances.

"You two should come over for dinner tonight," says Riah. Her spontaneous suggestion surprises herself and both ladies.

"That's a lovely offer," says Laine. "We did have other plans tonight." Laine casts a sideways glance at Hana.

"Which we can cancel," says Hana.

"Wonderful!" says Riah, clasping her hands together like she has seen Anjali do a few times before. She is conscious that Brandon won't like her deviating from the plan, but she doesn't have much to do tonight and doesn't want to be alone. It will be nice to have company and reunite with her old friend, Parshana. "How about you two come over for about seven?"

"Sure!" says Laine. "I will close up the café, and we'll come by afterward."

"Do you know the address?" asks Riah, realizing she doesn't know if Laine has ever visited Anjali's apartment before.

"Yes. I still have it from a few weeks ago when I dropped off those papers for you to sign."

"Yes, I remember. Okay, see you two later." She moves toward the door to usher them out. "Oh, Laine, I'll be leaving in a bit—I have some errands to run—"

"Sure boss! I know the drill," says Laine over her shoulder. Hana grins at Riah and mouths 'goodbye' as they descend the stairs.

Riah closes the office door and leans against it to calm her nerves. She hasn't realized until now, but she has been running on adrenaline. She can't believe she has met Parshana—her shorter name, Hana, suited her new life. Parshana did everything she used to say she was going to do. Parshana has worked hard on her English; even back then, she would take every opportunity to read and speak it. She remembers how Parshana used to buy every Sidney Sheldon book she could get her hands on to teach herself English. She also remembers how several girls made fun of her in Punjabi. But Riah had encouraged Parshana to ignore them because they were jealous of her ambition. Riah can't help but think about what her life would be like if she had stayed in India. Riah nudges herself out of nostalgic thinking—there is no point in dwelling on what might have been. She has a job to do, a gig to make her enough money that she'll never have to steal another dime.

EIGHTEEN

Tuesday, September 20th—Afternoon

Riah holds her breath as she enters the code for Anjali's apartment. She presses the *enter* button, the electronic lock beeps, and the tiny light at the bottom of the keypad flashes green, signaling success. Hearing the lock click, she turns the doorknob and opens the door. The apartment is in immaculate condition, gleaming in the brilliance of the mid-day sunlight. It looks the same as every other time she has been here, but today it appears extra flawless—she commits the room to her memory as if this is just another one of her *in-and-out* thieving jobs. Today, however, she has time to enjoy the amenities. Perhaps after her dinner date with Laine and Parshana, she'll open a bottle of champagne and run a long bubble bath in the whirlpool tub upstairs to celebrate her wins this week.

Anjali had given her a detailed walkthrough of the entire apartment, and Riah had made multiple mental notes during the *tour*. She had noticed Anjali's jewelry, locked in glass cases in her walk-in closet, and estimated these were likely the most valuable items in the apartment. The locks don't look too complicated for her skills—nothing she can't pry open with ease. But her first job is to find Anjali's laptop. Anjali had mentioned she wouldn't be taking it with her, but it wasn't in her office at the café, so it must still be in the apartment.

Riah scans the main floor and checks the office nook in the kitchen—no luck. She is about to head upstairs when there is a knock on the penthouse door. Shit—who's that? Her first instinct is to hide, but after a nanosecond of hesitation, she realizes she's Anjali. She peeks through the peephole. It's a woman facing the elevator, blonde spirals caressing her back. Her dress hugs the curves of her body—clearly, she isn't wearing underwear. Riah opens the door wide.

Sienna turns, her smile dropping at the sight of Riah. Was she expecting Michael?

"Hi," says Riah. "What's up?"

Sienna appears puzzled for a split second but redeems her expression. "Hi Anjali, I was hoping to talk to Michael for a few moments," says Sienna. "It's about my father's estate."

"Michael isn't here. He's out of town," says Riah. Hadn't her *lover* told her? Interesting.

Sienna's expression drops, sadness clouding her face. "Okay, I'll call his office and have someone else take care of it."

"Yes, you should do that." Riah hopes she has conveyed the same level of coldness she suspects Anjali would have displayed if she were here.

Sienna mutters a goodbye and turns toward the elevator.

Riah shuts the door with a slam. Peering through the peephole, she catches a shade of sadness on Sienna's face as the elevator doors close like curtains being drawn at an off-Broadway play.

"Wonder what she wanted," Riah mutters to herself as she resumes looking for Anjali's laptop. Upstairs, she happily discovers it, sitting in plain sight on the nightstand on Anjali's side of the bed.

Riah takes a seat on the bed and turns on Anjali's MacBook Air. It comes alive and displays the login screen. There are two options to sign in: as Anjali, and as Guest. She picks the Guest option as she figures it will be too challenging to guess Anjali's password.

The screen flickers and displays a classic mountain scene. Riah clicks on the Wi-Fi indicator and views the list of possible connections. She selects the *Anje&Mic* option. She holds her breath and hopes it connects with ease. A pop-up box appears, asking for a password. Damn, there has to be an Internet router box around here. She heads toward Michael's office.

Anjali hadn't shown Riah his home office, but she intuitively knows its location. She turns the doorknob but finds the office door locked. Squatting to the eye level of the keyhole, she assesses the challenge. She places the laptop on the floor and removes her thunderbolt-shaped earrings. Twisting the malleable metal of one earring, she inserts it into the keyhole and uses the other one as a lever. Hearing the desired click thirty seconds later, she turns the knob and pushes the door open. "Voila!" Riah says as if she has just performed one of Houdini's greatest escape tricks to an audience of more than herself.

The office is dark and does not have any windows. Riah finds the light switch and flips it on—the pot lights in the ceiling go from low mood lighting to bright white. Michael's office is cozier than she had anticipated.

On the left side of the room, bookcases span the entire wall from floor to ceiling. In the corner, beside the dark mocha Lazyboy armchair, a small round coffee table is littered with a stack of law magazines. On top of the stack rests a scotch glass with some remains of a brownish liquid in it.

On the right side of the room is Michael's desk. Riah looks underneath the table for the Wi-Fi router. Nothing. She places Anjali's laptop on the surface and opens the cabinet door on the right side of the bureau. The cabinet contains many tech gadgets, among them the router. She lifts it up and points the flashlight on her phone toward it to better see the password. She enters the password into the pop-up box and presses enter. The laptop chimes—she is connected. "Now we are in business," she says as she takes a seat in Michael's chair.

Riah searches for the First Republic Bank website and clicks on its online banking icon, pulling out Anjali's new bank card from the back pocket of her phone case. Riah had secured it from the bank earlier this afternoon. Fortunately, Debbie was working and had been expecting her. The visit to the bank had been incredibly productive in many ways. She enters the card number into the computer and logs in.

Ten minutes later, Riah leans back in the chair, pleased with herself. She has completed the first part of her plan. She closes her eyes and takes a deep breath—to savor this moment. She is so close to having it all. She opens her eyes, gazing leisurely at the wall of books.

How much time does Michael spend here? Has he read all these books, or is he a hoarder? Between his career as a lawyer, being a husband, and having Sienna on the side—when would he have the actual time? As Riah fixates on the books, a red one catches her line of vision. It reminds her of the painting Anjali had shown her last week—*Sisters*. Anjali had said, *if you stare at something long enough—you're bound to see the truth*. Something about the hardback looks off.

Riah rises and saunters toward the bookcase, keeping her eyes locked on the spot as though it could vanish without warning. She crouches and pulls the text from the shelf. An ivory fragment of paper sticks out from it. She opens the book, discovering its secret hollowness. It's a home for a colorful bouquet of resting origami flowers.

She takes a seat in the leather armchair. Mesmerized by the delicate floral art, she plucks one and studies its intricate architecture. Bringing the pink blossom to her nose, she takes a deep breath in. The scent of sandalwood, apple, cinnamon, and caramel tickles her nose, beckoning her into a warm autumn night. Had Anjali gifted this array of elegance to Michael? Are these souvenirs of the early days of their romance? Is their passion for each other tucked deep in the crevices of these little floral treasures? As she ponders the origin and the attachment these paper flowers carry, her eyes are drawn to what lies beneath them—tiny translucent paper squares.

Riah unfolds each pastel-colored diamond. Her heart thumps faster as she reads each one—one by one.

Michael, where have you been all my life?
Michael, you are the love of my life.
Michael, I want you.
Michael, I need you.
Michael, I love you.
Michael, be mine. Only mine.
Michael, wait for me in my apartment, 220689 xoxo.

Each lust note, transparent declarations of intimacy, is signed with the letter *S*.

Riah doesn't need to guess who this sinuous *S* is——*Sienna.*

How long has this affair been going on? Is it more than a fling? Why is Michael saving these letters? And has Anjali already discovered them? Riah is shaken by all these unanswered questions.

A supercut of memories flashes through her head. She hasn't known Anjali for long, but her sister's pain breaks through in a montage of scenes: Anjali, dropping Michael's baseball bat and duffle bag on the floor, unstated annoyance shadowing her face; Anjali, wrapping herself with a shawl, covering up purple and blue fingerprints; Anjali, admitting that Michael didn't know that she had found her birth mother and twin sister, unspoken fear on the tip of her tongue. All these breadcrumb clues now stepping into the light. Anjali has been harboring secrets of her own, with no one to share her pain. She wants to call Anjali and console her—she wants to ask her if she is *okay.*

For a moment, she feels guilty for stealing Anjali's money and is tempted to put it back. But that would be silly. She'll find another way to make it up to her sister. Anjali deserves justice for Michael and Sienna's betrayal, and they have both earned Riah's retribution for deceiving her sister.

NINETEEN

Tuesday, September 20th—Evening

Riah checks on the lasagna in the kitchen, delicately pulling the tray forward and turning it to ensure an even bake. She glides it back into the oven, setting the timer for another ten minutes. It's fifteen minutes past seven. She takes a generous sip from her glass of rosé wine as if she is taking a last deep breath before going underwater. Have Laine and Parshana changed their minds about coming over? There is a flaw in her impromptu dinner plans—she doesn't have Laine's number. If they were to cancel, they would text Anjali—the real Anjali. The distant buzz from the intercom at the front door puts her qualms at ease. She hurries over and presses the button, giving them access to the private elevator to Anjali's penthouse.

Riah opens the apartment door and anxiously anticipates their arrival. Thirty seconds later, the elevator dings, and the doors slide open. Laine and Hana spill out of the elevator, hand in hand, laughing.

"Hi!" says Laine. She giggles and glances over at Hana.

"Hi, come in," says Riah, stepping back to let them in. "What's so funny?"

Laine giggles again, and Hana, in an unenthusiastic tone, says, "Oh, she's making fun of me because I get dizzy on elevators."

"Oh—I don't get the humor in that," she says.

"I know, right?" says Hana, giving Laine a mock look of discontent.

"I'm sorryyy," whines Laine. "It was cute when you kissed me—did you actually think it would get rid of your dizziness?"

"Right, because kissing you should make me dizzier," laughs Hana. "I get it now!"

"Okay, enough with kissing and dizziness," interrupts Riah. "Who wants something to drink?"

"I'll have some of that," says Laine, pointing to the open bottle of wine.

"Great!" says Riah. Earlier in the evening, Riah had familiarized herself with the bar area and kitchen—she doesn't want to appear as though she is in a stranger's home. She pours two glasses of wine and hands them to her guests.

"Oh, none for me," says Hana.

"More for me," says Laine. She seizes both glasses and clinks them together.

"You don't drink?" Riah asks Hana, trying to mask her surprise.

"Oh, I do, but none of the fruity stuff, I only like the hard stuff."

Laine lets out a half-suppressed laugh.

That's the girl Riah used to know. "So, what can I get you, then?" asks Riah.

"A gin and tonic—light on the tonic," says Hana.

"Coming up," says Riah. She reaches for the bottle of Bombay Sapphire and a small liquor glass.

"Whatever you are cooking smells delicious!" says Laine.

"Oh, I'm making lasagna, I—" Riah stops herself. She had almost stupidly blurted out that the recipe was her own creation while she had lived in Italy. "I'm going to check on it. Do you want to see the kitchen?" she asks brightly, masking her nervousness about leaving them alone.

"You don't need to ask me twice," says Hana. She follows Riah into the kitchen, leaving Laine no choice but to trail behind.

"Wow!" exclaim Laine and Hana in unison as they walk into the kitchen.

Riah smiles. "Do you like the kitchen?"

"Yeah," says Hana. "What's not to like? Dude, I could live in your kitchen!"

Laine and Riah laugh. Although Parshana has lost her Indian accent, she hasn't lost her love of using Californian slang. When they were teenagers, everyone was a *dude* to Parshana.

The oven timer dings, and Riah reaches for the oven mitts to retrieve their dinner.

"Oh! It smells delicious. Where did you learn to cook, Anjali?" asks Hana.

"Yeah, Anjali, you've sworn up and down you don't know how to cook," adds Laine.

"Guys, come on, it's not hard to put a pre-made lasagna in the oven."

The three of them laugh.

"Cheers to that," says Laine, extending her wine glass. Riah swipes her glass and clinks it with Laine and Hana's. She has dodged a bullet, but she should've known Anjali doesn't cook from the first night she had been over for dinner.

"Shall I set the dining table in the other room?" asks Laine.

"Sure. I believe there are some fancy placemats here," Riah says, yanking one of the drawers open.

Laine pulls a few placemats from the drawer and takes the plates and cutlery to the dining room area.

Hana takes a seat on one of the kitchen chairs and smiles at Riah.

Riah cuts through the lasagna with a knife and starts to feel self-conscious. Hana is watching her. "So, you were raised in India?"

"Yes," answers Hana.

"Where about?" asks Riah—she hates small talk.

"Come on, Anjali, you know where I was raised. We grew up together."

Riah halts what she is doing—Hana's face is deadpan.

"Or should I say Riah?"

Before Riah can respond, Laine comes bouncing back into the kitchen. "Alright, we are all set! Let's eat. I'm starving."

❧

Dinner is quiet at first. The three ladies make small talk, which Riah finds unbearable. From the moment Hana asserted her knowledge of the truth, Riah has wanted nothing more than to escape. Hana's words continue to swim in her head. In a way, she shouldn't be shocked that Hana figured it out. Parshana, her oldest, dearest friend in the world, recognized her in a heartbeat. In an odd twist of fate, there is a comfort in being remembered, and maybe even missed.

Riah rises from her chair and strolls over to the bar area. She pours another glass of gin and tonic, making sure the drink has plenty of gin. She grabs the bottle of rosé from the canister and glides back to the dining table. Riah pours more wine into Laine's glass and places the gin and tonic in front of Parshana. Riah winks at Hana when she sideways glances at her. It is time to test Parshana, to determine if she will still be on her side *or* if she will out her.

"So, Hana—I want to know more about this person you thought I was when you met me this morning. What did you say her name was?" She takes a sip from her glass of water.

"Riah. Her name was Riah, and she was my best friend. But she went missing," says Hana. She takes a measured gulp from the fresh glass of gin and tonic.

"Missing? Wow, you never told me this, hon," says Laine, as she puts her hand on top of Hana's. "What do you think happened to her?" asks Laine.

Riah is silent. Waiting.

"I don't know," says Parshana. "But there were so many rumors circulating around in town."

"Like what?" Riah asks.

"Oh, like the typical type of gossip one might expect to hear in Delhi—it's where I was raised," she adds, shooting Riah a knowing look.

"Yeah, you told me how people treated you there," says Laine.

Hana continues. "Many of the stories had to do with Riah running away from home with a boyfriend. But it didn't make sense because I was her *best* friend, and she *never* told me she was seeing anyone, let alone planning to run away with him."

"What other rumors were there?" Riah asks. She is interested to hear more but doesn't want to appear overzealous.

"The usual ones, really, like she ran away to Mumbai to be an actress, but she couldn't make it, so she became a prostitute. And there were also weirder ones like she was murdered by her *Dādī* and was buried in her family's wheat fields."

"What?" asks Laine. "That sounds plain crazy!"

"The weird part is, after Riah went missing, her mother and uncle left too. Riah's *Dādī* was left all alone."

"Where did they go?" asks Riah, wondering if Parshana is telling the truth or if she is playing her—trying to trick her into confessing. Only Riah knows the facts: she and her mother fled Delhi together that horrendous night. And they left her uncle there. Dead. Why hadn't *Dādī* told the police?

"No one knows for sure." Hana takes another swig of her drink. "The police said, Riah's mother reported her missing. When they came to see me, they asked me all sorts of questions."

"Why?" asks Laine.

"I was the last person to see her alive." Hana finishes her gin and tonic and leaves the half-melted ice cube in the glass.

"And?—What did the police ask you?" asks Laine. Laine seems even more captivated than Riah.

Riah tilts forward in her chair, hanging on every word Hana is about to utter. Hana reclines back in her chair, quiet for an extended, drawn-out moment.

On a whim, Riah rises from her chair. "You need another drink." She strolls over to the bar area, pulls out the Bombay Sapphire bottle, and grabs a new clean drinking glass. She places the glass and the bottle of gin in front of Hana.

Hana pours herself a shot. Laine pushes her wine glass toward Hana, signaling she wants some too.

"It's Gin, boo," says Hana. "You're a lightweight." Hana shoots Riah a look of trepidation.

"I can handle it," says Laine, slurring her words.

Hana pours a one-ounce shot for Laine in her wine glass, and Riah instantaneously fills Laine's glass with water, diluting her drink.

Laine titters. "I can't imagine what you think of me," she says.

"I think you are the best, Laine. Don't ever feel judged."

Laine's eyes become teary. "Do you really feel that way, Anjali?"

"Why wouldn't I?" Riah can tell Anjali has a soft spot for Laine. She feels Laine deserves to know how valued she is—as an employee and a friend.

Hana puts her hand on top of Laine's and pats it. "She *is* the best."

Riah shifts in her chair, feeling ill at ease for veering away from Hana's story. "So, you were telling us about the police visiting you in India?" asks Riah. She's hopeful Hana will continue, but she also remembers how Parshana loved to stretch out a story. In their childhood days, she'd often give Riah a few tidbits to pique her interest and delay revealing the story's end. Luckily for Riah, Laine is also curious about Hana's missing friend.

"Hon, you are keeping me in suspense! What did the police ask you?"

Hana takes another sip of her drink. A shadow of solemnity pales her face as she continues her story. "The police came by my parents' shop a few days after Riah disappeared. They wanted to know the precise time I'd last seen her. The officers asked specific questions, like when she had come around and what we did when she was there. They also demanded to know what time Riah had left and if I was sure she had gone home. They insinuated I was a bad friend because I hadn't walked her home after she'd been drinking."

"You told the police that Riah was drinking?" asks Laine.

"She *was* drinking—we both were." Hana glances at Riah and flushes hot pink. "I lied to the police. I told them Riah had brought the moonshine and the smokes."

"Aww, hon! Do you blame yourself for Riah going missing?"

"I do feel guilty I lied to the police."

"I'm sure you had your reasons, Hana." She drills her gaze into Parshana, but her friend is unwilling to make eye contact with her.

Riah rises from the dining table and gathers their empty plates.

"So, that's it? You never found out what happened to her?" asks Laine.

Hana is quiet for a moment; she fidgets with her cutlery and bites her bottom lip. "No. They never figured out what happened to Riah because they couldn't establish with certainty *when* she had disappeared. I not only lied about the drinking, but I also told them I had seen her the next day and the day after—that she'd been hanging around town, but I hadn't spoken to her."

Riah halts.

"I didn't want to be the last person to see her alive."

Riah stands there, holding the dishes, staring at her old friend.

"I guess when I saw you, Anjali, I wanted you to be Riah so badly—if only to clear my own conscience."

She starts to say something but decides it's better left alone—better to leave the dead where they belong—buried in the past. Riah carries the dirty stack of dishes to the kitchen, letting their clamor fill up the silent void.

TWENTY

Wednesday, September 21st—Late Morning

Riah stares through the peephole, anxious for Sienna to leave her apartment. After Laine and Parshana left last night, she finished cleaning the kitchen, restoring it to how Anjali had left it. Although it gave her hours to ruminate about the mini bombshells Parshana unleashed on her, her thoughts still hampered her sleep. She needs to leave it all behind, as she decided yesterday. She blinks her eyes hard, giving her head a little shake; she re-focuses her mind.

After a few minutes, Riah hears the lonely creak of Sienna's condo door opening. It bangs shut with a vexed thud of finality; then comes the hollow click-clack of Sienna's high heels on the marble floor of the hallway. She comes into Riah's view.

Today, Sienna's stark white stiletto pumps match her curve-hugging white office-tailored dress. She's carrying her oversized Louis Vuitton purse on one shoulder and holding a medium-sized storage box with the opposite arm. Sienna struggles to press the elevator button.

As she waits for the elevator to reach the penthouse floor, Sienna turns to look at Anjali's apartment door as if she senses Riah's hypervigilant eyes itching for justice. Sienna takes a step forward.

Riah inhales sharply and holds her breath.

Sienna adjusts the box under one arm and raises her free hand to knock. She halts—her hand hanging mid-air, tethered to her invisible hesitation. As the elevator dings to signal its arrival, Buster, ceremoniously hiding in her purse, yelps at the sound. Sienna drops her hand as if the cord holding it up has been magically severed. She pivots abruptly and strides into the lift.

Riah lets the breath she was holding hostage escape with relief. She's glad Sienna has changed her mind; she can't imagine what she wants, anyway. On second thought, Riah knows exactly what Sienna yearns for—Michael. All of this is about Michael. How long has Sienna been Anjali and Michael's neighbor? Did they meet here in the apartment building and start having their affair later? Or had it begun before? Either way, Riah has an important detour assignment that will conclude this minor obsession with them.

Riah turns from the door and watches the security monitors. Seeing Sienna on the screen leaving the elevator, Riah observes as Sienna heads toward the underground garage and disappears off camera. A few minutes later, a black Mercedes with the top lowered pulls out of the garage. Sienna is wearing dark sunglasses, and her hands clutch the steering wheel. She waits for a car to pass and turns left onto the main road.

Riah watches the screen for another moment. Satisfied with a high degree of certainty that Sienna has left, Riah focuses on fulfilling her revenge plan. She wants to make things right for Anjali and put Sienna and Michael in their place. Reaching into Anjali's purse, Riah retrieves the indecent stack of photographs from Anjali's desk and the lust notes from Michael's hollowed-out book. She'll show them that Anjali isn't their fool. In a small, fractured way, this is her attempt to retrieve the power back from Michael and Sienna on behalf of Anjali.

She leaves the apartment and heads across the hall toward Sienna's apartment. Standing in front of the door for a moment, she knocks on it. After a minute of silence, she enters the code: 220689. She holds her breath until the keypad flashes green. She turns the door handle and cautiously opens Sienna's apartment door.

Riah slides into the apartment and closes the door noiselessly. She takes a long look at the suite and contemplates whether she should wreck the whole residence or leave the main floor as is. Does she want Sienna to know instantly that someone has been in her apartment, or is it better to drop the bombshell once Sienna enters her bedroom? Riah decides to go with the shock factor.

Sienna's apartment is nearly identical to Anjali's. It seems like the guy who designed Anjali's apartment, especially for her, used the same layout for this one. Riah spots the stairs and climbs them two steps at a time.

The second floor is noticeably different from Anjali's, with the bedroom being significantly smaller. Riah tours the second floor as though she were considering buying or renting the place. She browses the bedroom, taking in Sienna's space, before perusing the rest of the second story, including Sienna's walk-in closet and the ensuite bathroom.

The bathroom is lavish and feminine, with a Calcutta marble floor and countertops. The sparkling oval bathtub is the main attraction of the ensuite. Instead of tiles around the tub, as one would expect, the walls are lined with mirrors. Does Sienna like to watch herself when she takes a bath? There is a small shower in the ensuite, which is still wet with tiny beads of moisture. Perhaps the bathtub is for special occasions only. She leaves the bathroom through a second door that leads into a foyer. Riah spots a door to another room and opens it cautiously. The room is a personal gym. It's likely how Sienna stays fit, on top of whatever she does with Michael. The entire space is lined with mirrors. What is Sienna's fascination with mirrors? Riah closes the door to the gym and starts on what she had intended to do. She descends the stairs and stops at the bottom. Yes, this is an excellent place to start.

She sorts through the snapshots and picks the most innocent ones first. She tapes them to the stairs, one image on every third step. Once she reaches the top of the stairs, she takes one more harmless-looking picture and tapes it to Sienna's bedroom door. She re-enters the bedroom and lays all the lewd and not-so-innocent prints of Sienna and Michael on the bed. She places each one strategically. She scatters the love notes in front of the bed like rose petals.

Riah takes the last remaining picture of Sienna—the one of Sienna walking through a street, perhaps the *very* first one snapped of her—and enters the bathroom. She tapes the image to the vanity mirror. Riah snatches a tube of lipstick and opens it. Ruby-red—a perfect cliché! She draws a crimson circle around Sienna's image, followed by a line through it. Underneath the photo, she writes the word *whore*.

Riah smiles to herself. Sienna will be mortified when she discovers Riah's masterpiece—maybe even scared. Riah's grin widens.

Riah is pleased with herself. She believes Anjali would be proud of her handiwork too.

⁓

In Anjali's apartment, Riah rummages through the closet. There literally isn't anything here without a designer label. Chanel, Gucci, Hermès, Prada. They'll have to do, she reassures herself. Tugging on an array of silk blouses and chiffon dresses from the hangers, she lobs them into one of Anjali's empty suitcases. She'd need new clothing in California regardless, and it made zero sense to waste her newfound wealth on frivolous things like over-priced clothes.

Riah intends to live a quiet and simple life—now that she has enough money to live comfortably. She can even buy a new identity; she'll have to anyway, as she's not likely to get hers back from her sister. Once Anjali discovers she's been duped—that their mother was no longer alive—Anjali will be furious. Her twin will be even angrier when she discovers that Riah has stolen thousands of dollars' worth of clothes and jewelry from her. Anjali will be livid when she discovers Riah's ultimate betrayal—that all the money from her safety deposit box is gone too. Who keeps so much money in cash, anyway?

Riah wouldn't have known about the safety deposit box, had she not gone through Anjali's online banking statements and seen the yearly payment come out of one of her accounts. And then, this morning, when she was clearing out Anjali's jewelry, she found the key underneath the lining of one of the glass cases. Riah was going to the bank anyway and decided to check the safety deposit box. She was sure she would find documents but was ecstatic to discover cash—stacks and stacks of hundred-dollar bills. And now it is all hers.

Riah comes across a box hidden in the back of the closet. It's covered in ivory satin fabric and tied with a black ribbon. Like the box she found in Margaret's luggage last week, the package urges her to open it. She glances at her watch. It is getting way too late, and she should've already left the apartment and been on the road headed to Los Angeles hours ago. But her curiosity gets the best of her. Again.

She unties the ribbon and opens the box. Inside are several receipts and papers. Disappointed at not finding more, Riah dumps the remaining contents onto the ground. On top of the pile is a thin wallet, and as Riah picks it up, she realizes it's a passport holder. She flips it open to the first page. Her eyes scan the text, but her brain doesn't register the information at the same speed. Her hands begin to tremor, and she drops the book to the ground. A tsunami of unwanted truth pummels over her, leaving a debris of questions in its wake.

Why did Anjali tell her that she didn't have a passport?

Did she forget she had one?

This has to be a mistake—there has to be a logical explanation for why Anjali has this passport. She peers closer to the issue date on the travel document—it was issued two years ago and is valid for another three years. Anjali had lied about not having a passport. What else had she lied about? Anjali unequivocally wasn't anyone's fool—not Michael or Sienna's—nor Riah's!

Riah's ears perk up as the apartment door opens downstairs. All her senses become hypervigilant for a long-drawn-out moment.

"Anj! Anj! Are you home?" yells Michael.

Riah's whole body stiffens as a deep chill, creeps through her soul. She suppresses a shudder.

Holy Fuck—what is he doing here?

She tosses everything into the suitcase, pushes it further into the closet, and throws a blanket over it. Riah composes herself before hurrying out of the room. She arrives at the top of the stairs as Michael ascends. She needs to get out of here, but how?

Michael spots her, and a shadow of relief passes over his face.

"Where have you been?" he asks as she descends the stairs.

"Well, that's obvious, I'm here," she says. "Where else did you expect me to be?"

Michael is standing at the bottom of the stairs, with a small suitcase in one of his hands. Why's he back so soon?

"I thought you'd still be at the café," he says. He drops his suitcase with a dull thud.

"Oh, I had come home to grab something—some paperwork for the café," says Riah, hoping it sounds like a reasonable explanation. "How was your trip?" she asks, changing the topic. She needs to tread lightly until she figures out what is happening.

"It was okay—I'm worn out, though."

"Oh, you should rest," says Riah as she reaches the bottom of the stairs. She is face-to-face with him. He is much more handsome in person; she can see what other women might find attractive about him. His dirty blonde hair is tousled, and he has a bit of stubble along his jawline and chin, but he's still good-looking. What is he thinking? Does he notice a difference in his Anjali?

He leans in to give her a kiss but is interrupted. A light knock on the front door of the apartment diverts his attention.

Riah lets out the breath she didn't realize she has been holding.

Michael walks over to the door and checks who it is through the peephole. He pauses a moment before opening the door wider to reveal who is standing there. It's Sienna.

What is she doing here? It's as though she knew he is back home. It seems like she knows more about Michaels's whereabouts than Riah or Anjali combined.

"Hi," says Sienna.

"Hey, what's up?" asks Michael.

Sienna glances past Michael and spots her. "Hi, Anjali," says Sienna. Riah stares back at Sienna through cold eyes, making no attempt at concealing her displeasure. Turning her attention back to Michael, Sienna asks him: "Can you look at something in my apartment?—I think one of the pipes in my kitchen is busted."

Michael turns to Riah, who is still standing at the bottom of the stairs.

"Go," says Riah. "You should help our neighbor out," she says with a smile.

"Okay, babe, I'll be right back," says Michael as he follows Sienna to her apartment.

As soon as the door closes, Riah races up the stairs. She trips at the top of the landing and half sprawls to the floor.

The money and the jewelry are the only things on Riah's mind now. Luckily, she has packed those in a separate weekender bag. She'll have to leave everything else behind. She should grab the bag and get the hell out of here before Michael comes back. Likely, Sienna has been in her apartment and seen the surprise Riah left for her. Sienna seemed calm, but she is probably freaking out and wants to show Michael what has happened.

She grabs the bag from behind the closet door and pounds down the stairs. The agreement forms and keys to the rental car are in the kitchen. Passing by, she overhears Michael and Sienna's heated, hushed voices in the hallway as she heads toward the kitchen. It isn't hard to guess what they're arguing about.

Riah grabs the keys and papers and stuffs them into the front pocket of the weekender bag. The apartment door opens, and then the hollow click of the door shutting reverberates through her heart. She is out of time! She opens one of the island's large cupboard doors and tosses the bag in. Something catches her eye, but she hears Michael's footsteps coming closer. She slams the door and faces the kitchen sink. She turns on the water and pretends to be absorbed in washing the dishes. Fortunately, she had left a couple of drinking glasses in the tub earlier.

Michael comes into the kitchen.

She can feel him standing there—his eyes drilling into the back of her skull.

"Did you help Sienna with whatever she wanted?" Riah asks over her shoulder.

He doesn't say anything.

Riah stops the water and reaches for a dishtowel. As she dries her hands, she turns to face Michael. He looks much paler now, bordering on sallow. "What's wrong?"

His hands are clenching the top of the kitchen island, his knuckles turning white. He stares at her with contempt. "Do you know what you've done?" he asks.

Riah feigns bewilderment. "What are you talking about, Michael?"

"Don't play stupid with me, Anj!" He steps around the island and comes closer to her.

Riah stumbles backward.

"You couldn't leave it alone, could you?" he asks. His tone is dangerously quiet. He steps closer to Riah.

They are face-to-face again. His face now carries a heavier, meaner shadow; his previous handsome charm has vanished.

"Leave what alone?" Riah spits out. "Leave alone the fact you've been cheating on me? Leave alone that you're clearly in love with her? Leave alone your whore?"

Michael's eyes grow wide with surprise. She has caught him off guard. What is he shocked about—that she knows everything, or because she has dared to question him? He shoves her hard against the countertop. The surprise in his eyes is rapidly replaced with anger. There's evil in his enraged appearance—she has seen this look before.

The realization of the grave danger she has put herself in morphs into visceral reality in a split second. She tries to push him back, but he does not budge. He wraps his hands around her neck and squeezes tight. Panic has risen into her throat, but she is caught in this choke. She struggles to grab something from the counter—anything she can get her hands on to defend herself from this unhinged lunatic. But there's nothing.

"Do you like this?" he asks. He exerts more pressure. Excruciating pain reverberates through her as if her heart is hammering in her throat.

She grabs at his hands and digs her nails into his skin. He squeezes her throat tighter. She's losing consciousness as she falls to her knees. With as much effort as she can muster, she lifts her hand and punches him in the crotch—once, twice, three times.

He falters and releases hold of her throat. She tries to rise, but he strikes her with the back of his hand, disorienting her again.

Digging her nails into the floor, she attempts to crawl toward the kitchen island. She remembers seeing a baseball bat in the cupboard.

"Anj, don't make me hurt you more," he says. He sounds shocked that she's fighting back. He punches her in the head.

She hits the ground hard, her head smashing against the cold, tiled floor. He kicks her in the stomach, over and over again.

Why won't he stop?

She tries to scream, but her protests escape her throat like the low moans of an injured animal. Then, everything goes black.

TWENTY-ONE

Wednesday, September 21st—Late Evening

Sadie Harper loves the TV show *Crime Scene Investigation* (CSI). As a teenager, she would binge-watch an entire season over a weekend, often watching the same episode twice. Her parents had thought it was a phase, but much to their surprise, this obsession with solving crime and forensic science became the foundation of Sadie's career.

In college, Sadie studied Forensic Science, and she was one of the only students who didn't cringe when they saw their first dead body in the lab. Professor Ward had five cadavers shipped to the lab, and the students had to work in groups of three. Unfortunately (or luckily for Sadie), two of the other students who were supposed to be in her group became sick when they saw the dead body. The corpse was of a woman, in her mid-twenties, not much older than each of them. Her two male peers asked to be excused. Professor Ward wasn't happy, but he'd rather have productive students than sick ones in his class. He asked the rest of the students who wanted to be paired with Sadie, but she told him she preferred to work alone.

This cadaver was their semester-end case study. The trainees had one week to study the body, and they were to write and submit an examination report by the end of it. She studied the cadaver and decided to name her Lizzy—she looked like a *Lizzy*. As these bodies were donated to the University, Sadie knew it couldn't have been anything terrible that killed this girl. She tried to picture what Lizzy's life had been like. Sadie often talked to herself when she worked and didn't care about the strange glances she received sometimes.

Many of Sadie's mannerisms hadn't changed in the last ten years. She still preferred to work alone, muttered to herself, and felt socially awkward in most situations. Often, she felt the pressure to be someone else—to hide a part of her personality. Take, for example, the concept of working with others. She knew crime-solving took a team because everyone saw things from their own perspective. But this is where Sadie felt she was different. She thought she could remove her biases and see the crime scene from another angle. It's like Sadie had a knack for putting herself in the killer's, victim's, or witness' shoes. She often knew what had happened at a crime scene before the forensic evidence was examined—like a sixth sense, or something like it.

Her mother liked watching shows like *48 Hours*, where they depicted real-life crime stories. Her mother hated it when Sadie ruined the ending and revealed the wrongdoer in her matter-of-fact tone in the middle of the show.

"Sadie, why do you always do that? I want to watch the whole show and come to my own conclusions."

"Mom, it doesn't work that way. They are going to tell the story based on the evidence discovered. Technically, you can't draw your own conclusions. You have to follow what the science tells you."

"Okay, dear, but you ruined a good two hours for me."

Although she had told her mother that a good investigator followed the science, she could envision what had transpired. She never disclosed this ability to anyone; she thought people—especially her colleagues—would believe she was a freak. She wasn't sure when it had started; perhaps it was with the first body she was given to study: Lizzy. She took one look at Lizzy and knew she had committed suicide. Of course, she had no way to prove it. All Sadie could do was call it a hunch. However, using the different techniques she had learned throughout the semester, including DNA profiling, Sadie was able to argue that suicide was the cause of death for her case study. Sadie earned the highest grade in her class; some of her peers whispered rumors that Professor Ward likely felt sorry for Sadie because she worked on the case study on her own, without any group partners. But she knew she had earned it, and the others were, simply put, jealous.

Now it was different. You were expected to work as part of a team. Yet, over time, Sadie had learned how to fly under the radar. There was often a high level of emotional intelligence required for situations that involved others. Her mother called her a sponge once—she was speaking to her primary grade schoolteacher, inquiring about enrolling Sadie into a gifted program. Sadie remembers the teacher raising her eyebrow and asking her mother which child was hers again. "Sadie Harper?" asked the teacher, not even hiding her surprise that anyone would consider enrolling Sadie in a program for the gifted. *Average*—she had gleaned the word from her teacher's lips. "My child, Sadie Harper, is anything but average," was her mother's response. Her mother had taken her hand and escorted her off school property, and Sadie was homeschooled for the following four years. All these experiences had led her onto a particular path—today's destination.

Detective Sadie Harper arrives at Anjali and Michael Murphy's apartment building in Pacific Heights in the early evening hours of Wednesday, September the twenty-first—it's 7:15 p.m. to be exact. She's working the night shift this week. Often it is hectic during the beginning part of the evening but tends to taper off, with idle time usually spent doing paperwork. Today, however, she knows she'll spend the better part of the evening at the Murphys' apartment collecting crime-scene evidence. As soon as she arrives at the apartment building, she takes numerous mental notes. She finds it best not to make notes in her police notepad in heightened situations like this—it makes people nervous. And curious.

The older security guard by the desk is pale and visibly upset as he wipes his brow and dabs his eyes with a navy handkerchief. Two other uniformed officers from her division are questioning him. Either he's nervous about being questioned by the police or knows the victims. She nods at one of the police officers as she walks by. There was a death on the scene—it's why she has been called in. She's alone tonight; her regular partner, Detective Broly, has called in sick for his shift today—likely on another *Monique-bender*. She has been intending to have a discussion with her lieutenant about it. She doesn't like ratting on her colleague, but she can see he has been struggling recently. She is concerned for him; his drinking coincides with his girlfriend, Monique, who keeps coming in and out of his life. Broly is *good* when Monique isn't around—actively at the gym, eating healthy, and staying off the booze. When Monique is around, he becomes the worst version of himself.

Sadie approaches the elevator, moving her jacket to the side to expose the police badge on her belt. "Detective Harper," she says to the third police officer, who is blocking the elevator marked *private*. He moves to the side and presses the button to summon the elevator. He holds the door open for Sadie, and then leans into the lift and presses a button.

"Penthouse 2B," he says.

"Got it," she says. She catches a glimpse of his baby-blue eyes as the elevator door closes between them. He's a hottie—she'll have to find out his name later. The elevator dings its arrival on the second floor of the penthouse suites. Sadie steps into the hallway and faces a door labeled Penthouse 2B in gold chrome script. Fancy!

The apartment door is ajar and roped off with standard police tape. Sadie takes out a notebook from the side pocket of her blazer and jots a note: *Talk to 1st-floor penthouse occupants.*

Sadie slides on a pair of booties and nitrile gloves, and then pushes the apartment door open. A police officer turns to look at Sadie as she ducks underneath the police tape. Sadie flashes her badge, and the officer nods her head.

"Harper! It's about time you got here. Where's Broly?" asks her lieutenant as he waves her over.

"He's out tonight, sir," Sadie says, walking toward Lieutenant Washington. "What do we have?"

"One dead male, early thirties—he's still in the kitchen. And one in critical condition—a woman, in her thirties too—we called in a bus to take her to the hospital. She's on her way to Saint Francis."

"Was she talking?" asks Sadie as she jots things in her notebook.

"No, she was unconscious with a faint pulse. Looks like domestic violence, but no conclusions until CSU collects and analyzes all the evidence."

"Hmm, who's working the scene?"

"MacDonald and one of his newer guys. They're collecting DNA and dusting the main scene of the altercation—the kitchen."

"Where do you want me?" she asks. She silently hopes the lieutenant says she can help anywhere but the kitchen, though she knows she can't avoid Brett MacDonald forever. Brett and Sadie had a *very* brief fling a month ago. One night of too much rum, tequila, vodka, and some heavy flirting led to a hot one-night stand. Sadie enjoyed herself, and although they both agreed they wouldn't be weird about it on the job, there has been an unspoken tension on Brett's part ever since. Sadie believes Brett wanted more and was disappointed when Sadie made it clear it was a one-time arrangement—no strings attached. Guys were so weird—Sadie would have thought the type of fling that she and Brett had was every guy's dream. She couldn't figure it out, nor did she have the time. She'd dodge Brett until the awkward situation blew over.

"The team has been concentrating their efforts in the kitchen. They might be here all night before taking the body to the morgue. No one has had a chance to collect evidence in the rest of the apartment, and there was a witness—sort of—she'll need to be interviewed."

"Who is it?" asks Sadie.

"Neighbor from Penthouse 2A." He glances at his notebook. "Sienna Nash—an officer is calming her down—she made the 911 call."

"Was she here?"

"Not sure. You'll have to interview her."

"Okay, I'm gonna look around here first, make notes about where to dust, and see what the rest of the apartment has to tell us."

"Sounds good, Harper," he says. He turns away and hurriedly answers his ringing phone.

✤

Sadie scans the main floor of the apartment. There isn't much to go on—no indication of a struggle here. Nothing appears to be out of place on the pristine floor—either the cleaners have been in recently, or one of the residents has a severe OCD for cleanliness. She observes the single picture in the living room. She assumes these are the penthouse owners, and leans closer to the image, careful not to touch anything. The man looks familiar—Sadie knows him from somewhere but can't put her finger on it. She scribbles in her notepad before replacing it in the back pocket of her pants.

She pulls out a fresh pair of disposable gloves from her blazer pocket and puts them on. Her mind wanders to the crime scene in the kitchen. But it will have to wait—Brett will have to wait. She heads to the stairs, guessing the couple's bedroom is on the second floor. Climbing the stairs, Sadie methodically scans the area for evidence. She truthfully likes the investigative part of her profession—tedious to some of her colleagues—but she enjoys it.

"Damn, Mr. and Mrs. Richie-Rich," she says out loud. Her eyes dart around, relieved no one else is there. If she had overheard one of the other uniformed officers say something similar, she would reprimand them without hesitation.

She takes in the entire second floor. She's still young, and there's still time for her to save money and accumulate the wealth it would take to own a quarter of this apartment. Yet a part of Sadie can't help but be jealous. She shakes her head as if to dispel her wandering thoughts.

Her eyes scrutinize the bed—king size, and it looks like it hasn't been slept in today. It wouldn't seem important to some, but details like this help establish a timeline. It demonstrates precisely what the couple was—or wasn't—doing at the time of the altercation. She wants to go into the kitchen. She knows that if she visually discerns the scene there, she will not need to assume so much here. Convincing herself to take notes on the rest of the second floor before going downstairs, she braces herself for how she'll feel when she faces Brett.

Sadie examines the rest of the master bedroom and then walks into the large walk-in closet. The scene appears more haphazard here. Finally, some action. She takes note of the glass presentation cases—ten of them, aligned on individual pillars, all empty. They are like the ones she has seen in high-end jewelry stores. Each of them is closed and locked—Sadie peers at one of them closer. The lock is intact. She pulls out her notebook and scribbles a reminder to have them dusted for prints. The glass boxes may have been empty to begin with, or perhaps they were recently installed. Or someone who has access to them has cleared them out—another possibility.

Only someone who had access and time to spare would have left the impression that these were untouched.

Sadie spots something sticking out from underneath the row of dresses at the far end of the closet. She steps closer, swishing the clothes aside to inspect what had caught her eye—it's a suitcase. She kneels and tugs the bag toward her. The case isn't zipped and appears as though it has been shoved out of sight. The suitcase is filled with clothes—*unfolded and messy*, jots Sadie in her book. She lifts some of the clothing and spots an American passport. Opening it, she verifies the passport is in the name of Anjali Murphy—the same female in the picture in the living room downstairs. So Mrs. Murphy was packing to go somewhere, and she was interrupted—but by who? Sadie is even more curious about what was kept in these glass display cases—perhaps they weren't *always* empty. Was Anjali Murphy preparing to leave her husband?

Sadie takes a quick look into the ensuite bathroom—nothing out of the ordinary. As Sadie heads downstairs, she becomes aware of another room off in the corner. The door to the room is shut. Sadie steps closer, tilting her ear against the wood; she doesn't hear any sounds coming from the other side, but she must be sure. She cups her right hand around her gun and draws a deep breath. Turning the doorknob with her left hand, she pushes the door open and stands to the side. The room is empty and dark. It appears to be a home office; she steps in and searches the wall for the switch. The pot lights turn on, illuminating the room. It indeed is an office. Again, no sign of a struggle in here either. Sadie makes a couple of notes in her notebook and leaves the room.

Sadie decides it's time to see the kitchen and the scene of the homicide—it's time to see Brett. Her lieutenant's voice comes booming from the kitchen as she heads downstairs. The female cop is still standing by the door, likely responsible for ensuring no unauthorized individuals enter the apartment. A compact carry-on suitcase sits at the foot of the stairs—was it coming or going? The residence is oddly serene for a homicide scene.

Sadie pushes the swinging kitchen door open. The kitchen is massive. She speculates which one in the couple was the gourmet cook— it's evident this room was designed with the food connoisseur in mind. Past the island, she can see the body—male. Both Brett MacDonald and Lieutenant Washington glance at Sadie as she enters the room. The lieutenant, in mid-sentence, continues speaking, but Brett's eyes jam-lock onto her. Despite Brett wearing a Tyvek suit, she feels a familiar thud in her chest.

Sadie comes around the kitchen island and squats to the floor. She studies the body and the visible signs of trauma. His face is bruised and bloody, with blood splattered all over his clothes and the floor. The body is already outlined with white tape. Sadie becomes aware of the baseball bat on the countertop—still in the process of being bagged as evidence. It appears they're done with the body and will be taking it to the morgue soon. One of Brett's assistants is taking pictures of the window and door on the far side of the kitchen, which seems to lead outside to a rooftop terrace.

"Want to fill me in?" she asks, looking remorsefully from the Lieutenant to Brett.

The lieutenant nods at Brett. "MacDonald, update Harper, and let's get the body to the morgue—it's beginning to stink in here." The lieutenant's phone rings again. "Washington here," he says in a gruff voice as he heads out of the kitchen.

Brett clears his throat and waits till Lieutenant Washington is out of hearing range. "Hi Sadie, how are you?"

Sadie smiles. To look at them, one would think they were at a bar instead of a brutal crime scene. "Hey MacDonald," she says, trying to sound professional and unexpectedly conscious of the other person in the room. "Want to tell me what we have?"

"Yeah, Harper," he says. Trying to sound casual and professional, he continues. "I'll let Ridgefield take the lead on this one." He gestures toward the young man dusting a doorknob with a broad brush.

Ridgefield glances sideways, realizing he's being called over. "Let me finish here," he says. His voice cracks like a bashful schoolboy.

"I think you're making him nervous." Brett leans in closer. "What are you doing later tonight?"

"I'm on nights this week, and I'm not off until morning," says Sadie. Stepping back, she stares hard at the body. Her lieutenant was right—the kitchen reeks of death.

"I can wait," says Brett. "This poor guy is going to get me some OT today," he says, shaking his head at the victim.

"Killed by the bat?" she asks.

"Looks like it," he says. "Although I'm gonna need to examine him at the lab to conclude that in the death report."

"Did they find any ID on him?" Sadie asks.

"Yeah, his name is Michael Murphy—the guy owns this penthouse."

"Looks like a couple lived here. What did the girl who was taken to the hospital look like?"

"She was brown—of South Asian descent, I think."

"I heard she was unconscious?"

"Yeah, but she'll live. She didn't look as beat up as much as this guy," says Brett. His glance ricochets from the body to her. They lock eyes.

"You think she did it?" Sadie asks.

"Hard to say," he says, scratching his head with one of his gloved knuckles. "The dude looked like he fought back, though—his knuckles are bruised, and he has scratches on his hands and wrists."

"Did anyone take any evidence off of her?"

"No—there was no time. The woman was still breathing, so they rushed her to the hospital."

She glances at Michael Murphy. She doesn't want to call him the victim—not yet, at least.

"What are you thinking?" Brett asks.

Before she can say anything, her lieutenant comes back into the kitchen. "Harper, I need you to take a statement from the neighbor who called 911—Sienna Nash," he says. "Let's go." The kitchen door swings behind his abrupt disappearance.

As Sadie starts to leave the room, Brett touches her arm. "Try to come back later," he says.

As he winks, her heart leaps with a solid thud, desire shading her cheeks pink. She flashes him a tight-lipped smile and retreats out of the kitchen after her lieutenant.

~

Sadie stands in the hallway outside the open door of Penthouse 2A. A beautiful blonde is pacing the floor, and a couple of police officers are standing around. The blonde's eyes shoot up when Lieutenant Washington enters the apartment.

"It's about time," the woman says. "What took you so long?" She places one hand on her hip and glares at the lieutenant like a stern, annoyed schoolteacher.

Sadie raises her eyebrow, her interest piqued by this woman who has some chutzpah to talk to her lieutenant with annoyance— oblivious to who he is.

"I'm sorry for keeping you waiting, Ms. Nash," says Lieutenant Washington, seemingly extra accommodating. *Is she someone famous?* If she is, Sadie doesn't recognize her. One of Sadie's guilty pleasures is reading online gossip news feeds like TMZ—sure, one could say she was raised in the digital age and, therefore, normal for her generation. The gossip feeds and fake news are all about entertainment—and escaping from the harsh reality of police work.

"I'd like to introduce you to Detective Harper. She's the lead criminal investigator on the case," he says. He cues Sadie to enter and come forward. "Detective Harper is going to take your statement." He nods at the officers, and they pass by Sadie, leaving the apartment. "Why don't you have a seat," he says.

"Okay," she says. "Will you stay?" She blinks back at Lieutenant Washington; her attitude is seemingly more demure as she shrinks into the red leather couch.

"Of course," he says. He takes a seat in one of the armchairs, square opposite the witness.

Sadie's instinct is to go hard on this woman, but she needs to ease into it and gain her trust first. She pulls out her notebook and flips it to the first empty page. "Hello, Ms. Nash. I'm Detective Sadie Harper." She glances at her watch and scribbles *Sienna Nash   8:15 p.m.* at the top of the page.

Sienna dabs her eyes with a tissue in what appears to be a dramatic ploy. "I will tell you everything I know. It's not much, though."

"Let's start at the beginning," says Sadie. "I understand you called 911?"

"I did—" She's about to say more but pauses, remaining silent.

"Okay, walk me through what led you to call 911."

"I went over to Michael's apartment to thank him—he had come over earlier to check the kitchen pipe that I thought was leaking. The apartment door was open, which I thought was strange. But then I heard Michael and Anjali arguing in the kitchen, so I left."

"Anjali?" asks Sadie.

"Yes, Anjali—Michael's wife."

"And what were Michael and Anjali fighting about?"

"I wouldn't say they were fighting," Sienna says. "They were arguing. I didn't think anything of it—it's why I left—I let them have their privacy."

"Did you hear what they were arguing about? What words were exchanged which led you to believe they were arguing?"

Sienna stares back at Sadie. A coldness appears to wash over her face as the color drains from her skin. She turns toward Lieutenant Washington and says with deliberation, "I think they were arguing about Michael having an affair."

Sadie searches her lieutenant's face for a clue to his reaction before jotting several keywords in her notebook. "So, you came back to your apartment and called 911 because you heard them arguing about his infidelity, and you were worried about it escalating?"

"No, I didn't call 911 right away," she says, dabbing her eyes with the tissue. "If I had called right away, Michael would still be alive." Her voice cracks despite her efforts to contain herself.

Sadie leans in closer. "I know this is difficult, Ms. Nash, but I need to ask you these questions. It's essential to establish a timeline."

"I know, I know," mumbles Sienna in between tears.

"So, you came back to your apartment. And what did you do then?"

"Nothing, really. I put leftover meatloaf in the oven to warm it, and I went upstairs to change. I came back downstairs about ten minutes later to eat. I read some work emails, so it took me a bit longer to finish my meal."

"How much time had passed since you had left your neighbors' apartment?"

"I don't know. About forty-five minutes or so."

Lieutenant Washington's mobile phone starts ringing. He yanks it from his blazer pocket and answers it as he rises from his seat. He nods at Sadie, signaling she should continue without him. "Captain," he says. He rushes out of the apartment, but Sadie can hear him conversing in the hallway in a brisk and hushed tone. He sounds like he is getting reamed out for something.

"Okay, what happened next?"

Sienna takes a deep breath. "I went back to Michael's apartment. Honestly—" she takes a long pause. "I wanted to talk to Michael. I needed to tell him something. The door was still ajar. I knocked, but no one answered, so I opened the door further. I thought they had gone upstairs—but then I heard a strange noise from the kitchen."

"What kind of noise?" Sadie leans in closer, sitting on the edge of the armchair. She's hooked on every word Sienna Nash is telling her. This is the part she enjoys—hearing words, listening to every detail of the witness account, and tying it back to the evidence at the crime scene.

"It was a moan—like someone was hurt—so I went into the kitchen," says Sienna.

"What did you see?" asks Sadie.

"Anjali was standing by the kitchen sink. She was kind of leaning against the counter, and she was breathing hard. I thought she was heaving in the sink, but then she turned around. When she saw me, she dropped the bat and keeled over."

Sadie scribbles in her notebook, accumulating Sienna's account word for word.

"I came around the kitchen island to help her—that's when I saw Michael on the floor. I was so scared. I didn't know what to do. I went over to Michael right away." Sienna throws her face in her hands and weeps—heavy and raspy.

This is the part Sadie hates; she can deal with someone who's angry, but she recoils from anyone in tears—real tears. It is awkward; Sadie doesn't like emotions—especially crying. Perhaps this is why she isn't in a real relationship—one-night stands are more natural.

"It's okay," says Sadie. She rises and takes a seat next to Sienna. "What happened next?"

"He wasn't breathing. I checked for a pulse," Sienna says. "You know how they do on television, but I couldn't find it." She continues to sob. "I ran back to my apartment and called 911. I told them to hurry!" Sienna fixates on Sadie's face as if searching for confirmation she had done well. With her tear-stained eyes and ruined make-up, Sienna is damn compelling.

Throughout Sienna's account, not once does she seem concerned about Anjali's safety. Anjali passed out in front of her, but she went straight to Michael. *Why?* Earlier, after listening to the 911 call, Sadie had thought there was only one person in the kitchen—only one injured person. At this point, this is just a story—the fingerprints, hairs, and fibers will uncover the facts; later, these will corroborate or refute Sienna's statement.

TWENTY-TWO

Thursday, September 22nd—Afternoon

Anjali takes another sip of her cappuccino. She draws a deep breath in—the autumn air, crisp in her lungs. She holds it there for as long as she can and then gradually exhales, feeling all her reservations evaporate into the Paris air. She puts on the dark Prada sunglasses she bought at the airport en route to France. Sitting in the sunny part of an old Parisian café, she notices how warm the sun is for the early evening, even though it's the beginning of fall. She likes it—no—she loves it, all of it. She supposes the warm weather is an aspect of her new life she'll get used to. Michael always warned her of the dangers of the sun, indicating he didn't want her to get darker. *You are just the right shade of brown*, he had once said. She had tried not to be offended, but inside she had been.

She will have to get used to many new facets of her new life— her new life without Michael. A smile dances on her face as the realization of her freedom settles into her bones. She is finally free of that man. Closing her eyes, she relaxes at the thought of getting used to this beautiful life of her own. She'll have to find her own way of mourning him, because she knows she didn't always feel this hatred for him.

Anjali's mind travels back to when she first met Michael, sitting at the bar in the Beretta restaurant at the hotel where she was staying. It was her first time in San Francisco, which was odd since she'd traveled worldwide for work. She was in town for a conference as a guest speaker. She had passed the restaurant several times in the last three days, but had decided to check it out and have a quick drink that afternoon. She often judged restaurants she hadn't been to before by having a cocktail—usually a Dirty Martini with extra olives. If the martini was appetizing, usually the food was too.

The bar was empty except for Anjali and another customer sitting a few seats away—a handsome man preoccupied with his phone. The bartender brought Anjali her martini and placed a bowl of mixed nuts near her glass. Anjali was about to thank the young man when he winked and mumbled, "No problem."

Then he turned his attention to the other customer. "Mr. Murphy—did you want another?"

The man responded with a nod. He gave her a slight glance but then focused his attention back on his phone. Anjali reached into her purse to retrieve her notebook but paused and decided against it. She needed to unwind, so no work, she told herself as she took the first sip of her martini. She liked the way it felt on her tongue, cold and salty, and as the liquid trickled down her throat, she could feel the tension in her shoulders relax.

"Hey!" she said to the man a few seats away. "Is your name Shaun Murphy?"

The man distractedly glanced up at the bartender and then shifted his gaze to Anjali. He seemed taken aback by her seemingly random question. "No, my name is Michael."

"Oh, okay, sorry to bother you, I used to know a Shaun Murphy when I was a kid, and I thought maybe—" she said, letting her words linger and giving him a tiny shrug of her shoulders.

Michael's eyes held hers, taking her in. He abruptly shut off his phone, slid it into his pocket, and moved one seat closer to Anjali.

She was pleased that she had captured his full attention, as if she had drawn him in with her magnetic pull.

"Well, this Shaun Murphy, whoever he is, is missing out."

"Oh?"

"Were you just as beautiful when you were a kid?"

Anjali let out a little laugh. It wasn't the cleverest pick-up line she'd heard, but she was enchanted by this stranger's charm. She and Michael had sat in the bar talking for hours—the electricity of attraction pulsating between them. She was delighted by how easy their conversation had been—they talked about why each of them was in San Francisco, what they did for a living, where they were raised as children. The bartender was discreetly attentive but slowed his check-ins when the bar became busier. At one point, Michael asked if she wanted to have dinner, but feeling woozy after three martinis on an empty stomach, she feigned having other plans. Although Anjali had enjoyed herself and felt an instant connection with Michael, her anxiety about moving too fast got the best of her. She told Michael she had dinner plans with work colleagues for eight p.m. and needed to go upstairs to her room to shower and change. She felt terrible about leaving, but he seemed gracious about it.

As she reached into her purse to get her wallet, Michael slipped his business card into her hand and said, "You're going to be late—drinks are on me."

She appreciated his kindness and felt guilty about lying to him; it was the first of many lies she'd tell him. She took the card and put it in her wallet before she had a chance to change her mind. "Goodbye, it was nice chatting," she said. She left the bar without looking back.

The following day, to her surprise, Michael was waiting in the lobby—she hadn't expected to see him. Although she was late for the last day of the conference, she slowed her pace, so when Michael turned around, she had reached him. He gave her a big boyish smile and held out two takeout coffee cups.

"Well, good morning, Anjali," he said.

"Good morning! Gosh, I hope one of those is for me."

"You know it!" he said, handing her one of the cups, "I'm not sure how you take it—"

"Anything is fine."

"Do you really need to go to your conference event today?" he said as he passed her one of the coffees.

"What did you have in mind?" she asked, hoping to convey her interest in his question.

"I had one meeting early this morning, and now I am free until my flight this evening. I thought we could explore the city together, as cheesy as it may sound."

"No, sounds great," she said, surprising herself at how fast she answered. "I haven't had the time to see much of the city since I arrived, and my flight home is also this evening."

"Well, it's settled—we are spending the day together!"

They ended up not only spending the day together but also delaying their flights and enjoying the entire weekend in their spontaneous new romance. For Anjali, it was a whirlwind from the moment they met; they got married eight months later. In their wedding vows, Michael had written that she was his unexpected plot twist—the one he hadn't seen coming. It's also hard to believe it all happened seven years ago—it felt much shorter. Other times, it was like she had known Michael all her life.

Their life together was significantly different now—like an unconscious uncoupling. Or perhaps it was more conscious than she wanted to believe. She's not sure when things changed; maybe it was gradual—maybe it wasn't. But they *had* changed. Anjali wipes the tears away. She could manage the cheating and dishonesty because she knew he couldn't fall in love with anyone the way he fell in love with her. However, on the fateful day when she lost the one thing still missing from her world, she knew she could no longer be with him. After the *incident*, the years were unbearable.

It had been like any other day—like how any of their other fights started. She was tidying up the kitchen before he got home. He was in a jovial mood, coming behind her and hugging her while she was emptying out the fridge. Since she'd become pregnant, her sense of smell had heightened, along with an acute awareness of Michael's indiscretions. The perfume of another woman, clinging to him, overpowered her.

"You should take a shower," she said as she stormed out of the kitchen.

"Why? Do I smell?" Michael asked, trailing behind her.

"Yes, you smell like the cheap whore you've spent the afternoon with." She glared at him as she straightened the pillows on the couch.

"Well, if you fucked me once in a while, Anj, I wouldn't be attracted to other hot women who want me."

"I'm pregnant, Michael—how do you think I got this way? I must have fucked you!"

"How do I even know it's mine?"

She dropped the pillow she was holding and proceeded to the stairs. Michael grabbed her arm as she tried to brush past him.

"How do I know it's mine?" he asked again in a much lower tone.

She yanked her arm away from his grip. "Well, unlike you, my love, I don't have time to be with anyone else. And why would I? I cherish the vows we made."

He stood there, staring at her.

"Michael, you're projecting your own sins on me. Of course, the cheater would think he's being cheated on." She turned to climb the stairs.

He grabbed her by the hair and swung her to the floor. It was so unexpected and happened so fast that she didn't have time to react. He kicked her repeatedly. And as quick as it had begun, it was over. She didn't have time to protect herself, let alone her baby.

"You shouldn't say such mean things to me, Anj," he said. "I'm going to take that shower you suggested." And with all his bitterness, he climbed the stairs.

She had laid there, face down, her tears pooling on the cold hardwood floor. She doesn't remember how long she lay there, but she had passed out at some point.

She woke up in bed the following day, stiff and sore, but she knew something else was wrong. When she stood up, she almost fainted at the sight of the bloodstain, stark against the white bedsheets. Later that day, her obstetrician confirmed what she already knew—*she* had lost their baby—*he* had murdered their baby.

That was over two years ago. Had her baby been born, he or she would be starting their terrible twos. What kind of parent would she have been? Deep inside, she knows she would have made a good one. Sadly, she resigns herself to the thought that the best outcome for her lost baby was to never have been born. Her child would not become accustomed to the pain Michael caused.

Her café had, in a way, replaced her loss and become her new baby. She misses her café. Her mother had assured her she'd take care of it and everything else she left behind for a clean start. She had told her mother she didn't want to know the details of what would happen afterward. She had decided to distance herself from the fray—done with the visceral violence that came with it.

Anjali feels the faint buzzing of her burner phone, drawing her back into the present. She doesn't need to check who is calling her—only one person has this number. She decides to ignore it, her instincts guiding her to stay under the radar for the time being. Now, her only desire is to bask in the setting sun for a while longer.

TWENTY-THREE

Friday, September 23rd—Late Afternoon

Sadie chucks the half-empty disposable coffee cups into the garbage bin nearby. She collects the haphazardly strewn file folders from her desk and stacks them neatly in a corner. Taking a seat, she rummages in the drawer for disinfectant wipes, grumbling to herself. She detests the night shift sometimes exclusively for this reason—the day officers aren't as considerate about keeping the surfaces clean as she is.

"One of the new recruits was parked there today," says her partner, Detective Broly. "I kicked him out for you." He smirks from the desk adjacent to hers.

"You should have told him to clean up after himself," she says.

Broly chuckles and takes a sip from a Peet's coffee cup.

She had left the precinct Thursday afternoon, almost pulling a double shift, and her lieutenant had instructed her to take the night off. She knew Broly hadn't been in yesterday either. "Where were you the last two nights, anyway?" she asks.

"Why, did you miss me?" He avoids glancing up at her.

"Hardly," she says. "But Washington did. You're going on desk duty the next time you skip out on work like that—so I heard," she scoffs.

"Nah, Washington loves me," he says. He's slouched in his

chair, squinting at his computer screen and absent-mindedly biting on the plastic lid of his coffee. He looks exhausted, like he's nursing one of his epic hangovers. "Ah man, I missed a homicide the other night. And in Pacific Heights—why didn't you tell me?"

"Oh, what—you would have come in?" She raises an eyebrow.

"Yeah, what detective doesn't like a good mystery," he says.

"Did you bring me one of those?" she asks, nodding toward his hands.

"I got your back, partner—black with a gazillion sugars."

She rises from her seat, leans over, and grabs the other untouched coffee. The cup is warm to the touch—he must have just arrived at work. "You could have led with that," she says. She leans back in her chair, flips the lid off, and savors a long sip from her cup. "Yeah, you missed out on taking a statement from a blonde hottie."

"Aww, man! Is she a suspect?"

"No, she's a witness. And the one who found the body and called 911." She pauses. "Yeah, one body, and another in the hospital." She tosses a folder onto his desk. "It's all in there."

"Wow, did you go home at all?" Broly asks. He takes the elastic band from the folder and flips through the typed pages.

"No, she had to do the job of two detectives," says Lieutenant Washington as he walks by their desks en route to his office.

Broly straightens his back and flushes with embarrassment.

"Harper, I need an update on the Murphy case," Washington says, changing his tone. He doesn't treat her like the other male police officers or detectives—he seems to go softer on her. Sometimes he speaks to her in his usual gruff tone, but she believes he does this for the sake of others—so they didn't pick up on the disparity in his approach to her.

He reminds her of her father, who was also a police officer. Her father is retired, but he spent the latter half of his career serving as a Captain. In his younger days, he was also a homicide detective.

Most people thought Sadie had followed in her father's footsteps. But not many people knew one of her father's nuances, something he would never admit if he were confronted about it—he didn't like dealing with dead bodies. Her father would often say to Sadie and her mother that he didn't have the stomach for it. He kept it to himself. But on homicide cases, he let the junior Detectives take the lead. "It builds character and experience," he'd say. But Sadie and her mother knew the truth. He had objected when Sadie told them she had been promoted to Homicide a few years ago. She loved it, and was eager to talk about the cases with him, but he didn't like hearing about it.

"Did the Medical Examiner make his report yet?" Lieutenant Washington asks her when she and Broly enter his office.

"No, I called him," she says. "He said likely later this morning."

"Alright. I'll need you two to stay on him. See if he'll give you any indication of which way he is leaning."

"Will do," she says. Lieutenant Washington is an involved boss, but he seems abnormally close to this one. Something is off—does he know the victim, or the parties involved? She'll ask Broly afterward. He usually has good instincts when it comes to these sorts of matters.

"Oh, and I need one of you to see the other victim in the hospital—Anjali Murphy. See if she's awake yet. We need to get her statement and figure out what happened."

"Yes, Lieutenant," says Broly. "I'll check with the hospital—which one did they take her to?" he asks.

"Catch up will you, Broly!" he responds.

Lieutenant Washington's phone rings, and he waves them away.

"Damn, he's in a bad mood," says Broly as they head back to their desks.

"Really? Seems like *Catch up will you, Broly* is his catchphrase," she says with a chuckle.

"Very funny!" says Broly. He grabs his jacket and tosses it over his shoulder.

"Do you want me to go with you to Saint Francis?" she asks.

"Yeah, so you can catch me up!"

◆

Detectives Harper and Broly enter the hospital a few minutes past six p.m. Broly approaches the information desk to inquire about Anjali Murphy's room. Sadie doesn't like hospitals much; they give her a sick feeling in the pit of her stomach. Oddly, she has no qualms with dead bodies, but hospitals make her feel dejected. She has never told anybody, but somehow Broly knows. On the way over, he thanked her for tagging along. She had rolled her eyes at him, but he'd still asked if she wanted to wait outside. She'd told him she'd go with him but didn't want to admit she was curious about Anjali Murphy and wanted to be the one to take her statement.

After taking Sienna Nash's statement, Sadie had gone back into the Murphys' apartment for a more thorough investigation of the scene. She captured extensive notes and used them to make her report. Ridgefield followed her around the condo, took pictures, and dusted for fingerprints with Sadie's instructions. She had a feeling Brett was jealous she hadn't asked him to collect and document the evidence with her. She had told him he should stay with the body. She had felt the spark as soon as she saw him again. The first time they had been together, she had attributed their undeniable chemistry to the alcohol they had consumed. But at the crime scene, the mutual attraction was still there—something she wasn't ready for.

Broly approaches Sadie. "She's on the third floor," he says.

"Is she awake?"

"No, but Washington assigned a couple of officers to watch over her."

"Really? He didn't tell me." She doesn't bother hiding her puzzlement, but reflects on *why* the lieutenant hadn't told her this last night.

"Don't worry about it," says Broly. It is as if he senses her thought process and her tendency to dwell on unimportant details.

"I'm not—but doesn't Washington seem a tad more invested in this case?" she asks. They head toward the bank of elevators.

"No more than usual," says Broly.

They enter a large elevator and ride in silence—the lift dings, and the doors open to reveal a busy intensive care unit. Sadie walks to the reception desk and flashes her badge to the nurse.

"Room 3019?" she asks, glancing at the nurse's name badge.

"Down the hall, to your left."

"Thanks, Diana," she says.

The nurse smiles back. Although Sadie doesn't like hospitals, she likes nurses. She remembers visiting her grandmother in the hospital the night she passed away. Sadie was nine. She didn't understand what the word *cancer* meant, but she'd heard it a lot in the hushed conversations between her parents. She heard things like *the cancer got her, the cancer was getting worse*, and *the cancer took her*. She had heard so much about *the cancer*, she believed it was a person. "I don't like the cancer," she had told her mom that night. One of the nurses who overheard Sadie's protests brought her chocolate pudding.

"This is it." Broly points to Anjali Murphy's room.

One police officer sits in front of the door. Another one is further down the hallway, talking on his cell phone. As they approach, Brett MacDonald and another nurse step out of the room.

"Hey, man," Broly says to Brett. "What are you doing here?" he continues, as if he can read Sadie's mind.

"Came to take some notes on this victim," he says. He nods in the direction of Anjali Murphy. "She's not awake yet, but we needed to collect evidence before the seventy-two-hour mark."

"Oh, is she a suspect?" asks Broly.

"There was only the two of them in the apartment, and we found her with a baseball bat in her hands," says Brett. "Can't rule it out."

"Alright, man, keep us posted when the M. E. is done with his report. Our Lieutenant is on our ass about this one," says Broly.

"Well, yeah, I'm not surprised," says Brett. "The vic was the Chief's nephew."

"Oh, wow! No one told us. No wonder," says Broly. "Well, thanks for shedding light on lieu's pressure." Broly slaps Brett on the shoulder before making his way into Anjali's hospital room. Sadie hangs back to talk to Brett.

"Your lieutenant didn't tell you?" asks Brett.

"No," Sadie shrugs.

"Ah, don't overthink it," he says, giving her a soft smile. "Are you off for a couple of days after your shift tonight?"

"I am. Going back on days as of Tuesday."

"Let's try to get away—think about it. I'll call you in the morning," he adds before she can object.

"Sure, call me later, and we can chat about it."

He winks at her, turns around, and heads toward the elevators.

Sadie is smiling as Broly comes out of the room.

"She's still out," he says. "Let's get out of here. I'm hungry."

"When are you not?"

TWENTY-FOUR

Sunday, September 25th—Morning

Riah hears the beeping, faint but constant. Staggering through the darkness, she makes a vain attempt to open her eyes, but they're heavy with the haze of sleep. It has been days since she has been lost in this endless maze, stumbling through empty hallways leading nowhere. This place is familiar, yet so unfamiliar to her. Often, voices hover over her like faint and garbled murmurs, but every now and then they are crisp. She pauses and listens. She slows her breathing, a feeble attempt to concentrate on what they're saying. But as quick as the words become coherent, these voices disappear. And she is left alone again to wander in this labyrinth of confusion.

Beep . . . beep . . . beep—*where is that coming from?* It has always been here, relentless and unnerving. She walks forward, and as she does, the sound fades. She turns around in the dark and walks back in the direction she came from. The beeping becomes stronger. She continues forward and arrives at a door. The door thumps like a heartbeat under her hand.

As she leans forward, the door pushes open with ease. Through the hazy gloom, she can see a tiny blood-red light flickering in sync with the beeping. With arms outstretched, she walks toward it. She stumbles over something, and without warning, the sound becomes deafening—BEEP! BEEP! BEEP!

The room floods in fluorescent white light as shapeless figures shrouded in pale blue garments come pouring through the door. "She's awake," one of them yells and flashes a bright light into her eyes, causing her to wince in pain.

She wants to speak, but her lips, crusty and cracked, feel as though they are glued shut.

"It's okay, Anjali. You are in the hospital."

Who is Anjali? They think my name is Anjali.

The nurse checks her vitals and taps something into a tablet. "The doctor will be by in a few minutes. We just paged him." She steps outside and is approached by two male police officers.

Riah tries to listen to their conversation, but they speak in hushed whispers. *This is bad.* One of the police officers takes a seat in the chair outside of Riah's hospital room. The other officer and the nurse saunter through the hallway, disappearing from Riah's line of sight.

∽

Sadie and Brett are entangled in bedsheets. After her shift ended yesterday morning, they met for breakfast and ended at his place. She would have preferred her home, but she knew her parents would be around, and she didn't want to explain who Brett was. She wasn't ready to introduce him quite yet.

Brett's place is in the same neighborhood as the restaurant they had breakfast in. When he asked if she wanted to go back to his apartment, she smiled and said *yes*. She felt very comfortable with him. She knew this was drastic, spending the weekend with someone she thought had been a one-night stand.

Sadie's phone rings. She glances toward the nuisance, bolting to a sitting position when she realizes who's calling. Sadie answers it with urgency.

On the other end, Broly says, "She's awake."

꩜

Riah opens her eyes and glances around the room—she must have dozed off. She's still in the hospital but no closer to remembering what landed her here. There's nothing in her mind but darkness. They had called her Anjali. The name sounded familiar, but she intuitively knew it wasn't her name—*what is her name?* She squints at the hospital bracelet on her wrist: *A. Murphy*. Why couldn't she remember anything?

She presses the grey button hanging on the right side of her bed, releasing a faint buzz in the hallway. And waits. A nurse appears in the doorway, pausing to look at the police officer sitting in the chair before entering Riah's room.

"Hello, dearie!" she says in a cheerful voice. "I see you're awake again."

"I need to go to the washroom."

"Oh, I think the doctor is coming back—he really should check you first," the nurse says. "Besides, you have a catheter in."

Riah surveys the plastic tube running along the side of the bed.

"Don't worry, he'll be here soon. I'll get you water in the meantime," she says, retreating from the room.

Riah touches the bandages on her head. A razor-sharp pain sears through her temples. Without warning, images come rushing at her like shards of glass. She's on the outside of a café window, staring at a woman. She's sitting on a bench side-by-side with the woman in a crowded place. She's with the woman in a well-decorated apartment. Then there's a man. He's frowning. He's angry now. Then it's blank. She winces in agony.

"Mrs. Murphy, I see you're awake."

She opens her eyes to a man towering over her.

He pulls over a small rolling stool and takes a seat. "My name is Doctor Marajaan. We've been worried about you." The doctor pulls out a small device from his pocket and leans closer. He flashes a light into her left eye and then her right one. "But you seem to be doing better now. Do you know where you are?"

"In the hospital—isn't it obvious?"

"Good. And do you know your name?"

Without hesitating, she answers. "Anjali." Riah decides it's easier to be who they think she is.

"Anjali?" His question lingers in the space between them.

"Anjali Murphy," she says with conviction. She shifts in her bed, propping herself into a comfortable position.

"Great! And Anjali Murphy, do you know what day of the week it is?"

Riah shakes her head. There is only so much she can fake.

"It's Sunday," he says.

"Oh," she says.

"Do you remember what happened to you?"

"I don't have the faintest clue," she says. "Seems like I hit my head."

"Yes, you had a serious head injury and were unconscious when they brought you in. But there doesn't appear to be lasting damage. Memory loss can be frustrating and scary after a traumatic event, but usually, it's temporary. Give it time."

The smile in his eyes puts her mind at ease.

He clears his throat. "Anjali, there's a detective here from the San Francisco Police Department. She would like to talk to you. Do you think you may be ready for that?" he asks.

"I'm not sure. What do the police want from me?"

"It's alright," Dr. Marajaan says, patting her hand. "I will be here the whole time."

Riah has a bad feeling in her gut, but she half-smiles at his reassurance.

He walks to the door and pokes his head out into the hallway. "You may speak with her now," he says to someone in the corridor.

Dr. Marajaan steps aside as a short woman in her early thirties strolls into the room, exuding confidence with every step. She's wearing dark grey pants with a matching suit jacket over a black t-shirt. Her police badge is conspicuously poised on the left side of her belt. Her brunette hair is wavy and damp-looking, as though she had rushed out of the shower to be here. She's sporting a natural, no-make-up look.

"Hi, Anjali. I'm Detective Harper from SFPD."

"Hello, I understand you want to talk to me?" Riah asks, glancing over at Dr. Marajaan, lingering by the doorway and staring at his tablet.

"We're glad you're awake," the detective says, moving to the foot of the bed. "How are you feeling?"

"I think I'm okay," she says hesitantly.

"I know you recently gained consciousness from the injuries you sustained, but as the lead detective on your case, I need to understand what happened. Can you tell me how you got injured?" The detective slides a notebook from her back pocket.

"No, I don't really remember how I got here. My memory is all jumbled up."

"You and your husband, Michael Murphy, were hurt in your penthouse apartment. So anything you recall will be helpful."

"My husband? Michael?" asks Riah.

"Your husband sustained significant injuries," says Detective Harper.

Riah frantically assembles the confusing thoughts in her head. They think she's Anjali. She doesn't know who she is. She doesn't know what happened to her. She doesn't remember Michael. While she struggles to make sense of this chaos, somehow, *being* Anjali feels familiar. "Where is Michael?" she asks.

"I'm sorry to inform you, Michael is dead."

"Dead?" Her voice becomes a hoarse, panic-stricken croak. "How?"

"Anjali, this is where your memory of what happened is key to our investigation."

She feels a knot in her chest tightening. She didn't even know Michael, yet the tears were hovering, threatening to break through the surface. "But how did Michael di—die?" She mouths the last word, unable to utter it out loud.

"Michael sustained significant injuries to the head and chest. He was pronounced dead on the scene. But we don't know who did this or why. Hopefully, we can piece this together with your memory of that night."

Riah leans her head back on the pillow, closes her eyes, and lets the tears rivulet down her face.

"I'm sorry, Anjali, I know this is hard. You must be confused and in shock."

Riah nods but doesn't open her eyes. "My head really hurts."

"Maybe that's enough for today—she's exhausted," says Dr. Marajaan.

"Okay, I will come back tomorrow once you've had time to rest, and we can walk through what you *do* remember."

Riah opens her eyes and fixes her gaze on the detective. Can Riah trust her? Trusting her gut, Riah decides it's best to wait for her to regain her memory and figure out what has happened to her and whoever Michael is. "I'll tell you what I can," says Riah as she turns on her left side.

She feels Detective Harper's eyes on her for a never-ending minute, then she hears the detective snap her notepad shut and exit the hospital room.

TWENTY-FIVE

Monday, September 26th—Morning

Riah falls in and out of consciousness. What is this dreamlike state? She hasn't experienced anything like this before; it's equivalent to being mesmerized by soft ethereal murmurs stretching across the glowing expanse of eternity. She lingers in this condition, letting the cloak of safety swaddle her. Floating, oblivious, free. For most of her life, she has felt a lack of protection and freedom. But in the last few days, she has felt nothing but unbound. Free of anxiety, free of remorse, and most of all, free of the obligations of living to the expectations of others. *Where are these feelings coming from?* Instinctively, she knows these are not her own emotions—it's as if she has harnessed someone else's exhilaration, someone else's elation, someone else's freedom—not her own, but some other piece of her. There's a comfort in the vastness of this space.

Riah comes to again. The faint illumination of morning filters through the window shades. It appears to be very early in the morning. *What day is it?* She uses her elbows to prop herself up and scans the semi-dark room. She realizes there's someone hunched over, fast asleep, in a chair in the corner. She gropes around her bed for the call button. Finding it, she presses hard, hoping the low buzzing from the nurses' station at the end of the hall is from her device.

A minute later, a nurse approaches her bedside. She reaches behind the bed and turns on one of the lamps to a low setting.

"Hi, dear," whispers the nurse. "Are you okay?"

Riah tries to speak, but her mouth is too dry. "Waa . . . water."

The nurse reaches over and hands Riah a large styrofoam cup. She removes the paper covering the straw in the container. "It isn't cold, though. It's been sitting here all night,"

Riah drinks from the straw. Her throat is raw, as though she has been screaming all night. The water stings as it hits the back of her throat. "It's fine. Thank you."

The nurse takes the cup and is about to place it on the tray beside Riah's bed but seems to change her mind mid-action. "This is too warm—I will get you some cooler water."

"Okay," says Riah. "Who is that?" she asks as the nurse is about to leave.

The nurse glances at the young woman in the chair. "Oh, she's your friend—Laine," she whispers. "She came in late last night and has been here since—poor girl must have fallen asleep."

Riah observes the young woman, willing her mind into recognizing this stranger. Her memory is still a black, hazy void. Hopefully, this sleeping stranger can shed light on what happened to land her in the hospital. All she knows is what the policewoman had told her. What was the detective's name? Riah remembers that she had left a business card on the tray by the bed. Reaching for the ivory-colored card, she reads the name: Detective S. Harper, San Francisco Police Department. What does the 'S' stand for? Is it a simple name like Sue or Susan, or something more exotic like Savannah or Sienna? Sienna—why does the name sound so familiar? Did the detective mention her first name?

The young woman stirs for a second, shifting the position of her arm underneath her head, but falls back into stillness again. It's beyond Riah's understanding *why* someone would choose to sleep in such an uncomfortable position. The nurse said the young woman is a friend of hers. God willing, this friend of hers—Laine—will understand if she doesn't remember her. Laine must be a good friend if she's willing to sacrifice her own comfort to be here for Riah.

Riah stares at her with piercing intensity. If she fixates on her long enough, hard enough, perhaps the memories will start to flow. Or they could hit unexpectedly. As if on cue, there's an acute pain inside her head—a penetrating affliction turning her vision inky black. She grabs her head in her hands to steady the excruciating throb.

"Ohhh," she moans. The room becomes a kaleidoscope of grey coils.

"Anjali? Anjali! What's wrong?" a voice asks from beyond her fog of suffering. "Anjali, it's me—Laine."

Riah lifts her head, and Laine's concerned face glares at her with fierce intensity, searching for any sign of recognition. "Are you okay?" she asks.

"Can you call the nurse to come in?"

"Sure, I can," says Laine, as she presses the nurse call button. "Someone should be here in a minute." Laine pulls a chair closer to her bedside.

"I'm sorry, I don't remember much. Are we friends?"

"Kind of," says Laine. "I'm your assistant at the café."

The same nurse enters the hospital room. "I brought you a pitcher of cold water. Did you need something else, dear?" she asks.

"Yes, she's having severe head pain," says Laine. As Laine rises, her chair scrapes backward against the linoleum tiles.

"Well, I'm surprised you're not in more pain. You took some nasty blows to the head," she says, going over to the machine on the other side of her bed. "I'm adjusting the setting on your pain meds, and I'll page Dr. Marajaan—I think he's still on call."

"Thank you," says Laine. "Do you know how long the doctor will be?"

"It's hard to tell," she says, glancing at her watch. "Press the call button again if the pain becomes too much," the nurse says before exiting the room.

"Okay, thank you," says Laine, pulling the hospital chair closer to Riah's bed again. "When was the last time you ate?"

"They brought some dinner last night, but I didn't have much of an appetite," says Riah. "I ate a bit of the rice and vegetables, and the Jell-O," she adds.

"I can get you something to eat from the coffee shop downstairs," Laine says, peeking at her phone. "I think it's too early for them to serve you breakfast."

Riah musters a smile. "I can wait."

"Anjali, what happened to you?" Laine asks, leaning forward.

"To be honest, uhm—"

"Laine."

"Yes, Laine," Riah says, flushing red for a second. "To be honest, Laine, I don't remember much. When I woke up yesterday, I didn't know where or how I got here. Hell—I didn't even remember my own name."

"Anjali, this must be so difficult for you. I'm not sure what to even do."

"Laine, can you help me figure out what happened here? How did you find out I was in the hospital?" asks Riah.

"I got worried about you because you hadn't been to the café since last week Tuesday. The three of us had dinner on Tuesday night—"

"Three of us? You mean you, Michael and me?" she asks.

"No, Michael was out of town—it was you, me, and Hana."

"Hana?"

"Hana, my girlfriend—I wouldn't expect you to remember her. You only met her on Tuesday."

"Oh, okay, so we were having dinner on Tuesday night."

"Yes, nothing out of the ordinary—other than I quite possibly had too much to drink," she says, blushing pink. "You told me you wouldn't be coming in on Wednesday. You said you had a lot of things you had to take care of, and you needed a personal day."

"Did I say what those things were?"

"No, not really. You were super vague."

"Was it normal for me to be vague with you, Laine?"

Laine is quiet for a moment. "No, it wasn't, and I did think it was strange."

"Strange? In what way?" Riah asks.

"Well, I felt you were acting strange over the past week or so. You didn't seem as interested in the café as you ordinarily were, and you'd come in but then suddenly leave on mysterious errands."

"And you have no idea where I went?"

"No, Anjali, I don't—I'm so sorry," she says. "I wish I had asked more questions—I didn't think it was my place, though."

"Don't be sorry. I *need* my memory to come back." Riah stares ahead, coercing her mind to remember something. She grasps at fragments of what potentially could be memories, but somehow, they feel more like splinters.

"Give it time, Anjali," says Laine, sighing and leaning back in the chair.

"So, you were saying Tuesday night was the last time you saw me. And on Wednesday, I took a personal day. When did you start to worry?"

"When you didn't come in on Thursday, I called your mobile number several times that afternoon, but it kept going to your voicemail. On Friday morning, Hana suggested we go to your apartment to ease my worry. We asked the head security guard in your building. And it was only then that we learned you were in the hospital. Hana pressed him for more information, but he said he couldn't say anything more because of the active police investigation. Once he told us that, Hana and I went to your café. Hana used one of the upstairs offices and made calls. She somehow found out you were at Saint Francis Memorial. And we came here. They confirmed you were here, but they wouldn't let us see you because we weren't family. Hana made more calls—she's a criminal defense lawyer," says Laine, pausing to catch her breath. "She discovered that the active police investigation at your apartment was because Michael was killed, and you were in a coma."

Riah takes a deep breath. She thought she would have felt something a moment ago when Laine told her Michael had been killed. Even yesterday, when the detective came by and informed her of Michael's death, she didn't feel anything. Although she had shed a few tears—which were more for the benefit of the detective—she hadn't felt any real emotions for him.

"I wish I knew how to help you regain your memory. You need to figure out what happened to you—and Michael."

"I know that!" Riah rests her throbbing head on the pillow and stares at the ceiling. "I'm sorry, I didn't mean to snap," she says. "I am *so* frustrated right now. You don't understand, Laine. I don't remember anything—it's not only the last couple of days I don't remember—I don't remember me. I don't remember my life. I don't even remember Michael!" She covers her face and her hands and starts to sob. "Why is this happening? What did I do to deserve this?"

Laine moves to Riah's side, mutely putting her arm around her.

There's a light knock. Riah and Laine simultaneously glance toward the door.

"Hi, I'm sorry to interrupt," says a woman, awkwardly showing off two coffee cups in her hands. This must be Hana.

"Oh, yes!" Laine rises from the bed and meets the woman halfway across the room.

"I figured you could use some java."

"You were so right, hon," Laine says, giving Hana a quick hug.

Hana sneaks a glance at her over Laine's shoulder. "How is she?" Hana mutters.

"She's doing better," says Laine, turning to face Riah. "Did you want my coffee? I can share Hana's." Laine takes a seat on the edge of the bed, handing her the cup.

"Are you sure? I can wait until my breakfast comes."

"Not a chance—drink."

"So what's going on?" Hana asks, taking a seat in the chair.

There's a comfort in Hana's casual approach that puts her at ease. "Well, I'm drinking your girlfriend's coffee, and I have no clue what I've been doing this past week. And let's not even mention that I don't remember my life or my dead husband." She isn't sure why she spewed her business to a total stranger, but there's something familiar about Hana.

"Yeah, you've got a lot to deal with," says Hana. She takes a sip from her coffee cup and then passes it to Laine. "I called the detectives on your case and tried to obtain an update on the investigation, but since I'm not your lawyer, they didn't tell me anything."

"Yes, one of them came to see me yesterday—a woman detective. She also wanted to know what happened, but I wasn't feeling well, so she said she'd come back today." She pauses to grab Detective Harper's card, handing it to Hana. "Laine said you are a criminal lawyer. Do I need a lawyer?"

Laine gasps. "Anjali! Why would you need a criminal lawyer? You've done nothing wrong!"

"Well, I don't know—maybe, because I don't remember anything?"

"Anjali, I'm not going to lie to you. I've got some friends who work at the CSU—the crime scene unit. They gather all the evidence at the crime scene, like fingerprints, hairs, and fibers—regular DNA evidence. They said the only evidence found in your apartment is yours and Michael's." Hana pauses. "They found zero evidence of anyone breaking in. There's nothing suggesting there was anyone else in the apartment except for the two of you." Hana leans back in her chair.

"I don't remember anything—I don't know what happened. There must have been someone else there," she says, tears welling in her eyes.

"They're still doing their investigation—they haven't concluded anything yet. It's best to cooperate with the detectives and the police," Hana says, leaning forward to touch Riah's hand.

"I will—but it's hard because I can't remember anything. I don't want them to think I'm not co-operating."

"Don't overthink it," says Laine. "Let it come back to you naturally—the universe has a way of revealing the truth when the timing is right."

"Yeah, but the quicker you remember, the better," says Hana. "The investigation isn't going to wait for you to recover your memory. In cases like this, the sooner detectives charge someone with a crime, the better."

"Hon, you're scaring her," Laine says. "You're scaring me."

"I'm being realistic," says Hana. "But don't worry, I'll try to be here for you when Detective Harper comes back to question you."

"Are you going to be her lawyer?" asks Laine.

"Hopefully, I won't have to be," responds Hana, with a grim but determined expression.

"Thank you, Hana. I do feel a little better knowing you'll be here."

"Well, I can tell Laine really cares for you, so any friend of hers is a friend of mine. You must be one hell of a boss!"

Laine chortles. "She is!" Then Laine clears her throat. "Anjali, I didn't know when the right time would be to tell you this. But . . . we were both worried about you." Laine glances at Hana and then at Riah. "So, I went into your office to see if I could find any information about your family, so we could contact them."

"Okay," says Riah. She stares at both women, waiting for the rest of the story.

"We called your mother yesterday. We told her what we knew, and she's on her way here from Seattle."

"My mother?" asks Riah. Suddenly she has a shooting pain in her left temple. She closes her eyes, bracing herself against the torture. A flash of an image overcomes her—she's wearing a traditional white cotton *salwar-kameez*, her head covered with a white chiffon scarf. The smoke from a charred body wafts into the welcoming arms of a darkening sky. "My mother is dead. I cremated her body."

Both Laine and Hana look at her, stunned.

"My mother is dead," she repeats again as if in a trance.

"Dead? Your mother certainly isn't dead!" says a voice from the hallway.

The three women turn to face the older woman standing in the doorway of Riah's hospital room.

"I can assure you—I am alive and well," says the woman.

TWENTY-SIX

Monday, September 26th—Morning

Riah stares at the woman, trying to comprehend what she has uttered. The woman enters the room and places her oversized Hermès bag on the empty chair in the corner. She takes off her lilac, Italian cashmere pashmina in one fell swoop and throws it on the bag.

"Anjali, darling, let me look at you," says the woman in a British accent.

"Are you Mrs. Patel?" asks Laine as she springs from Riah's hospital bed.

"I most certainly am, and who are you?" she asks authoritatively. The woman casts a judgmental glance toward Laine as if she was assessing and categorizing her as friend or foe.

"Oh, I'm Laine. Anjali's assistant." Laine stretches out her hand but drops it when Mrs. Patel indicates zero intent to return the gesture. "I was the one who called you about your daughter."

"Well, thank you," she says, turning her attention to Riah. "My love! I was so worried. I jumped on the first flight I could catch from Seattle when, uhm—"

"Laine," interjects Laine helpfully.

"Yes, when Laine called me and told me you were in trouble." She reaches over and pulls Riah into a tight hug.

Riah awkwardly embraces her back. She stares at the woman

trying to connect with her—any emotional trigger that would verify that this is indeed her mother. Based on Riah's flash of cached memory, moments ago, she's positive her mother is dead. She has no reason not to believe this woman, but her gut tells her something is wrong here. Riah decides to go with it. In a way, it's comforting to know she has family and friends standing by her side. Even though she can't remember anything, she isn't alone. They—these people want to help her remember what happened as well. She remembers how lonely it felt in the murkiness of her coma, lost in a maze of hollow emptiness. But she's awake now and determined to piece her memory back together, putting the darkness behind her. She is confident these people can help her do it.

"I'm glad you are here . . . Mom," she says. The word, *Mom,* sounds so foreign to her.

"What happened, my love? Tell me everything."

"I wish I could—"

"She doesn't remember anything," says Laine, jumping in.

Her mother peers over her dark-rimmed glasses at Laine and Hana. "Can you ladies go downstairs and get me a coffee?"

Laine and Hana look at each other and gesture toward the door.

"How do you take it—your coffee?" asks Hana.

"Black," says Mrs. Patel, giving them a tight smile. And then, finally, as an afterthought, she adds, "Please."

"We'll be back soon," says Laine in a chirpy tone.

Anjali's mother waits until she is sure Laine and Hana have left the room. "Do you *really* not remember anything?" she asks, giving Riah a hard stare.

"No—frankly, I'm not sure. I've been having visions, but I'm not sure if they are real."

"What do you mean?"

"I don't know how to explain it—it's like everything is a blank slate. I met Laine and Hana this morning, and although they say they know me—I don't remember them," she says, pausing. "I don't even remember you," she says, looking into Mrs. Patel's eyes.

"What about Michael? Do you remember Michael?" She pauses to scan the room. "Anjali, where is Michael? How come he's not here?"

"Michael is dead."

"Wh-what do you mean, my dear?" she asks with terror-filled eyes.

"Michael was killed, and I'm afraid they think I did it." Tears form at the corner of Riah's eyes again.

"I don't understand—I think you need to start from the beginning."

⚏

Laine and Hana stand in the long line-up at the coffee shop on the lower level of the hospital.

"This is so crazy," Laine says. "I'm not even sure what I should do."

"It's okay, boo—don't freak out, okay?"

"Hana, what if she did it?" she asks, on the verge of tears.

"Let's not jump to conclusions—let's see what she remembers over the next couple of days."

"I hear you, hon, but I am a little freaked out," Laine says. "You must see this all the time in your line of work, so it's easy for you to be calm, but this is my friend."

Hana takes a deep sigh. "Look, let's give it a bit of time. And God willing, her memory comes back—if it already hasn't."

"What do you mean?" she asks, surprised at Hana's suggestion. "Do you think she is lying?"

Hana stares forward.

"You think she is lying, don't you?" Laine asks in a hushed tone. "Why do you think that?"

"Isn't it obvious?" They move ahead in line.

"No—it's not. Do you have something against Anjali?"

"What?" asks Hana, appearing to be taken aback by Laine's question. "I barely know her, boo. What would I have against her?"

"I don't know."

"Let's give it some time—what is it you said earlier? The universe has a way of revealing the truth when the timing is right?"

"Yeah, but I was referring to her memory."

"But you can apply it to many things—everything, in fact. Regardless of what happens, I'll help in any way I can. I know she's your boss and friend, so I'll do my part."

"Next!" says the barista.

Laine and Hana order four black coffees. Hana pays the barista, and Laine grabs the coffees from the other side of the counter. As they walk, Hana peeks at her watch.

"Wow, it's already nine o'clock. I need to get to the office."

"Oh, okay," says Laine, handing one of the coffees to Hana. "I'm going to see if Anjali wants me to open the café and keep it going while she's in here."

"Good idea—it might be best to keep your mind occupied with other things. I'm sure Anjali will appreciate it as well. Besides, her mom is here now—she's clearly the overbearing type," Hana adds.

Hana and Laine giggle, as they both know those types of mothers. They share a goodbye kiss and go their separate ways.

❧

Sadie stands in the doorway of Anjali's hospital room. Anjali and an older woman are too absorbed in their conversation to notice her, so she knocks louder, startling the two. Sadie walks into the room and gives them a warm smile.

"Hello, Anjali. I'm glad to see you are feeling better and seeing visitors."

The older woman stands and extends her hand to Sadie. "I am Sangeeta Patel, Anjali's mother."

"It's nice to meet you, Mrs. Patel. I'm Detective Harper of the San Francisco Police Department." Sadie lets go of Mrs. Patel's hand and turns her attention to Anjali. "So, how's our patient?" she asks, glancing between Anjali and her mother.

"She's fine, given the circumstances," says Mrs. Patel. "Detective, I want to know what you are doing to find out who is responsible for this—for putting my only baby in the hospital, and for killing my son-in-law, Michael." Perched on the edge of Anjali's hospital bed, the mother crosses her arms.

Sadie takes a seat in an empty chair. "Mrs. Patel, I want to start off by saying I'm so sorry for your loss. I understand your need for answers. I want to assure you we're doing everything we can to figure this out—"

"And exactly what have you done so far?" asks Mrs. Patel abruptly.

"Well, we've collected and analyzed all the evidence we could from the crime scene, and we've reviewed the Medical Examiner's report on the cause of death—"

"What was the cause of death?" asks Anjali, barely audible.

"Blunt force trauma. There was a baseball bat at the scene, and we have examined it for DNA."

"And? Did you find the killer's DNA?" asks Mrs. Patel. "Do you know who did this?" the older woman asks, on the verge of sounding desperate.

"This is where we need your daughter's help."

"She doesn't remember anything," says Mrs. Patel. "I've already gone over this with her. She doesn't remember anything about the accident." Mrs. Patel peers at Sadie with sad, teary eyes. Is Anjali's mother trying to play on her sympathy?

Anjali seems uncomfortable with this conversation. Perhaps

Anjali is glad her mother is here to buffer the questions. Sadie hoped to avoid this. She likely isn't going to get anything out of Anjali, especially while her mother is around. Is Anjali telling the truth? Does she truly not know what happened on the afternoon of Wednesday, September the twenty-first? If Anjali is dishonest about her memory, she can't lie about it forever.

"I understand it's a challenging time for you, Anjali," says Broly, strolling into the room. "We don't have to do this now. I think my partner is overzealous in her pursuit to get you and your late husband justice." He puts his hand on Sadie's shoulder.

"Oh, and you are?" asks Mrs. Patel.

"Oh, I'm sorry for barging in and *not* introducing myself." He extends his hand out to Mrs. Patel. "I'm Detective Broly." He shakes her hand and then extends his hand out to Anjali. "I'm the other lead detective on this case."

"Well, like I told Detective Harper here," says Mrs. Patel, "Anjali doesn't remember anything about last week. My poor baby has been in the hospital in a coma. For God's sake, she only came back to us yesterday!"

Broly addresses his words to Anjali. "We're very mindful you're still recovering. Like my partner here, I only want to gather as many facts as possible to arrest whoever did this."

"I assure you, she is doing her best to remember," says Mrs. Patel. "As soon as she remembers anything, you will be the first to know!"

"Fair enough," says Sadie, rising from her seat. "We appreciate your time."

"Please, do let us know if you remember anything which may be helpful to the case," adds Broly. "Or even if you want to follow up on our progress on the case, do not hesitate to give Detective Harper or me a call." He flashes the ladies a smile and leaves the room.

Sadie follows him out, disappointment weighing heavily on her.

Laine approaches Anjali's room but halts when she realizes additional people are standing inside. They appear to be police officers in plain clothes. Apprehension pokes her as she recalls what Hana had said a short while ago. What if Anjali *does* remember what happened to her and Michael? She doesn't want to think about it, but what if Anjali did kill Michael? After all, she doesn't really know them as well as she likes to believe. The few times she saw them together, she recalls that Anjali seemed anxious around Michael. Laine considers Michael. He never did say more than a few cursory words to her, and she often felt weird around him. Uneasy, nervous—she'd even go as far as fearful.

The male police officer comes out of the room first. He's good-looking—in a masculine, rugged way. Sure, she's with Hana, but she can still appreciate looking at a handsome man. He flashes her a boyish smirk, and her cheeks flush. The female officer trails after him. After surveying Laine as if she's performing a CT scan, she reveals a disarming smile.

"Those coffees smell good," says the woman. "You going to see your friend?"

"Yes. I'm glad Anjali is finally awake."

"Yes, us too. I'm Detective Harper," the woman says, extending her hand.

Laine shifts the tray of coffee and donuts from her right to left to shake the detective's hand. "I'm Laine. I'm Anjali's assistant at the café." She regrets saying the last comment. Is she giving too much information away? She'll have to ask Hana about the protocol for talking to detectives.

"Oh yes," says Detective Harper. "The Art Café owned by Anjali Murphy."

"It's called *The Artists' Café*," she corrects the detective.

"I think I went there once when I was dating a broke painter—it didn't work out, though," says the detective.

"I only started working there about six months ago," Laine says. She doesn't know what it is about this detective, but she is pleasant to chat with.

"Listen, I'll let you get back to the recovering patient. But I wouldn't mind chatting with you later. Detective Broly and I will be hanging around the main floor for a while," Detective Harper says, nodding at her partner.

"Oh, sure," says Laine, a little bit surprised. What do they want to talk to her about?

Detective Harper smiles at Laine one last time, and then they head toward the elevators.

Laine takes a deep breath and turns to Anjali's room. As she enters, Anjali and her mother are watching her in suspense.

"Hi, I brought the coffee and some donuts," she says, hoping to sound cheerful, ignoring that the police were there only a minute ago. This is all so surreal—it feels as though she's caught in a murder mystery novel, and she can't get out.

"So? What did they say to you?" snaps Sangeeta.

"Who? Those detectives?" she asks. "Nothing much. Why? What did they say to you?" She hands Anjali one of the coffees.

"Well, they obviously came here asking questions," says Sangeeta. "I don't understand why they won't let up. Don't they understand what my daughter has been through?"

"What kind of questions were they asking? There are likely standard questions they ask in these scenarios," says Laine.

"They wanted to know if I remember what happened," says Anjali in a subdued tone.

"To which I told them—Anjali does not remember anything!"

"They said Michael's cause of death was blunt force trauma. They have a baseball bat with DNA on it." Anjali turns to Laine with tears in her eyes. "I think they think I did it."

Laine gasps. "Anjali! They can't think you had anything to do with this—do you really think it's possible? That you killed Michael with a bat?"

"Anything is possible," says Sangeeta.

Anjali and Laine gasp in unison.

"Anything is possible when you don't remember anything—maybe you need to at least come up with a plausible story," says Sangeeta.

"What are you saying?" asks Laine. "Do you think she should lie and create a story?"

Sangeeta is mute for once.

Laine glares at Anjali. "Anjali, don't do it. I don't know what happened while I was gone, but whatever you are thinking, don't lie because you don't remember." Anjali and her mother gaze at each other. They don't say anything, but Laine can tell there's something they aren't telling her. "Is there something I should know?"

"Laine," says Anjali, pausing to take a deep breath. "There's a lot you don't know—"

"Okay, then tell me." What doesn't she know?

Sangeeta turns to Laine. "Where did Hana go? I understand from Anjali that Hana is a criminal defense lawyer."

"Yes, she is. She had to go into the office." Laine doesn't like the sound of this. Feeling agitated, she asks, "Do you want me to call her and ask her some questions for you?"

"Look, I can tell you care very much about my daughter, but can you stay out of it? It may be easier for you this way."

"What do you mean?" asks Laine, raising her voice.

"Laine," says Anjali. "The police won't harass you if they believe you don't know anything."

"Are you afraid I might say something I shouldn't?" Laine is on the brink of tears. "Because you don't need to worry about it—I don't know anything. I have no idea about what's going on here!"

"Call Hana and ask her to come back. She may need to represent Anjali as her defense attorney," says Sangeeta with an air of resolve.

"Excuse me while I go and call her." Laine leaves Anjali's room feeling defeated.

TWENTY-SEVEN

Monday, September 26th — Late Morning

Sadie and Broly linger outside of the hospital in their unmarked police cruiser. Broly finishes his coffee, crushes the cup, and tosses it in the small plastic garbage bag near Sadie's feet on the car's passenger side.

"How many does that make for you?" she asks, jotting details from earlier that morning in her notebook.

"I'm hurting, Harper. Still getting used to the day shifts this week. How do you do it?"

"Do what?"

"Transition from days to nights, and nights to days. Do you ever sleep?"

She chuckles. "Of course, I sleep. I don't know. I guess my body is used to it."

"Hmm, well, I need to get better at it."

"You can start by drinking less." She pauses writing. "It'll make it easier to get out of bed if you're not hung over."

He groans. "Come on, is that the best you got for me?" He runs a hand through his thick head of hair. "If I wanted to be judged about my lifestyle, I'd talk to my mom."

"She'd give your ass a beating too!"

"Yeah, she would," Broly guffaws.

Sadie admires Broly's mom. She's the captain of another police division and a no-nonsense woman. Captain Broly had taken Sadie under her wing a few years back when she'd first made detective; she taught Sadie a lot about how to have confidence in herself while she was on the job. One of her primary lessons was to tell Sadie never to take any flak from anyone, especially any men on the force. Though times had changed, there was still the male egotistical attitude in the agency. She had told her to watch out for those who pretended to be her friends—those were the worst kind of people. Although Broly's mom was her mentor, Sadie never knew she had a son on the force until they ended up as partners, which may not have been a coincidence if Sadie knew anything about Captain Broly.

"Hey, isn't that the girl who was visiting Anjali Murphy a little while ago?"

"Yes, it is," says Sadie, closing her notebook. "Give me your pack of smokes, quick!"

"What do you have in mind?"

"To win her over," she says, grabbing the pack of cigarettes and exiting the car.

Sadie pulls out her phone and acts as though she's talking on it. As she approaches the walkway, she raises her voice. "Look, I told you I'd try my best—you don't have to tell me a million times." She abruptly ends the call, feigning frustration at whomever she was talking with. Pulling out her cigarette pack, she makes a desperate show of searching in her pockets for a lighter. "Fuck." She fakes her sudden realization that she isn't alone. "Lost my lighter," she says, noticing Laine's tear-stained cheeks.

"Oh, I think I can help you there." Laine rummages in her purse, pulls out a silver lighter, and passes it to Sadie.

"Oh! You're a lifesaver. Thanks." Sadie passes the lighter back.

Sadie had seen Laine earlier in the morning with another woman. She had noticed Laine light the woman's cigarette and put the lighter in her purse. Sadie guesses the woman Laine had been with is Hana.

Brett had told Sadie that Hana Thakur had been calling around the CSU department to get information on the Murphy case during their intermittent pillow talk. She did a quick background check on Hana, discovering she's a criminal defense lawyer. It seems like a lucky coincidence that Anjali's employee and friend has a girlfriend who is a lawyer. But if it's a fluke, then Anjali is one lucky woman. Although the SFPD hasn't yet decided whether to arrest her, Anjali is the number one suspect at the moment for Michael Murphy's murder.

"No worries," says Laine as she throws the lighter back into her bag.

"You okay? You look a bit upset." She takes a long inhale of the cigarette.

"Oh, I do?" Laine asks, flushing pink. "No, I'm okay," she says.

"Hey, I know I'm a cop. But I am a good listener," says Sadie. Laine eyes her phone and slips it back into her pocket. Does Laine have somewhere else to be? "Sorry, I didn't mean to pry."

"Oh, I'm sorry—I'm distracted." Laine points to the hospital.

"Yeah, I get it. You must be worried about your friend."

"I hope she gets better and remembers what happened."

"I can't imagine what it feels like for Anjali. But luckily, she has you and her mother to help her through this."

Laine glances at the ground, not saying anything. Sadie revels in the uncomfortable silence—she was trained for this. She knows the friend of a suspect is harder to crack. But she knows Laine will soften—she doesn't seem strategic or manipulative with her relationships. Laine appears to be a 'what-you-see is what-you-get' type of person. Sadie will have to ensure she is there when Laine is ready to talk more openly. Sadie puts out her half-smoked cigarette in the public ashtray when she detects Broly approaching the walkway.

"Harper, the lieutenant wants us back at the precinct—ASAP."

"Sure, boss, let's go!" Sadie is about to thank her again for the lighter when Laine interrupts.

"Can I get your card?" Laine asks.

"Oh yeah, sure," says Sadie, as she pulls a black cardholder from the inside pocket of her blazer. She draws out a card and hands it to Laine. "All the ways I can be reached are there," she says as she walks away.

"Thanks," mumbles Laine.

As Broly pulls out of the parking spot, Sadie catches a glimpse of Laine in the side mirror. Even from a distance, Laine appears to be torn about something, still standing there, inspecting the card Sadie has handed her.

"She knows something," says Sadie—her face is deadpan.

"What? You didn't win her over?" asks Broly, momentarily taking his eyes off the road to glance at Sadie. "Or you didn't have enough time?"

"She asked for my business card. It's a start—they never voluntarily ask for the card unless they want to talk to you later."

"Well, I hope she tells you whatever she knows soon. The captain's badgering the lieutenant on this one. And you know what it means for us." Broly puts on his left indicator and waits in the turning lane.

"Yeah, they want this homicide solved yesterday."

"Yesterday," Broly repeats.

Brandon paces the floor of the hole-in-the-wall hotel room he had chosen. Not expecting to have been staying long in Los Angeles, he had picked the cheapest hotel in West Hollywood. And texted Riah the address four days ago. He has called her multiple times in the last two days—his hope that she'd answer waning with each call that went straight to voicemail: *'Hey, you got me, leave a message at the'*—Beep. Her voice, and the thought that she should've been here by now, vibrate in his head.

They would have completed the deal and moved on. They'd planned to hawk Anjali's jewels, splitting the money sixty-forty—she'd get the larger cut. He was okay with that arrangement because he had a bigger deal in the works. But now that's gone to shit too. After the job, he wanted to head further south to Brazil or Cuba. And Riah's intent had been to travel back to Europe after she had gotten a new passport.

But it's Monday now, and check-out is at noon. Any hope of Ri-Ri showing up now was unlikely. He needs to face the truth—she must have double-crossed him. Who is he to her anyway? She duped her own sister—her own flesh and blood—so what would stop her from cheating him out of his forty percent? Her smiling, lying face sashays in front of him.

The sharp buzz of his burner phone jolts him out of his rattled thoughts, giving him a second of newfound hope. But his optimism is crushed as soon as he realizes it's the *other deal* calling. He eventually has to talk to this woman—it's a wonder he has managed to avoid her for this long.

"Hello?" he says in his raspy American accent.

"What the fuck happened?" asks the British voice on the other end—no preamble, straight to the fucking point—

"Sangeeta."

"You've utterly botched the job! Our arrangement was to keep it clean and simple. He was supposed to be alone. This is the exact opposite! And now the detectives are badgering Riah about what happened—they think she is Anjali! The police have no evidence of anyone else in the apartment—and believe she murdered him!"

"I didn't do it—" No payout was worth taking the rap for this.

"How convenient."

"No, Sangeeta—you don't understand. I didn't do it! I got there, and the place was already crawling with cops and paramedics. I didn't know Riah was still there. How is she?" he asks, relieved Riah hadn't betrayed him after all.

"Well—she has a concussion. She doesn't remember anything and thinks she is Anjali."

"Isn't that convenient for you and your daughter—you got Anjali her clean break after all."

"But I'm left cleaning up this god-damned mess."

He's about to say something, but the phone goes dead. The bitch hung up.

"Fuck!" he yells, throwing his phone against the wall.

He glances at the clock radio on the nightstand. It's time to check out—of the hotel and this situation. He'll go south then. He doesn't want to leave Riah behind—but it is already too late for that. Besides, Sangeeta will handle it—she'll ensure Anjali's *name* is cleared. Riah is a smart girl—she'll figure it out.

❧

Sangeeta's blood seethes with anger as she slips her burner phone into a secret compartment of her purse. All men were the same— the horrible creatures—the entire lot of them! Brandon, Michael, and even her own late husband, Sanjay, were cut from the same cloth. She should have known better than to trust Brandon. She was wrong to believe he had the required experience to pull this off—even though she had given him everything he needed to get into Michael and Anjali's apartment undetected. He said he didn't do it, but did he *really* expect she'd just take his word for it?

She takes even breaths, inhaling deep and then exhaling long like she learned from her *Yogi-Mindfulness* app. The cool outside air will calm her down, and she convinces herself that the simple act of breathing with intent will open the spaciousness to think. She has to figure out her next move before going back inside to continue with the charade of Riah being *her* Anjali. Last week, she was hopeful that the situation with Anjali would work out perfectly. She had made all the appropriate arrangements and planned every detail meticulously. And with the Lord Shiva's blessings, her baby would finally be free! Even she had been surprised by her own ingenuity. Never had she thought any of it would go so wrong. Sure, a hiccup here or there. But this? This mess was a colossal shitstorm. She doesn't want to blame Riah, but at the same time, she does question her contribution to this chaos. Her mind dwells on when she first learned of the girl's existence.

The trip to Italy with Vibha and Rashmi started this whole chain of events. On that same trip, when she discovered Anjali's birth mother, Nisha, and learned that Anjali had an identical twin sister, she had also met Brandon. He had been around the villa helping Nisha with odd jobs, and he had even acted as a tour guide to the ladies—herself, Vibha, and Rashmi—chauffeuring them on their excursions to other Tuscan towns. He was charismatic, the words *belle ragazze* dripping like honey from his Italian tongue. It was sickening how easily Vibha and Rashmi were overcome by his charm. Vibha thought Brandon was like a breath of fresh air to her previously suffocated life. And Rashmi claimed that every time he helped her in and out of the car, his fingers sent currents coursing through her veins. The two widows were infatuated clichés! But not her. She saw him for what he was—a playboy swindler.

Last year, when she hired Leo to investigate and dig deeper into Nisha and Riah Arora, she also asked him to find out what he could on Brandon Russo. Leo found nothing of material value, except that Brandon and Riah were good friends. Sangeeta kept in contact with Brandon over the past year, stringing him along, feeding his ego, hinting at a lucrative future. She eventually gave him Anjali's name and address, knowing very well he'd share it with Riah and that the girl would find her way to San Francisco. She convinced Brandon to keep the source of the information a secret until she figured out a way to reunite the twins.

Riah was never supposed to be in Anjali's apartment that evening. The plan was to get Anjali out of the country with Riah's passport, and Riah was supposed to have left by Wednesday morning to meet Brandon in Los Angeles. Although Riah would believe Brandon had gotten a head start on their trip, he was—in reality—staying behind to take care of Michael. But somewhere, that scheme went awry. Somehow Michael came home early, and Riah hadn't left yet, getting caught in the crossfire. Michael's murder wasn't even meant to be so brutal. The idea had been to keep it clean and simple. The goal had been to make it look like a suicide. Brandon would enter the apartment once Michael came back. Brandon would drug him, staging it like an overdose, leaving a *Dear John* note tucked in Michael's hands. It would look like Anjali had left him, and he had committed suicide. It was a strategy that made sense at the time and couldn't have caused the mess they were in now.

Sangeeta inhales one last breath and rises from the bench. It is time to go back inside and deal with the precarious situation. The doctor is supposed to see Riah today; hopefully, he will have a good prognosis and give them the green light to release her from the hospital.

TWENTY-EIGHT

Wednesday, September 28th—Early Afternoon

Riah exits the taxi as Sangeeta pays the driver, an elderly, turbaned Sikh man. Studying the building towering over her, she guesses this is where she lives. The street is still. Evidently, the news of her release from the hospital hasn't made the headlines yet—unlike Michael's death, or on Sunday when Riah had come out of her coma. Afterward, the hospital was crawling with incessant news reporters looking for information to break the story. They all wanted to be the first to report on the details of Michael's murder and Anjali's accident. *Accident*—it's what they were calling it, momentarily.

Hana arranged for Riah to be released from the hospital discreetly, away from the media's prying eyes and ears. Hana, Laine, and Sangeeta had spent time chatting outside of Riah's hospital room many times over the last two days. Riah is curious, but at the same time, she doesn't want to know what they were talking about. She doesn't feel comfortable broaching her concerns with Sangeeta, but she knows something has been going on. Yesterday, Riah asked one of the nurses what items she had with her when they brought her to the hospital last week. The nurse said that there was nothing other than her clothes. Maybe the nurse is in on the charade.

Riah can't shake the feeling that everyone is conspiring against her. Of course, she has no memory of the events leading to her hospitalization, or any memories prior—so, intuitively, she knows her memory loss is causing her to feel the world is colluding against her. Or is there more to it? She senses that everyone knows something she doesn't. After her memory returns, will she still feel this way?

The taxi pulls away from the curb.

"Let's go inside, dear. You must face your old life, sooner or later."

"I know, Mom."

Is this a good idea? Initially, she suggested to Laine and Hana that she shouldn't go back to her apartment. She thought her mother would want to take her back to her home in Seattle. But her mother said they should stay in town. Riah had even suggested staying in a hotel for a couple of days. The Edwardian Hotel popped into her head for some reason, but she hadn't told the others.

"Is it even safe to go into my apartment? Aren't the police still doing their investigation there?" she had inquired.

But Hana and the detectives assured her she could return to the apartment. So there is no luck staying with Laine and Hana, or her mother, or even in a hotel. They tell her this will be good for her; being at the last place before her *accident* will possibly restore her memory. Once she sees her apartment, sees her things, and sees pictures of herself with Michael, her memory will come back; they are all hoping for it—even the police. But not Riah; she wants to run as far as she can from this nightmare.

As they walk through the large entrance doors of the apartment building, a pit of burden rots in her stomach. She doesn't belong here. A few people in the lobby stare at them—she reads shock on their faces. Riah lowers her head, conscious of how hideous she must appear. Anjali's mother guides Riah by the arm to the security desk. An older gentleman rises from his seat and comes out from behind the counter, arms outstretched.

"Anjali! I'm so glad to see you are out of the hospital," he says.

"Uhm, thanks," Riah says. She doesn't recognize him and takes a couple of steps backward.

Sangeeta intervenes. "Louis, I'm sorry but Anjali is having trouble with her memory," she says, handing him her overnight bag. "Can you help us get to her apartment?"

"Of course, Mrs. Patel. I didn't know you were in town."

Sangeeta glares at him. "Well, of course I'm in town! Where else would I be, other than beside my daughter in the time of her need?"

He cringes with embarrassment. "Follow me," he says.

Riah and Sangeeta follow him to the end of the hallway. He presses the button for the elevator and ushers them inside. They travel upwards in silence. When the elevator dings, Louis holds the door open to let the women exit.

Riah stands outside of a glossy white door. The letters *Penthouse 2B* are written in gold script. A piece of leftover police tape hangs from the edge of the door frame. Louis swiftly plucks it off, stuffing it into his pocket. Expectantly, he gazes at Riah, and she peers back at him, clueless.

"I don't suppose you remember your key code?"

"No, I don't remember. Is it the only way to get in?"

"Oh, no. I've got my extra keys here." He places Sangeeta's overnight bag on the floor and fumbles to pull out a small key wallet from his back pocket.

"Well, why didn't you say that from the beginning?" Sangeeta asks.

"So sorry, Mrs. Patel," he says, as his stubby fingers sift through the keys to find the right one.

He opens the door, passes Sangeeta her bag and waves them in. Sangeeta steps over the threshold and heads straight to the bar.

Riah stands in the doorway. She's hesitant to enter the apartment—what will the next few days hold for her? She glances at Louis, and he flushes red.

"Thank you, Louis. I'm sorry I don't remember you. But I'm glad you were here to let us in."

"Of course, Anjali! This is my job."

She turns to go in, but he stops her by cupping her arm. She winces; her whole body seems to be sore today. She reminds herself that she has been through something traumatic—even though she can't recollect it. She's positive something will come back to her soon.

"I'm so sorry for your loss, Anjali," Louis says and swallows hard. "Mr. Murphy was a good man. If you need anything at all, please do let me know."

"Thank you, Louis. I appreciate your condolences," she says. Suddenly, she feels weighed down, as if her tiredness is an ocean wave that has crashed into her. She retreats into the apartment and starts to close the door. "Oh, Louis," she says. "Do you mind if we change the lock on this door?"

"Oh, yes, Anjali. If it's okay with you, I can arrange for a locksmith to come in the morning."

"Sure, it would ease my mind."

"We'll have all the locks to your apartment changed," he adds.

She watches him waddle into the elevator and then closes the door. How many entrances does this place have? She'll explore tomorrow, and perhaps something will shake her mind out of this dark hibernation. She's as anxious as the police to figure out what happened a week ago.

Riah turns toward her mother, who is sitting on one of the bar chairs, nursing a half-empty tumbler. Sangeeta is fixated on her phone, absorbed with whatever is on the screen.

"What is it, Mom?"

Sangeeta doesn't answer.

"Mom, are you all right? What are you reading?" Riah steps closer.

"What?" Sangeeta asks absentmindedly. "How are you feeling?" she asks despite her preoccupation. "Perhaps we should have brought something to eat on the way home. I'm starving—how about you?" Sangeeta downs the last sip of her drink and rises from her chair.

Riah touches her stomach, realizing she hasn't eaten since last night's hospital dinner of bland meatloaf and mashed potatoes. Even though they brought her breakfast this morning, she hasn't had anything but the coffee. She doesn't feel that she is a breakfast person, but isn't sure if that is who she is all the time, or if her lack of morning appetite is due to her hospitalization over the last few days. She should've eaten breakfast, she tells herself. It took the hospital a long time to process her paperwork and check her out of the hospital. And then the detectives were there inquiring about her memory again. Thank God for Hana! She had assured the detectives that Riah would visit them at the police station tomorrow. Hana had advised Riah she should cooperate as much as she could with the police. Otherwise, they could turn on her and accuse her of hiding the truth. Laine and Hana suggested she not read anything on the Internet or even watch the news on television. Clearly, there is something they don't want her to see—and what has her mother been reading on her phone?

Riah saunters to the bar and caresses the bottle of Bombay Sapphire. "Do I drink?" she asks.

Her mother scoffs. "Who doesn't drink?"

She stares at Sangeeta, unsure of what to say. "Well, the doctor did advise me *not* to drink."

Her mother takes off the top of the bottle and tops her glass. "I will get you a glass of juice instead," Sangeeta says as she turns toward the fridge.

Riah brings Sangeeta's glass to her nose and takes a whiff. The bitterness of the alcohol hits her nostrils with a punch. She places the glass on the counter and stares into the transparent abyss, admiring how the liquid dances under the illumination of the apartment's pot lights. And then, as if it had always been there, another shard of her memory steps onto the stage.

Like the vignette from the other day, it's a crystal-clear moment. Riah is in a store's backroom; rows and rows of beautiful Indian silk outfits hang on portable racks around her. The gold and silver gems shimmer off the costumes like the light glittering off the glass of gin. Hana is here too. It's a much younger version of Hana, but unmistakably it's her. Hana's uncontrollable laughter suffuses Riah's ears. Hana giggles so hard that she falls off the couch they're both sitting on. She gazes at Hana, who has landed on the floor, howling like a crazed person. Riah extends her hand out, pulling her back onto the couch. Hana takes a deep inhale from her cigarette, lifts her chin, and puffs out a series of circle puffs. She bursts out in laughter again, and Riah joins the din of madness.

"Are you okay?" asks Sangeeta, yanking her out of the past.

Riah, all at once, becomes conscious of where she is. She's back in this apartment, which does not feel like her own. There's no connection to this place or this woman standing in front of her.

"I'm fine," she says.

"You look pale, and all the color from your face is gone. Did you remember something?" Sangeeta asks with curiosity.

"No, not really." Riah's head whirls with nausea. "I should lie down."

"Do you want me to take you upstairs?"

"No, I'll rest here. For a bit."

Riah stumbles toward one of the white leather couches. The room spins as if she's on an unceasing carousel. She closes her eyes and eases into the void of her mind. In the dark, there is comfort here—where she knows no one, and no one knows her. She wants to stay here forever in this inky abyss of blissful slumber.

Riah stirs two hours later to find herself covered by a fuzzy mink blanket. Someone has also placed a pillow underneath her head. She rises from the sofa and scans the enormous apartment. Although the apartment is clean, the decorative pieces in the living room look out of place. Riah plucks a picture frame that has been left face-down. She ponders over it—her voice inside her head says it's a picture of herself and Michael in Hawaii. How does she know that? She caresses Michael's face behind the glass. Riah closes her eyes and tries to conjure up his image. She sees nothing. She feels nothing, except for an estrangement of sorts from a life that does not feel like her own. Putting the picture down, she decides to walk around the apartment. She can hear a faint murmur of voices coming from another room.

Riah walks over to the balcony door and slides it open. She steps onto the expansive patio and peers over the railing to see the city below. In the distance, she squints at a red bridge. She knows this bridge is famous but can't remember its name. The brazen sun meets the azure ocean on its descent across the horizon, leaving scattered hues of orange and pink on its atmospheric canvas. The view is breathtaking. How often has she seen this kind of sunset against this ocean before? Has she been awestruck each time, or has she begun to take it for granted?

"It's beautiful out here, isn't it?"

Riah turns to see Laine standing by the balcony door, holding a glass of rosé wine. How long has Laine been standing there watching her? Riah walks across the deck to meet her by the door. Over Laine's shoulder, she spots Hana and Sangeeta sitting at the bar. They are both having drinks.

"Hi, Laine. When did you get here?" Riah gives her a brief hug.

"A little while ago. You were asleep on the sofa, so I put a blanket on you."

"Ah, thanks for that."

"We brought you some take-out dinner," says Laine as she steps back indoors.

"Oh, so thoughtful of you," she says, smiling at Laine.

"Besides . . ." Laine leans in. "I don't think your mother cooks," she whispers.

"I think you're right," says Riah.

Hana rises when she catches a glimpse of Riah and Laine approaching. "Hi Anjali, how are you feeling?"

"I'm alright, considering," she says, touching her head. "But—I am starving."

"We were hoping you would be! We brought takeout."

"I heard," says Riah. She doesn't see any food but does notice the almost empty bottle of Bombay Sapphire. She is sure it was half-full earlier. She wonders if her mother has drunk it all or if she had help from Hana, who is also nursing a half-empty glass.

"It's in the kitchen," says Laine. "Should I bring it out in the dining room here?"

"Why don't we eat in the kitchen," says her mother, as she lowers herself from the bar chair and heads toward the kitchen. Laine follows Anjali's mother.

Hana, by her side, asks, "Are you sure you're okay? You look pale."

"I think I'll get more color back when I eat something other than hospital food."

Like the rest of the apartment, the kitchen is massive, beautifully built and decorated. Riah takes a seat at the kitchen island between Laine and Hana, and Sangeeta chooses a place at the head of the table. It occurs to Riah that this is where *it* happened. This is where they found Michael—dead. And where they found her injured and unconscious.

Hana places a plate in front of her. Watching the others serve themselves from white Chinese take-out containers, Riah grabs hold of one and takes a modest portion of fried rice.

"Try this," says Laine, handing Riah some noodles.

It's bizarre to Riah that everyone seems to be comfortable having dinner here, in the kitchen. After all, isn't this the scene of the crime? From the minute Riah stepped into this apartment, she has felt nervous about how the place would look—she didn't know if there would still be remnants of that night. She has anxiety about something else, too, something she can't quite put her finger on.

"Does anyone want any wine?" asks Laine as she walks over to the other side of the kitchen. She snatches the bottle of rosé and fills her wine glass.

"None for me," says Sangeeta. "I never did like the pink stuff."

"Yeah, the hard stuff for me, boo," adds Hana.

"You know, Laine," says Sangeeta. "If you like wine, you should do a tour in Italy—such exquisite landscapes and extraordinary wines, especially from the Chianti regions."

"Sounds awesome! Oh, hon, wouldn't it be so cool to do?" she asks, turning to Hana.

"Sure, anything for you, boo—I think I might pig out on all the different cheeses."

The two of them laugh.

The mention of Italy tugs at Riah's heart—no specific image comes to mind, but the twinge tells her she's connected to Italy somehow.

"Mom," says Riah. "Did I go to Italy with you?—Or have I ever been there?" she asks.

"No," says her mother, "I went with my friends a few years ago, after your—Why do you ask?"

"Oh, no reason. I was merely wondering. You haven't told me much about my life, especially my younger days."

Her mother places her fork beside her plate in a smooth,

measured approach. Sangeeta is quiet for a moment, as though she is buying time to craft the perfect answer. "I do not want to influence your memory, my dear. I suppose I wanted to see what you would remember when your memory returned." Sangeeta grabs her fork and continues to eat.

"What if my memory never returns?" Riah asks. Before she can stop them, tears pool in her eyes. She lets the tears streak her face and doesn't bother wiping them away.

Hana and Laine both stare at Riah; she can feel their sympathy.

"I mean, it happened a week ago—it happened right here—in this very kitchen. What if I don't *ever* remember what happened? What am I going to tell the police? How am I going to ever get closure for Michael's death?"

Hana is about to say something, but Sangeeta cuts her off.

"Well, it's not exactly bad karma if you can't remember anything. Why don't you take this as a sign that you *can* truly have a fresh start?"

"I don't want a fresh start—I want my old life back. I want my memory back."

"Be careful of what you wish for, my dear."

"What are you *not* telling me?" She glares at her mother from across the island.

"Whatever do you mean, my dear?" Sangeeta asks as she clutches her pearl necklace.

Riah sets down her fork. "I feel like all of you have been hiding something from me," she says.

Laine jumps in. "Anjali, no! We are not hiding anything from you. We're only trying to protect you."

"Protect me from what?" she asks.

"From yourself," says her mother.

Before Riah can say anything, Hana puts her hand on Riah's arm and glowers at Anjali's mother from across the island. "What

Mrs. Patel *means*—is we are protecting you from worrying too much about what will happen in the future."

"And we want you to be able to recover your memory, Anjali," says Laine.

Sangeeta is silent. She takes the final sip from her glass of gin and places it with a thud. The noise vibrates through the silence. She rises from her chair, leaving her half-eaten plate of food. "I'm going to bed," she announces, leaving the kitchen door swinging behind her.

Riah sits there tight-lipped, waiting to be sure her mother has left. She gives Laine and Hana a grateful look and pats their hands. "I appreciate you guys being here for me. Honestly, I'm not sure what I'd do without you."

Laine rises from her seat and leans over to give Riah a hug. "Don't worry. Everything is going to be okay."

"Thanks, Laine. So, is my mom always like that?"

"Like what?" Hana asks.

"Cold, distant. So absolute." Riah casts a lingering glance between Hana and Laine, waiting for an answer.

Laine shrugs her shoulders. "We wouldn't know—we only met her the other day."

Hana casts her eyes downward and appears to be in a reflective mood. She mutely rises from her chair and starts clearing the kitchen island.

"Speaking of cold mothers—I need to call mine," says Laine. "She rang me a while ago, and I missed her call. I'll be out on the patio," she says, gripping her glass of wine.

Hana seizes the near-empty bottle of rosé and pours the remainder into Laine's glass.

"Thanks, hon!"

Riah hears a door open and then close.

"She found the side entrance leading to your outdoor patio

from this side of the penthouse. This place is huge," says Hana as if she has been reading her mind.

Hana is trying to make small talk, but it seems something else is bothering her. Riah is glad they are alone—it gives her a chance to ask Hana what she has been wondering about since she had the flash of memory a few hours ago.

"Hana, can I ask you, what is your real name?" She is sure her question sounds odd and isn't even sure why she asked it.

"Parshana." Hana stops clearing the dishes and stands there, eyes fixed on Riah.

"How do we know each other?" asks Riah.

Hana pauses as if digging deep for an appropriate response. "We met last week, Anjali. Laine introduced us."

"Oh, so we haven't met before?" asks Riah. "Like perhaps—when we were younger?"

Hana gapes at Riah and swallows hard. She appears to be heedful in choosing her words. "Define *younger*."

"Younger, like, maybe as teenagers."

"Anjali—did you remember something?" asks Hana, now wide-eyed.

"Hana, I trust you—I'm not sure why, but I feel close to you as if we've known each other in another life or something. I had a vision earlier this evening."

Hana comes around the kitchen island and pulls out one of the chairs. She takes a seat facing Riah and motions for her to continue.

"I think it was a memory—I'm not sure. It felt sort of like a waking dream. We were sitting on a sofa in a storage room, and there were rows of clothing all around us. You were laughing uncontrollably. I'm not sure about what, but I think you were smoking, and I was drinking."

"Riah?" Hana is undoubtedly in shock.

"Who is Riah?"

"I think it's you." Her eyes fill with tears. She throws her arms around Riah and hugs her. Hana begins to sob. "I can't believe it," she says between sobs. "You're alive, Riah—you're alive."

Without any warning, visions and images flood Riah's head. They all come rushing back to her like a tidal wave. Like a torrential downpour of information, the recollection of her life is overpowering.

Laine rushes into the kitchen from the balcony patio, frantic. "The police are downstairs," announces Laine. She doesn't appear to register that Riah and Hana have been hugging.

At that exact moment, Anjali's mother bursts into the kitchen. "You have to hide, my dear."

"Don't be crazy, Sangeeta. She can't hide! They likely want to ask Anjali a few questions for their investigation," says Hana in a calm and collected voice.

"At this hour of the night?—If they just want to ask questions, why can't they wait until the morning?" asks Laine.

Riah peers from Sangeeta to Laine to Hana. Their faces show different reactions that Riah doesn't know how to read. "What's going on?" she finally asks.

Hana grabs hold of Riah by the shoulders and stares her in the eyes. "Anjali, listen to me—this is procedure. If they arrest you and take you to the police station, don't say anything—"

"But—" objects Riah.

"Listen—don't say anything. Simply ask for your lawyer—me," says Hana with a confidence Riah hasn't noticed before.

"But you're here, can't you come with me?"

There is a knock on the penthouse's front door—the hollowness of the blow vibrates through the apartment. Sangeeta leaves the kitchen, trailed by Laine.

Riah turns to Hana again, with a worried look on her face. "They think I did it, don't they?"

"Don't say anything. Let them take you to the station, and when they put you in the interrogation room, your first task is to ask for me—I am your lawyer now, and we will figure this out together," Hana says, squeezing her hand and embracing her with a tight hug. "Let's go," says Hana. She steps out of the kitchen and holds the swinging door open for her.

Riah wants to follow her, but she is frozen. Moments ago, she had a flood of images from her past life, but she still doesn't remember how she arrived here. She desperately wants to remember more and connect all the jigsaw pieces of her fragmented memory. When did she change her name from Riah to Anjali? What has happened to cause her to be in this predicament? What has she done? Perhaps, she did kill Michael. She can't remember anything about him—was it possible she didn't love him? For all she knew, she could've hated him and was trying to leave him, and he attempted to stop her. Maybe the facts in front of the police point to her murdering Michael.

Still standing near the kitchen door, Hana exudes an air of calm confidence. Riah prays Hana is an exceptional criminal defense lawyer too.

Detective Harper—the woman detective who visited her twice in the hospital—comes through the kitchen door. Riah can see her mother and Laine standing next to each other in the living room, fear in their eyes. She wants to tell them everything will be okay—this is a big misunderstanding. She wants to console them. If she tells them it will all work out, then maybe she can convince herself too.

TWENTY-NINE

Wednesday, September 28th—Late Evening

Riah's knees buckle as the detective opens her mouth to speak. It's as though she knows what Detective Harper will say even before she utters the words. Her first instinct is to run; she desires to be anywhere except here. The kitchen begins to feel smaller by the second, as if the walls are closing in on her. In a flash, she catches a glimpse of her future—dressed in an orange jumpsuit. There's a massive lump in her throat; she swallows hard and tries to speak. Before she can say anything, another policeman joins the detective, an older man who carries himself like he's Detective Harper's boss.

"Anjali Murphy," says Detective Harper. "You are under arrest for the murder of your husband, Michael Murphy." The detective pulls out a pair of handcuffs from her belt.

The cuffs glint off shards of light, causing her eyes to grow wide. Bile burns at the back of her throat. She takes a deep breath in, but it feels like acid in her lungs, not air. Despite herself, she musters a response. "I'll go with you willingly. I don't think the handcuffs are necessary." Her composed voice sounds foreign to her ears.

"Precaution," says Detective Harper. The detective steps behind Riah and asks her to put her hands behind her back. As the detective places the handcuffs around her wrist and clicks them shut, Riah is read her Miranda rights. "You have the right to remain silent. Anything you say can be used against you in the court of law. You have the right to talk to a lawyer for advice before we ask you any questions. You have the right to have a lawyer with you during questioning. If you cannot afford a lawyer, one will be appointed for you before any questioning if you wish. If you decide to answer questions now without a lawyer present, you have the right to stop answering at any time."

Tears sting Riah's eyes, but she is determined to be strong. She tells herself repeatedly not to freak out or do anything stupid. She repeats Hana's instructions in her head—don't say anything, ask for your lawyer, ask for Hana, don't say anything. Although Hana hadn't told her to keep the name Riah to herself, she read between the lines when she distinctly called her *Anjali*.

Detective Harper escorts Riah out of the kitchen. As she is walked through the apartment, all the faces—her mother's, Laine's, Hana's, and the other police officers'—become a blur. Why are there so many police people here? It's not like she will run or even has the means to escape. Someone passes Riah's coat to one of the police officers, and he puts the jacket over Riah's shoulders. As they walk her out of the apartment, two police officers hold the elevator door open. She catches a glimpse of Louis, who would have needed to give the police access to this elevator. What does he know? If he is a witness, the police have already talked to him. A woman is standing beside Louis, clutching a tiny Chihuahua. She's beautiful in the traditional sense—tall, slim, and blonde—but appears to be unsettled. Perhaps they are friends? Riah abandons the idea—if they *had* been friends, this woman would have come to see her in the hospital, or at least when she returned to the apartment.

Riah and Detective Harper step into the elevator. The older officer in plain clothes also steps into the elevator with them. Before he presses the button to go to the lobby, he turns to Detective Harper. "It's crazy down there."

"I heard, Lieutenant. The press wants to have a field day with this one." She glances at Riah. "Do you want to cover your head with your jacket?"

Riah takes a deep breath. "No." Deep, deep inside, she knows she is innocent, whether she remembers her life or not. Let them do their worst.

They ride the rest of the way in silence. When the elevator dings, Riah takes another deep breath. The elevator doors open to mayhem. Cameras, microphones, and strangers are crowded in front of the private elevator. Riah winces at the flashing cameras and the cacophony of chatter from all these people. They are all talking at once, asking her and the detective questions. They walk through the lobby, and the mob follows. The assault of questions continues. Detective Harper says "no comment" a few times but remains calm. The detective appears to be enjoying this. Riah wants to tell the detective and reporters of her innocence—that they have the wrong person. But Riah remembers what Hana said a few minutes earlier, and she presses her lips together. She has to do this correctly, but will she get another chance to be in front of cameras like this?

Detective Harper escorts her out of the front doors of the apartment building. It is raining. Riah lifts her face to the dark sky and lets the raindrops hit her face. At first, each icy drop is relief on her hot skin; she hasn't realized before how feverish she is feeling. Then each raindrop feels like a tiny assault on her face and soul.

Detective Harper waves for the police car to come closer. The vehicle moves forward, and Detective Harper opens the back door. The cameras and the reporters have followed them outside to the front of the building; the rain will not deter them from getting the story. Riah turns to the cameras. Her hair is wet and matted to one side of her head, and her face is solemn.

"I'm innocent," she blurts into the cameras as though this is her last chance to plead for her innocence. "My uncle was trying to rape me, but I didn't kill him."

There is one millisecond of silence, as though the crowd takes a moment to process what Riah had uttered. Then the frenzy starts. The reporters stick microphones in Riah's face, and another assault of questions begins. The inquiries come all at once, rapid and overlapping each other. Everyone is confused, curious, and wants answers. Riah stands there, not saying another word. Her mind is jumbled; memories about what happened with her uncle eons ago are tangled with her current reality.

Growing impatient, Detective Harper turns Riah to face the open door of the back seat of the police car. "Watch your head," the detective says as she guides her into the cruiser. Detective Harper closes the door and waves the reporters back.

"That's it, show's over," Detective Harper says to the crowd. A second later, the passenger side of the police cruiser opens, and the detective slides in. "Let's get out of here, Broly." She leans back in her seat and pulls her hair back in a tight ponytail at the nape of her neck.

Her partner pulls the police car from the curb, honking the horn to disperse the reporters surrounding the vehicle. He inches forward, his hand steady on the car horn. "Geez, it's a circus out here," he says, looking over at Detective Harper. There's a gentleness in his profile as he asks his partner if she's okay. Detective Harper mumbles something as she glances back at Riah.

Riah turns her face to look outside. She agrees, it's a circus out there, and somehow, she has become the main attraction. When she came home earlier this afternoon, she couldn't have guessed she'd be leaving so soon. Riah shifts in her seat, finding it uncomfortable to sit up straight. She leans her head back and catches Detective Broly's eye in the rear-view mirror for a moment. Before Riah can stop it, she feels the pinprick of tears threatening to gush out. This is some mess she is in. How can she prove her innocence to them?

THIRTY

Sadie takes a long sip from her bottle of water. She observes Anjali through the one-way mirror as she sits there, waiting. From her profile, Anjali appears cool, calm, collected. Anjali inhales deep breaths with her eyes closed as though she's meditating. She likely does yoga and is fit beyond belief. "Anjali Murphy—you have to be the killer," Sadie mutters to herself, as though saying it out loud would make it true. She can't deny that something is off about this case. The situation has felt strange from the beginning, as if Sadie is missing something obvious. She can't put her finger on it, but there's a hollow, nagging feeling in the pit of her stomach.

Lieutenant Washington enters the fluorescent-lit observation room. He stands beside Sadie and gazes at Anjali as well. "So, who's going to go first?" he asks.

"I am, sir." Her lieutenant looks exhausted—she empathizes with his situation. "I'm waiting for Broly so he can observe from out here. We can update you in the morning." She glances at her watch. It's close to midnight, and they'll likely be here till dawn.

"Not a chance," he says. "Look, I know you got this, kid. But we have a lot of eyes on us—we can't afford to get it wrong."

"I understand, sir."

"Has she asked for a lawyer yet?"

"Not yet, but she will as soon as I step into the room and start asking her the tough questions. One of her friends is a defense lawyer." She gauges his reaction.

He continues to gaze at Anjali with his unwavering poker face.

"Shall we get the party started?" asks Broly as he enters. He seems to see Lieutenant Washington a little too late and flushes red in embarrassment when the lieutenant shoots him a look of disapproval. Broly clears his throat and passes Sadie two bottles of water.

"Thanks, partner," she says with a smirk. Broly is always good for a comical diversion.

Sadie enters the interrogation room without making a sound. As she puts the water on the table, Anjali gives her a questioning look. Sadie removes the handcuffs. Then she walks around the table and pulls out the empty chair, deliberately scraping it against the grey floor to unnerve her suspect. She takes a seat and faces Anjali.

Sadie is silent, taking a long, hard look at the woman across the table from her. Upon closer examination, Anjali looks tired—as though she hasn't slept in days. She probably hadn't. Sadie hopes to get the real story from her—and soon—before she lawyers up.

"The water is for you," says Sadie. Twisting the cap off her bottle of water, she takes a sip.

"Thanks," says Anjali.

"Where would you like to start?" asks Sadie.

"I don't know—where would *you* like me to start?"

Sadie leans back in her chair, tilting back on its hind legs. She must tread cautiously around this suspect and push her annoyance aside. They haven't even started, and already Anjali is playing games. "Anywhere you would like to start your story, Anjali," she says.

Anjali is quiet for a moment, and then she speaks. "Detective Harper?"

Sadie nods, waiting for her to continue.

"Detective Harper, like I told you when I woke up in the

hospital a few days ago—I don't remember anything. I don't remember what happened to land me in the hospital. Nor do I recall anything about my life before that day. It's a complete blank."

Sadie stays quiet. People—especially guilty ones—don't like silence. It's as though the silence is a void of torture, and so they fill it with words to cope with it. Sadie has learned to use it to her advantage—she revels in the silence.

"I tried over and over again to remember—to recollect anything that would explain this nightmare!" Anjali indicates to the room, raising both hands in the air. "I keep telling myself I will wake up soon—but no—it keeps going on and seems to worsen with every passing minute."

Sadie swallows. This is her moment to turn the tables and make her suspect feel uncomfortable. "How do I know it's true?" she asks.

"What do you mean?" asks Anjali. "Do you think I'm lying?"

Sadie ignores her question. "You said your uncle was trying to rape you but that you didn't kill him. Who were you referring to?"

"I don't know," says Anjali. "I wasn't thinking—it just came out." Her eyes are moist, on the brink of tears.

"Look, Anjali, I believe you when you say you want to remember what happened to help end this nightmare—but I don't believe that you don't remember anything about your life before your coma. It's impossible. Eventually, it all comes back. No one can hide from their past forever." Sadie leans back in her chair. She opens her bottle of water again and takes a sip.

Anjali starts to speak but seems to decide against it. Sadie knows she's getting to her. She'll make her talk soon and get her to confess what she *does* remember. Anjali opens her bottle and takes long gulps. She finishes three-quarters of it, then places it back in the same spot.

"I want my lawyer," she says.

Sadie rises and slides her chair back. "As you wish—it's your right."

"Hana Thakur," says Anjali.

Sadie steps out of the interrogation room, letting the door slam behind her.

Lieutenant Washington and Broly look at her; their disappointment is palpable.

THIRTY-ONE

Thursday, September 29th—Early Morning

Riah waits in the sparsely furnished interrogation room, her eyes fixed on the dingy wall in front of her. Except for the table and three chairs, the space is empty. The gloom of the confined cubbyhole matches her dejected mood. Turning her head to the left, she catches a glimpse of herself in the mirror. She looks horrid—blotched skin, murky dark circles under her eyes, scraggly hair. She appears not to have slept in days, unless one counts a coma as sleeping. She's conscious that the mirror is a one-way mirror. Who is on the other side of it? Watching her. Judging her. Is Detective Harper standing there, discussing Riah with the other detectives? Perhaps they are considering her fate and what will happen to her. What *will* happen to her?

She wishes Hana would arrive soon. She needs to talk to her about the events she remembered earlier. Hana seems to be the key to regaining her past now. It is as if her life is returning to her in fragmented bursts of color. So far, the memories are from her younger days, before this life—this terrible life where she is being accused of murdering her husband. Something about the thought of murder resonates in the depths of her muscles, making the notion of it plausible. The detective is right to think that she is lying or hiding something.

The interrogation room door opens, and Detective Harper and Hana stand in the frame. The light from the hall pours over Hana's shoulder, gifting her with a halo. Hana turns to the detective and says, "I'll need time to consult with my client—in private."

"Ten minutes," says Detective Harper. She steps aside to let Hana through.

Hana appears fresh and keenly alert. She must have gone home for a shower and a change of clothes. Hana is wearing a black suit jacket over a silk top, paired with a black pencil skirt that ends past her knees and accentuates her curvy figure. From her neck hangs a thin chain with a plain gold cross. Hopefully, she is as good a lawyer as she seems to be.

Hana struts toward Riah and places her briefcase on the table. Her eyes narrow as she zeroes in on the bottle of water. "Did you touch or drink from that bottle?"

"Yes, I did."

Hana opens her briefcase and places the water bottle in it. "If they want your DNA, they will have to ask for it," she says. Hana pulls a chair over and takes a seat beside Riah. "We don't have much time before Detective Harper comes back." She scans Riah like an MRI machine. "How did they treat you when you were brought in?"

"Fine. What will happen next?" asks Riah.

"Well, they should elaborate on the charges against you when they come in."

"They think I murdered Michael," Riah says.

"Yes, I know, but I want them to expand on those charges and tell us why they believe you are the killer. I must ask you—do you remember anything? Something which may cast a shadow of a doubt that you did this? Anything to suggest that they should be looking at a different suspect?"

Riah remains quiet—her mind like a heavy fogged-up windshield. She wishes she could remember her life with Michael.

Strangely, she can't even recall his face. Why can't she remember anything about him? "I wish there was something I could tell you, Hana, but I have nothing."

Hana leans back in her chair and stares at Riah long and hard, making Riah feel uncomfortable. "What about what you said to the reporters outside your apartment?"

"You heard about that?" asks Riah. She glances downward in embarrassment.

"It's all over the news—what were you thinking? I told you not to say anything."

"I'm sorry, Hana—it kind of just came out. I was confused for a moment. What are they saying?"

"It doesn't matter. Let's focus on getting you out of here."

"Why doesn't it matter? Hana, what aren't you telling me? Ever since I got out of the hospital, it's felt like you, Laine, and my mother have been hiding something from me."

Hana is quiet for a moment. "We didn't want you to know what they have been saying about you in the media. Right now, we should focus on preparing you for the detectives' questions—they are going to be here any minute." She lowers her voice. "We can talk about that later—when we get you out of here."

As Hana leans back, there is a knock on the door, and it flings open. Detective Broly walks in, followed by Detective Harper.

"Counsellor, hope you've had enough time to consult with your client?" asks Detective Broly as he pulls out the remaining empty chair and sits.

"Why? Did you get bored of listening outside?" asks Hana sarcastically.

"Oh no, I just got back from getting a coffee," he says, giving her a boyish smile. "But I can't guarantee that she wasn't listening," he says as he points over his shoulder to Detective Harper. She's standing in the corner, arms crossed.

This all seems too casual. Detective Broly and Hana banter back and forth while Detective Harper stands and leans against the wall, observing the room. Riah starts to become agitated; she wants to speed this along. She doesn't want to admit it, but she is scared. Her past is blurry and unclear, and now her future seems much the same.

Riah clears her throat and glances at Hana. "Can we get started?" she asks. She had meant to ask in a louder tone, but she seems to have lost her voice between the question being in her head and leaving her mouth. They must see that she isn't a cold-blooded killer—she must make them understand.

Hana shifts her attention from Detective Broly to Riah. She angles her chair toward the detectives. "We would like to know more about the charges against my client, Anjali Murphy," says Hana.

Detective Broly leans back in his chair. His demeanor suggests he will be the good cop, which means Detective Harper, who's still standing in the corner and has yet to speak, will play the bad cop. For some reason, Riah understands this—it isn't a memory but more of an instinct, as though she inherently knows about law enforcement and how to read it. How observant had she been in her old life?

"The charges are simple," he says. "We are charging you with first-degree murder."

"However, we can recommend a lesser offense to the prosecuting attorney if you cooperate with us," adds Detective Harper. She moves away from the wall and walks closer to the table.

Riah is about to say something, but Hana puts her hand on her arm to stop her.

"My client has been co-operating. She came here voluntarily after you yanked her out of her apartment tonight," says Hana.

"We couldn't wait until the morning," says Detective Broly.

"Why not?" asks Hana.

"She has access to funds—making her a flight risk."

"That's ridiculous—she's not going anywhere," Hana spits out.

Detective Harper puts her hands on the table and leans in, staring Riah dead center in her eyes. "Anjali, we want to know what happened. The evidence we found at your apartment on the night of Michael's murder tells a grisly story, but we also know, perhaps, there is more to that story—your story." Detective Harper takes her hands off the table and straightens.

"My client has been through this with you already—she doesn't remember anything," says Hana. There is a hint of annoyance in her voice now.

"Nothing at all?" asks Detective Broly, his eyebrows rising as he asks the obvious question, shooting her a suspicious glance.

"Nothing of value," says Hana. "Nothing to shed any light on what happened on Wednesday, September the twenty-first."

"But you are starting to remember things about your life?" asks Detective Harper.

"Things that don't quite make sense—like memories from my childhood," says Riah.

"What kind of memories?" asks Detective Harper.

Hana starts to say something, but Detective Harper raises her hand to indicate that she doesn't want Hana to interject.

"Memories—like dreams—things like drinking and hanging out when I was a teenager," says Riah. "Also, I've had flashbacks of events that couldn't have happened, like having a cremation ceremony for my mother."

"But your mother is alive, right?" asks Detective Broly. "We met her at the hospital?"

"Yes," says Riah.

"Again, my client does not remember anything about the night her husband died."

"Well then, we can't help your client," says Detective Harper.

216

"We are charging her with the murder of her husband, Michael Murphy."

Everyone becomes instantaneously quiet. The silence in the room is deafening—this goes on for a torturous minute.

"These charges are unsubstantiated," says Hana finally. "My client has nothing more to say."

Riah can't believe this is happening. Thank God Hana is here to speak for her.

THIRTY-TWO

Friday, September 30th—Morning

Sangeeta has rehearsed and is confident about her approach when she speaks to the detectives on the case. Sangeeta needs to get Riah out of this mess. Although she questions the girl's innocence, she owes Riah's mother at least that much. Hopefully, she can get them to recognize that Riah is the victim. And consider the possibility that someone else murdered Michael. But at all costs, avoid a trail that would lead them to the real Anjali. She can't risk being accused of lying to the police if they discover they have Riah and not her Anjali.

As she waits for the detective in the main lobby of the San Francisco Police Department, she remembers her own struggles with her late husband. When Anjali was a child, Sangeeta sheltered her from her father's abusive and cruel nature. She had prayed that Anjali would never witness or experience the emotional and physical abuse she had to endure.

However, in the end, Sangeeta took care of *that* problem. Over time, with every drop of poison in her husband's food, she reclaimed her life. As he deteriorated, she became more assertive. She recalls him on his deathbed—so frail and insignificant. She felt a nanosecond of guilt for what she had done, but flashes of what she had suffered were enough to disperse any thoughts of remorse.

Sangeeta never imagined Anjali would have to deal with the same abuse she had dealt with most of her life. When Anjali first married Michael, it seemed like they were perfect for each other, but then she noticed small cruelties—the kind she had endured with Sanjay—being inflicted by Michael on Anjali. She pretended not to notice when Anjali started losing weight or when she began covering bruises. When she had ultimately forced Anjali to tell her the truth, she realized the extent of the abuse and that Michael would never let her go. She decided that he'd pay for his sins against her daughter, and she would make sure her daughter was safe and free.

Sangeeta glances up to see Detective Harper standing in front of her. She must have gotten so lost in the past that she doesn't know when the detective arrived on the main floor. The other detective, the male one, is standing by the main reception area, flirting with a young female police officer. Sangeeta recalls his name—Detective Broly. Perhaps this would be easier with him, as it's hard to read his partner.

"Hello, Mrs. Patel," says Detective Harper. "I understand that you wanted to talk to me."

"Yes, Detective Harper, I want to speak to you—about my daughter." Sangeeta pushes herself up despite the aches in her ankles and wrists—a permanent reminder that she'd always be a battered woman.

Detective Harper steps back to give her more room to stand. "Sure, we can go upstairs to one of the private conference rooms—if you'd like."

"That would be ideal."

"Great, follow me."

As they walk, Sangeeta observes as Detective Harper catches Detective Broly's attention and points toward the second floor, indicating that they are heading upstairs. Detective Broly nods and continues his mild coquetry.

"I'm sorry," says Detective Harper, peeking over her shoulder. "We should have taken the elevator." The detective pauses to let her catch up.

"Oh, don't be sorry, dear. It's always a good idea to get some exercise, even in my old age," says Sangeeta. Facing Detective Harper now, she notices her striking green eyes and smooth olive skin.

"Do you want some coffee?" asks Detective Harper as they climb the stairs in unison.

"Sure, that would be delightful, just black, please," says Sangeeta as they reach the second floor's landing.

Detective Harper indicates one of the conference rooms. It's a small meeting room that can accommodate three or four people. Sangeeta places her purse on one of the chairs and anticipates the detective joining her soon. Sangeeta Patel takes a deep breath and tries to slow her heartbeat.

Detective Harper returns, placing two large mugs on the table.

"Thank you," says Sangeeta, reaching for the cup and holding it in both hands, letting the heat warm her skin. "What is your first name, dear?" Sangeeta asks.

"Sadie—Detective Sadie Harper," she replies politely.

"Oh, that's a pretty name," says Sangeeta. "What does it mean?"

"I don't know. I never thought about it."

"Oh, I'm sure it must have some meaning. Perhaps your mother never told you."

Detective Harper shrugs.

"Now, Anjali's name—Anjali's name has meaning. I don't know if you know this, but Anjali was adopted," she says, gauging the detective's interest. "We adopted her from an orphanage in India in 1987. We didn't pick her name—it was the one her birth mother gave her. We had planned on changing it, but then we found out what her name meant." Sangeeta pauses.

"What does Anjali's name mean?" asks Detective Harper.

"Anjali means *divine offering*," she says.

"A very nice meaning. So you took it that Anjali was a present from God?"

"Yes, she was," says Sangeeta, taking another sip from her coffee. "You see, I couldn't have children of my own. My husband and I yearned to be parents. While he worked for the Indian government as a dignitary, we were notified that there was a baby girl whose mother had passed away from traumatic labor. I loved the child the moment I laid eyes on her, and I knew she was meant for us—she was our divine offering."

"Interesting story, Mrs. Patel," says Detective Harper. "What does this have to do with the case against Anjali?"

"I wanted you to see Anjali for the pure soul she is. Anjali loved Michael very much—more than he deserved. She wouldn't have had the physical or emotional strength to hurt Michael, let alone kill him. She is the victim here, just as much as Michael. There had to be someone else in the apartment."

"Perhaps you don't know your daughter as well as you think." Sadie stares at Sangeeta with her feline-like eyes.

"Are you *so* anxious to close this case that you won't consider another possibility?"

"The evidence doesn't lie—"

"What evidence?"

"We have reason to believe they had been arguing earlier in the evening. Anjali's injuries were consistent with the marks found on Michael, which leads us to believe he caused them. More interesting are Anjali's fingerprints on the bat. The fact that Anjali had a bat in the kitchen and that the initial blow he sustained came from behind—leads us to believe she had intent. This was not self-defense—it was murder."

Bloody hell! This is going wrong in so many ways. She came here to protect Riah as best as possible and find out why they arrested her. How is she going to spin this? "I admit, the evidence against Anjali seems damning, but I am convinced someone else was there—you need to take another look at the evidence."

"Why don't we talk more about *why* you feel there was someone else in the apartment. You said something earlier that piqued my interest."

"What was that?" Maybe she could convince this detective that Riah isn't the killer.

"You said Anjali loved Michael very much—*but* more than he deserved. What did you mean by that?"

Sangeeta takes a deep breath. "Michael didn't treat Anjali the way she deserved—and he was cheating on her."

"Oh? Why do you think that?" asks the detective.

"Because Anjali told me of her suspicions a few months ago."

"Anjali must have been angry that Michael was cheating on her. How did she find out?"

"She didn't find out. I found out on her behalf. I hired a private investigator to follow Michael, and he obtained proof that Michael was having an affair with a woman in his apartment building—a neighbor of all people! I never told her—I kept it to myself." She's watched enough true crime dramas to know that the detective was steering her toward giving Anjali a motive.

"But could Anjali have discovered the affair in another way?"

"No—she would have told me."

"But what *if* she didn't tell you. Maybe she found out and confronted Michael about it. Maybe it turned into a heated argument, and it got out of hand—"

"You are wrong," Sangeeta says, leaning forward. "I'm telling you—Anjali is innocent—there *was* someone else there!"

Sadie starts to say something but then stops and is silent. They sit there, glaring at each other for a long, dragging minute. Deciding that she's done what she can for Riah, Sangeeta grabs her purse and stands abruptly.

"I guess you do not want to believe you botched this investigation. You have the wrong person in jail. Good day, Detective Sadie Harper."

THIRTY-THREE

Friday, September 30th—Late Morning

Sadie plucks the coffee mugs from the table and turns off the lights, closing the door behind her. Broly is standing by the top of the stairs, leaning against the railing, nonchalantly looking at his phone. He has been hanging around, waiting for her.

As she approaches him, he straightens up. "So, what did Mama Bear want?"

"Oh, you know the usual—she came to plead her daughter's case."

"Really! Well, we saw that one coming. What did she say?"

"Mrs. Patel is adamant there was someone else in the apartment that night. And she implied that we rushed Anjali's arrest. But I don't think she realized how much else she revealed."

"Oh, do tell," says Broly as they make their way to the lower level.

"Mrs. Patel said Anjali was suspicious that Michael was cheating on her. So, Mama Bear hires a private investigator and gets proof that not only was he cheating, but that the affair was with Sienna Nash."

"Ah, we already knew that," he says. "The Murphys weren't the perfect couple they appeared to be on social media!" As soon as they learned that Michael Murphy was the Chief of Police's nephew, they spent countless hours scouring the online pages of Michael and Anjali. Broly is right—they did appear to be the perfect couple, always arm in arm with big, bright smiles on their faces. Anjali looked perfect, and Michael—well, he looked beyond perfect.

"Yes, but Sangeeta Patel was helpful—she unknowingly corroborated Nash's allegations that Anjali knew about the affair," Sadie says.

"For reals? So, are you convinced we arrested the right person?" Broly asks.

She lets her mind linger on his question, replaying the whole conversation with Sangeeta Patel, wary of reveling too soon in this newfound information. "Not exactly," she finally says.

They pause at the bottom of the staircase. He narrows his eyes and motions with his hand for her to expand on the statement.

"Well, if Anjali knew Michael was cheating with the neighbor, it aligns with our motive theory. But why is Patel so unwavering in her belief that there was some mystery person in their penthouse? And that *we* got it wrong?"

"Well, Harper, it's her kid. What parent wouldn't defend their child?"

Is Patel just a distraught mother defending her daughter, or is there an element of truth to what she had said? "I know. But something still feels *off*—I wouldn't mind re-examining the wall one last time—for due diligence," she says.

His eyes light up like a child on Christmas morning. "Oh boy, my favorite part!"

Despite her apprehension, she lets out a relaxed chuckle. Broly is a good partner; he likes playing the devil's advocate, but she always feels he has her back. "Let's go," she says.

They head to the precinct's lower level, where they had turned one of the interview rooms into the home base for their evidence wall—Broly referred to it as his *Wonderwall*. Now he hums the chorus of that late-nineties pop song. They'll have to review the evidence with the Assistant District Attorney before Anjali's arraignment. Anjali will likely make bail, but they need to show she is a flight risk. And the ADA will make sure the bail is set high, even though they know, based on their investigation, that Anjali can afford it.

Broly fishes the key from his pocket, opening the door to their makeshift investigation room. Sadie flips the light switch, and the room is flooded with harsh lighting, like when they turn the lights on in a seedy club long after the last call.

Broly drags a metal chair closer to his *Wonderwall* with the back facing the board. "The floor is yours, madame," he says, waving her forward.

Sadie steps forward like a theater actor walking on stage. She eyes the board with the persons of interest, red strings stretching from their pictures to an image of Michael Murphy. Broly straddles the chair, his body language saying he's non-threatening, yet he'll be frank and attentive as she runs it through, reliving how they arrived at this juncture.

There were five prominent persons of interest when Sadie had started the investigation over a week ago. Anjali Murphy was among the five. The other four were Sienna Nash—the next-door neighbor and the owner of the other penthouse suite on the floor; Louis Watts—the security guard from the Murphys' apartment building; Peter Truffen—Michael Murphy's long-time partner at their law firm; and finally, Trent Wilson—the ex-husband of a client of Michael Murphy.

"Let's start with Trent Wilson," says Broly, coaxing Sadie out of her head.

"Yes, Trent Wilson," she says, launching into his story. "Lucy Marten, the office manager at Michael Murphy's law firm, told us that a week before the murder, Trent Wilson had come into their law office and threatened to kill Michael. In Lucy's and a dozen other witnesses' statements, we learned Murphy was the lawyer for Wilson's ex-wife. And Wilson was livid about the divorce settlement going in his ex-wife's favor. He felt he had lost more than half of his hard-earned estate to—in his words—his 'money-grubbing whore of a wife.' His ex-wife, Morgan Wilson, hired Murphy—a well-known divorce attorney—to represent her. Murphy was known as a shark with a reputation for representing women. He didn't only help them get a divorce, but helped his clients take their ex-husbands to the cleaners. And Trent Wilson was no exception."

"Remind me to never get married, Harper. So, what was the settlement?" Broly asks, although he very well knew. He just liked hearing this part of the story.

"Morgan Wilson was awarded three of the four houses they owned, two of the luxury cars, and an alimony settlement totaling fifty thousand a month. Although Wilson had accused his wife of adultery, the law firm's private investigator had uncovered Trent Wilson's many indiscretions. Although all of them were before he met Morgan, Murphy's law firm had them altered so they looked more recent. Morgan Wilson also had her own collection of tapes and photographs of Trent Wilson's alleged abuse. Based on numerous interviews with junior lawyers in the office, Murphy and his firm partner, Peter Truffen, were not above fabricating facts to get what their clients *deserved* from their ex-spouses. It was the firm's culture, and as junior lawyers, they were encouraged by the partners to do anything necessary to get a win for their clients, even if it meant telling *a few white lies*, as they referred to it."

"So was anyone shocked when Trent Wilson showed up at the Truffen & Murphy law firm, demanding to speak to Michael Murphy?" Broly asks.

"Well, Lucy Marten certainly wasn't. The firm had a protocol for these kinds of situations. When Lucy told Wilson that Murphy was out of town, he didn't believe her and walked past the reception area and burst into the conference room where the lawyers had their weekly finance meeting. Seeing Murphy at the head of the table, nearest to the door, Wilson grabbed him out of his chair and threw him against the door."

"Damn," says Broly, shaking his head.

"Luckily, Lucy had called security right away when Wilson had pushed past her. Two large security guards arrived before Wilson could do any real harm to Murphy. As the security guards dragged Wilson downstairs, he yelled several profane slurs at Murphy and a clear death threat. According to witnesses, Trent Wilson said, 'I'm going to kill you, Murphy, this isn't the last time you hear from me! I'm gonna kill you in your sleep, and then I'm gonna fuck your wife!' Apparently, everyone in the room was shocked at Wilson's reaction, but no one took the threat seriously, not even Murphy. In fact, Murphy even joked that it was one of the hazards of being the top divorce attorney in San Francisco."

"I'll say, but we took that death threat very seriously, didn't we?" asks Broly.

"We certainly did, and Wilson was our prime suspect because of the threat he'd made to Michael's life and Anjali's safety. Trent, surprisingly, was cooperative with us when we went to his beach house on the coast."

"At least he got the beach house," Broly mutters.

Sadie continues. "He willingly came into our precinct and answered questions about the day he made those threats against the Murphys. He didn't hide his hatred for Michael Murphy, though. In fact, Wilson said he wasn't shocked that someone had *murdered*—in his words—*the son-of-a bitch*. According to Wilson, Murphy had it coming. Yet Wilson had an alibi for the entire day of Wednesday, September the twenty-first—he was with his older sister and her family in Richmond, California. He had been there for a few days and hadn't returned to his beach house until Friday night."

"Did anyone talk to the sister?" asks Broly.

"His sister also voluntarily came to the precinct and corroborated Wilson's explanation. He had taken the ferry across the bay and then taken an Uber to her house. She found him sprawled on the doorstep of their childhood home—drunk and broken."

"Been there before," Broly says.

"Apparently, Wilson was upset by the outcome of his divorce. The sister said he was a good, hardworking man and the stories of him cheating on and abusing his ex-wife were all lies. She said he hadn't left the house for the five days he had spent with her. He was depressed and spent most of it in bed. She worked from home and was there the entire time with him. After an extensive background check on Trent and the conclusion he was nowhere near the Pacific Heights apartment based on his alibi for the evening in question—"

"He was ruled out as the murderer," says Broly, frowning. "Next!"

"Next, we have Peter Truffen. Lucy Marten had also disclosed to us that Murphy had been having issues with the other name partner of Truffen & Murphy law firm. She had seen Truffen and Murphy arguing over the last few months and heard rumors about Truffen trying to buy Murphy out. Truffen was older and ready to retire, so he wanted his son to come on board as a name partner."

"Nepotism at its finest," says Broly, nodding his head in approval.

"According to Lucy, Murphy had been livid about the Truffens trying to push him out. He believed he had made the firm what it was today, and his reputation as a shark is what kept the firm thriving. However, Peter was also ruled out as a suspect because he was away on a business trip and out of the San Francisco area."

"Convenient, another one out of town! Who's next?" asks Broly.

"Louis Watts," she says.

"Okay, I never got why this guy was on the board. Explain, Harper."

"According to some of the uniforms on the scene that night, Watts was acting agitated and nervous. I witnessed it myself. He repeatedly said that he couldn't believe a murder happened in his building and, more importantly, on his watch. He seemed, according to the officers, preoccupied and overly distraught. Watts was rambling on and wasn't making any sense."

"Yup, and you had me run background on him. He was just a regular old man who worked his entire life in the security biz. In fact, the poor guy was having dinner at a pub during the time of the altercation between the Murphys," says Broly.

"Maybe that's why Watts was so distraught—he was out eating during his *watch*," she says with air quotes. "But I admit, he was more than cooperative with us and handed over all the security footage from the apartment complex—everything from the cameras for the entrances and exits, the parking garage, and the two penthouse floors."

"Yeah, lots of boring, random footage of the comings and goings of San Fran's elite," he says with a melodramatic sigh.

"Speaking of high society," she says.

Broly perks up in his chair. His favorite star on the board is up next, and all he is missing is the heart emojis in his eyes.

"Fourth up—Sienna Nash. Nash was fascinating from the onset. And the initial interview in her penthouse suite the night of the murder was weird and, frankly, a bit baffling. Although Nash was the prime witness shedding light on what happened hours before the altercation, she couldn't be ruled out as a suspect right away."

"Yeah, I never believed she belonged on the board as anything other than a witness," says Broly. "But to be on the safe side, I did some extensive homework on her—just for you, Harper," he says, flashing a boyish grin.

"Do you want to go through this part?" she asks him.

"Don't mind if I do," he says, jumping up like an eager schoolboy.

Sadie turns the chair to the forward position and takes a seat. She is tired from all the pacing around on the floor.

Broly clears his throat as if he is about to launch into a valedictorian's speech. "Sienna Nash was the new girl in San Fran, originally from the heavens of high society in New York. Her father, Ezra Nash, was a successful land developer and had made his first million before he turned thirty. Her mother, Alexia Montgomery, had also come from money, old New York money, as they had called it, and met Ezra in her early twenties when she was studying literature at NYU. Ezra and Alexia married soon after she graduated and began having children right away. They had five children altogether, all named after beautiful cities; Sienna was the oldest of the five."

Sadie's not surprised he started from the very beginning. Clearly, the blonde is his type, and he is already on a first-name basis with her.

Broly continues. "Sienna spent most of her childhood and teenage life in boarding schools abroad, as did her brothers and sisters. They weren't sent to the same ones, though, as her father's goal was to give each of his children diverse experiences. Sienna's parents were both killed in a car accident ten years ago. A distraught Sienna sold everything in her parents' estate, divided it among the five siblings, and left New York to start a new life in California. She wasn't close to her siblings as they all spent their formative years apart. When Sienna arrived in California, she lived in an apartment in San Diego for a year and then made her way to Los Angeles. Sienna had moved from city to city along the coast of California for a few years. She then settled in San Francisco three years ago. What made Sienna settle in San Francisco after living in every other major area on the California coastline? Perhaps she ran out of places to explore and was like a million other souls—lost and looking for a place to belong. Although Sienna didn't need to work (she had inherited more money than most people would know what to do with), she opened a small publishing company. Sienna named the company Montgomery & Nash as a tribute to her parents. Her mother loved literature, and although she dedicated her life to her husband and her children, her love for books never receded. The logo for the company was a simple yet elegant letter 'M' intertwined with the letter 'N'—the perfect ode to her parents."

"Dude—how do you even know all of this?" Sadie cuts in. "You make stalkers look bad."

"Harper, I made it my job to know," he says.

"Well, let me take over to speed up the narrative here," she says. "The night I took Nash's witness account, I felt she was holding something back. Nash seemed a little too distraught over Michael Murphy's death, and I had my suspicions that something was going on between them. When I invited Nash to the station a couple of days later to revisit her statement and give her the news that Anjali Murphy had awoken from her coma with no recollection of what happened on the night in question, I was gauging her reaction. Based on the forensics report, I knew Nash's DNA wasn't found on the most important piece of evidence at the scene—the baseball bat. They did find some long blonde hair strands belonging to Nash in the kitchen, but nothing else to indicate she had anything to do with the murder. The hair strands found in the kitchen matched the story Nash told the lieutenant and me that night. She had been in the apartment and found Michael. Nash was probably so distraught at finding Murphy in that state she probably ran her hands through her hair or maybe even pulled at it. That's likely when her blonde strands fell out on the floor."

"Yeah, I remember when she came to the precinct—she only wanted to talk to you," says Broly, looking mildly sullen at the memory.

"I was curious and anxious to hear what Nash had to say. Nash was dressed casually in an oversized cream turtleneck sweater, a pair of jeans, and flat Gucci running shoes. There was something different about her."

"Yeah, she looked hot!"

Sadie rolls her eyes at Broly. "It was something more—Nash seemed more subdued, and although her face was glowing, there was sadness in her eyes. During our forty-five-minute conversation, she dropped several bombshells. She had begun by asking questions about Michael's body—whether they had figured out what happened and when his body would be released. I felt these were odd questions coming from Murphy's neighbor. I told her we were still holding the body so the forensics team could finish their investigations. I also added that the body could *only* be released to next of kin, which wasn't possible as Anjali Murphy was still in the hospital. Nash looked like she was trying super hard to blink back her tears. Nash even stated she knew who the killer was. 'It's as clear and plain as the day itself,' she said. I played my quiet card."

Broly smiles, leaning against the far wall of the room. "That's your trump card, isn't it?"

Sadie nods. "Nash was on the brink of letting it all out. And I was right, Broly! Ten seconds later, tears were streaming down her pretty face. You would have been putty in her hands if you had seen how she wiped those tears away—in such a privileged, refined manner."

"Be still," Broly says as he taps, mockingly, on his heart.

"But the woman is a shark! A second later, she's reaching into her purse and slapping out a stack of photographs on the table."

"I remember, Harper!" he says. "I was watching on the other side of the mirror with my bag of popcorn—you should have seen your face!"

Sadie sighs heavily and continues. "I sifted through the photographs, but before I could say anything, Nash placed her phone in front of me and told me to look at the additional pictures on her phone. I did as she told me to and just scrolled. They appeared to be pictures of Nash's apartment. The same photographs laid across the table were displayed on the staircase steps and scattered on her bed. The last picture on the phone was of a bathroom mirror with 'whore' written in red lipstick. And her whispered words—*she knew*—are still stuck in my brain, Broly."

"Yup," says Broly. "Anjali Murphy knew. We ran the finger-prints on Sienna's photographs, and they matched the ones on the bat," he says like Sadie didn't know.

"Nash explained that she and Michael had been having an affair for over six months. It's like she was trying to get my sympathy. She said it had started suddenly—and it wasn't something she had expected when she first sought legal advice from Murphy regarding a trust that was coming to maturity for one of her younger siblings. Nash said she had felt electric chemistry between her and Michael from day one when she moved into the penthouse next door, but she had ignored it because she knew he was married. But after she had gotten the legal advice from him, he hadn't billed her. So she had decided to treat him to lunch to thank him, which turned into an unexpected affair. She said she wasn't proud of it—but she and Michael were in love. Nash claimed Michael was going to leave Anjali. She explained that the pictures on her phone were photographs of the *gift-slash-warning* that Anjali had left for her on the same day Anjali had killed Michael. Nash asserted that Anjali was livid about the affair and knew Michael was on the verge of leaving her—so she murdered him. If she couldn't keep him, then *no one was going to get him*," Sadie mimics in air quotes.

"Yeah, I remember you asking Sienna how she knew Michael would leave Anjali. And how did she know it wasn't just something Murphy said to keep her at bay," says Broly.

"And then she dropped her bombshell—*I'm pregnant with his baby.*"

"What every non-committal guy wants to hear." Broly shakes his head.

"Yup. And there it was. The bombshell Nash had been hiding—not the affair, not the notion that Anjali was the murderer, but the fact that she was carrying the love child created from their six-month affair."

"Did Murphy know?" asks Broly.

"Nash said she told him that evening. He had come over to her apartment right after he had gotten back from his business trip. She showed him the mess Anjali Murphy had left in her apartment. She said she was afraid of Anjali—for herself and *their* baby. That's when she told him she was eight weeks pregnant. She claimed he would tell Anjali that he was leaving her, told her not to worry, and promised they'd be together. Apparently, he was thrilled she was pregnant with his child."

"I bet she wanted to know when you would arrest Anjali for Michael Murphy's murder."

"I told her I couldn't comment on the pending investigation. We needed to get Anjali Murphy's statement and couldn't do that until she had regained her memory. Nash was convinced Anjali was faking the memory loss—apparently, she was a good actress. And with those last comments, she snatched her phone from the table and asked if she was free to go. I told her she could leave but that she should stay in town if we needed to talk to her further."

"And out walked suspect number four!" says Broly.

After the series of confessions from Sienna Nash, they had ruled her out as Michael Murphy's murderer. Sadie knows Sienna Nash is far from morally innocent, but she believes the likelihood of Nash swinging the bat is unlikely. Besides, the only other DNA found in the apartment, in the kitchen, and on the murder weapon belongs to Anjali Murphy. She remains the final suspect.

A rapid tap on the door breaks the silence between Sadie and Broly. Broly strolls over, swinging it open. On the other side of the threshold stands a junior detective.

"Yo, Williams!" says Broly.

He peers over Broly's shoulder and asks, "Is Harper in here with you?"

Broly steps aside.

"Hey Harper," says Detective Williams. "I'm working on a theft case from the Edwardian Hotel and thought you might recognize this woman caught on camera."

Sadie rises from the chair, stepping closer to the door. Williams hands her a stack of glossy eight-by-ten photographs. The images are grainy, but the woman walking through the Edwardian Hotel bears a mysterious likeness to Anjali Murphy.

THIRTY-FOUR

Friday, September 30th—Late Evening

Sadie spends the rest of her shift poring over footage from the Edwardian Hotel. After viewing the recordings of the woman thought to be Anjali Murphy, she acknowledges an uncanny resemblance but isn't convinced that they are one and the same person. This woman dresses and moves differently than the Anjali from the apartment's security videos shared by Louis Watts. Sadie reviews the case file from Detective Williams and establishes that the investigation involves an alleged theft at the hotel over a week ago. At that time, Michael Murphy was still alive, and Anjali Murphy wasn't in lockup.

She interviews the officer who wrote the initial police report. A woman named Margaret Oxley was accusing the Edwardian Hotel of stealing an expensive necklace she'd purchased from the Tiffany & Co. store. Oxley had been visiting San Francisco from out East. According to the report, Oxley left San Francisco on Tuesday morning, returned home, and realized items from her suitcase were missing—designer clothing and, even more critical, an expensive Tiffany's necklace. According to her statement, she immediately called the hotel, but they did nothing about it. When Oxley accused the cleaning staff, the hotel told her she must have been mistaken and ignored her request for further investigation.

When they refused to take her subsequent calls, she flew back to San Francisco on the following Tuesday and went straight to the SFPD, filing a formal complaint.

Oxley had meticulously documented the entire story on floral, pink-lined paper. Details including her daily itinerary, shopping times, and the receipts for all her purchases were included in the case file. Once an SFPD officer logged the formal complaint, he assured her they would complete a thorough investigation and let her know the outcome. When Detective Williams was put on the case, he interviewed the hotel manager and the cleaning staff. Much to his surprise, they were more than willing to cooperate.

Detective Williams had conducted the first round of investigation by asking for the security tapes from the hotel. Now, sitting in front of the hotel manager, Sadie is glad she came along for further questioning. Following her sixth sense, she feels a linkage between hers and Williams's cases, like they are part of the same puzzle. And it is up to her to figure out how they fit together.

"We need to know everything about this guest," Sadie says to Enrico, the Edwardian's hotel manager, pointing to a photograph of the woman who looks strikingly like Anjali Murphy.

"Of course, ma'am," he says.

"It's Detective Harper," says Sadie, hating being called a ma'am. She was much too young to be called that—even her mom hated it.

"Of course, Detective Harper, my apologies," he says, turning to a filing cabinet behind him. He rummages through the credenza for some time. His office is small and cramped—not what one would expect from a boutique hotel like the Edwardian. "This guest stayed with us for fourteen days, and she checked out on Tuesday, September the twentieth." He lays out an open file folder in front of her. On top of the pile of papers is a copy of the woman's passport.

Sadie studies the piece of paper. "Riah Arora," she says.

"Yes, yes, Riah—she was a nice guest, quiet—kept to herself," he says, trying to be helpful.

"She's from Italy. Do you know why she was here in San Francisco?" asks Sadie.

"No, not really—Ms. Arora was private. She didn't divulge a lot of personal information," he says. "Unlike some guests who reveal everything about their lives."

"Like Margaret Oxley?" she asks, peering from the file in her hands.

"Yes, that woman talked to everyone about everything—complaining most of the time—she never stopped."

Detective Williams chuckles at Enrico's comment. "You got that right," he mutters under his breath.

Sadie clears her throat, sifting through the contents of the folder. She gleans that Riah Arora checked into the hotel on Tuesday, September the sixth; the original booking was made online and paid through a credit card. Then another sheet showed Riah had extended her stay. The final receipt in the folder indicates she checked out early on the morning of Tuesday, September the twentieth—one day before the murder of Michael Murphy.

"Can I get copies of these?" Sadie asks Enrico.

"Of course, ma'am—I mean, Detective Harper—I will make copies right away," he says, taking the papers as he exits the room.

Sadie calls Broly, who is still back at the precinct, and asks him to run a background check on Riah Arora. She spells out the name and gives him her date of birth and nationality. Once she disconnects the phone call, Detective Williams is about to say something, but then Enrico returns, interrupting them. "Here you go, it's all here," he says, handing Sadie the records.

"Can I trouble you for an envelope?" Sadie asks.

"Of course!" He pulls open one of the drawers of his desk and retrieves a large white envelope with the hotel crest and address on it. "Is Ms. Arora a suspect in the theft Mrs. Oxley reported?" he asks, handing her the envelope.

"She's a person of interest in another crime," she tells him.

"Oh, okay, and you will update us if you find out what happened to Mrs. Oxley's necklace? She has been writing bad reviews on our website, and our hotel can't handle the negative press."

"We understand, sir," says Detective Williams. "We are looking into the matter and dealing directly with Mrs. Oxley."

"Okay, because I have cooperated and given everything the police have asked for," he says.

"Yes, you have, and we appreciate you cooperating with us. It makes our jobs easier," says Sadie, smiling at Enrico, adding, "We'll be in touch."

Sadie and Williams leave the hotel manager's office.

Enrico follows them into the lobby. "The room she was staying in is empty—if you'd like a look around," he says.

Sadie stops. "It is? Have any other guests stayed in the room since Riah Arora?"

"To think of it—no. No one has stayed in the room since Ms. Arora checked out. It has been cleaned, but no one else has been there since."

"Then yes, we'd like to take a quick look," says Sadie.

"Of course, let me get the master key and pass."

Enrico guides the detectives to the tenth floor of the Edwardian Hotel. The hotel is quiet for a Friday evening. It's a beautiful old hotel, antique almost, but she's sure it has seen better days. Now that the fall season has begun and children are in school, families are not traveling as much. She thinks of the trip Brett had suggested the other day. He had proposed they escape the city, not too far, but enough to be affectionate with each other in public— somewhere where no one knew them—somewhere they could be themselves. She smiles at the lingering thought of them tangled up in hotel bedsheets. The elevator dings, pulling Sadie out of her reverie.

Enrico leads them to the room. "Here it is—1013," he says.

"Great. Thank you for taking the time to accompany us here," says Sadie, putting on a pair of white nitrile gloves.

"Do you want me to come in with you guys, or should I wait here?" asks Enrico.

"Might be best to wait in the hallway—we shouldn't be too long," says Detective Williams.

As they enter the room, she switches into investigative mode. The suite is simple, yet elegant, and ready for the next guest. On one side of the room, a flat fifty-inch television screen rests on the larger dresser. She opens the top dresser drawer, half-hoping and half-praying Riah Arora left something behind.

Sadie asks Williams to check the rest of the drawers and underneath the bed. "I'll check the bathroom," she says.

The bathroom appears to have been renovated and upgraded with dark wood trimmings and marble counters. It isn't over-the-top extravagant like the bathroom in Anjali's penthouse apartment, but it is still lovely. The bathroom is spotless and well stocked, with miniature luxury shampoo and bath soaps. Sadie peers into the large mirror, studying the dark circles underneath her eyes. She will get some well-deserved sleep after this case is concluded.

Sadie closes her eyes for a moment to refocus. When she opens them, her vision settles on a fragmented slice of Scotch tape stuck on the outer corner of the wood panel, as if forgotten and abandoned. Peeling it off the wood, Sadie observes the partial print on it. She places the piece of tape in the small plastic evidence bag from her back pocket. *This could lead to something.*

On a gut feeling, she grazes the back of the mirror's wood frame. Her fingers touch something smooth; she tugs at it and pulls out a piece of magazine paper folded many times over. Sadie unfolds the sheet and then smooths it over, laying it flat on the counter. It's a photograph and a newspaper article about Anjali Murphy.

This clearly is *not* a coincidence. Sadie pulls out her phone and snaps pictures of the article about Anjali, followed by more photos of the mirror and the rest of the bathroom. It appears the paper has been folded back, displaying only the image of Anjali. She holds up the photo against the mirror. She imagines Riah Arora standing right where she's standing, gazing at this picture and then her reflection in the mirror. Did this woman come to San Francisco looking for Anjali?

During Sadie's initial investigation, she learned Anjali had been born and adopted in India. Her family moved around most of her life before settling in Seattle. Sadie also discovered that Anjali and Michael met in San Francisco, and after dating for less than a year, they were married. Sangeeta Patel's earlier visit this morning hadn't disclosed anything new.

But now, there's this whole new development named Riah Arora—this Italian national could pass for Anjali Murphy. Except for the different hairstyle, their faces and features were identical. Riah could be her doppelgänger or her twin. Yes, her twin. Could Anjali and Riah be twins? This possibility hits Sadie as if she'd just been t-boned by a truck on a Sunday-morning country drive.

Detective Williams pops his head into the bathroom. "Did you find anything?" he asks.

"Something, yes," Sadie says distractedly. She has the sudden urge to leave the bathroom, the hotel room, and the hotel altogether. The desire to race to the precinct and discover everything she can about this woman, Riah Arora, overwhelms her.

As Sadie and Williams enter the hallway, Enrico stares at them expectantly. At that moment, her cell phone rings. "Harper," she says, already knowing it's Broly calling.

"I put in a rush request to get Arora's immigration and customs information—"

"Thanks, partner! We found something else—we're coming back now—call MacDonald from Forensics. Ask him to meet us at the precinct," she says, a whirlwind of emotions brewing inside her head.

Sadie glances at her watch—it is close to midnight. Part of her wants to go home and take a quick shower, knowing she'll have to pull a double shift. Likely she'll be at the precinct for the rest of the night, but she knows she has to solve this—she feels so close. The shower will have to wait.

THIRTY-FIVE

Saturday, October 1st—Early Morning

Sadie arrives back at the precinct within the hour. Detective Williams is driving, as they chose to take his car. He's a junior detective, promoted to the division a few months ago. They call him *Small Times*. It's a nickname they coined for the grunt work and the cases that most of the newbie detectives get assigned to—crimes that are more important than what the regular uniform officers deal with, but not as critical as what the detectives in homicide or drugs and trafficking departments deal with. None of the seasoned detectives like working with the newbies. But Sadie is sympathetic to the struggles of being a new detective, so she has tried to take advantage of the opportunities to mentor them whenever she can.

Williams didn't talk too much on the way to the hotel; perhaps he was nervous around Sadie. But she can't get a moment of silence on the way back. Although Williams keeps talking, her head is reeling with all the new information she has gathered at the hotel. The day seemed to turn on a dime from the conversation with Sangeeta Patel this morning to the discovery of Riah Arora, who could potentially be Anjali's twin sister. They would have to find Riah and bring her in for an interview.

As Sadie enters the station, she spots Broly and Brett standing by the front desk. They're chatting with Maggie Somers, one of the new officers fresh out of the academy. Maggie had told the department she loved desk duty more than being in the field, and someone higher up decided that desk duty was a good idea for her. But no one complains—all the officers like Maggie at the front desk because she is efficient at managing the coming and goings in the precinct.

Sadie bypasses the group and heads toward the stairs. She catches Brett's attention and points upwards. Brett nods, says something to Broly, and the men make their way to the second floor. Sadie is in the conference room waiting for them.

"So, what did you find on your little field trip?" asks Broly.

Sadie slides the envelope across the table.

"What is this?" Broly asks, pulling out a chair and dumping the envelope's contents out.

"Copies of Riah Arora's info from the Edwardian. And guess what else I found," she says, holding out two clear plastic evidence bags.

"What am I looking at?" asks Brett.

"Williams and I searched the hotel room where Arora stayed. There was a scrap of Scotch tape stuck to the mirror in the bathroom, and I found this article folded and hidden behind it," she says, handing the bag to Brett. "There's a partial print on the piece of tape and more on the glossy paper this article is printed on. Luckily for us, the hotel staff were not thorough in their cleaning."

"Oh, that looks like the *San Francisco Magazine* article on Anjali Murphy. We have a copy of it in her case file," says Broly. "What are you thinking?"

"A whole lot," she says.

"Could Anjali Murphy have a secret second identity?" asks Broly.

"No, I am convinced from watching the video footage from the Edwardian and Anjali's apartment building that these are two different women. I think they're related—they look so much alike that they could be identical twins!"

"Twins?" asks Broly.

"They're the same age and both were born in India," she says, pointing to the copy of Riah's passport photo.

"Creepy—if they're twins, do you think this Riah Arora had anything to do with the assault on the Murphys?" asks Broly.

"That's what we need to determine. If Arora's DNA is anywhere in the Murphys' penthouse apartment, then it will muddy the ADA's case—she'll never get beyond reasonable doubt with a twin in the picture," she says.

"Damn," Broly mutters under his breath.

"Can we get a rush on those?" she asks Brett.

"Of course, I'll go to the lab myself and run it through forensics," says Brett, turning to leave.

~

Brett could have stayed and watched Sadie work at the precinct all day—he is fascinated and in awe of her. He didn't add to the theories that Sadie and Broly were throwing around, but he has his own hypothesis. He wants to validate his hunch with the forensic evidence. If this woman, Riah Arora, is connected to Michael Murphy's murder, he will figure it out. He will give the evidence and reassurance to Sadie that she can solve this case with meticulous accuracy. And then she'll be one step closer to her ultimate goal of making it into the FBI. Maybe they both will.

Brett opens the evidence bag and takes out the piece of tape with a pair of long medical tweezers. He places it on a glass plate, gliding another layer on top. After putting the slab under the microscope, he adjusts the magnifying glass and peers inside. He presses several keys on his computer, and the image of the partial fingerprint displays on his screen. Simultaneously, he punches in a lengthy string of code, launching a search program on the second monitor. Brett pulls out the magazine article with tweezers as the application explores the database. He unfolds it, delicately smoothing out the creases. Next, he brushes the paper with a translucent powder and shines a fluorescent lamp over it, illuminating several thumbprints. Using the scanner, he adds the prints to the computer. He then follows the same process with the other side of the paper. Brett imagines a woman holding the article in her hands. The program runs rapidly for a full minute and then displays the words: *match found*. The matching prints are the same ones captured from the Michael Murphy murder scene—on the baseball bat.

Brett's heartbeat quickens as he makes an imaginary checkmark in the air—step one complete. Now the hard part will begin. A few years back, he published an article about this exact scenario in an obscure medical journal. He was fascinated by the idea of twins and the fact that they share identical DNA. Most people don't realize there is a way to tell them apart—apart from using a mother's intuition.

His mind wanders to his own twin brother. What would have happened if he had lived? Nobody really knew this about Brett, as he and his brother, Trace, were raised in a small town. Brett always wanted to escape the shadow of his older twin. He purposely tried to steer his life towards everything that was the opposite of Trace. When his brother started playing sports, he leaned toward books. Other than sharing their good looks, their personalities were worlds apart. They couldn't have been more different.

He considers telling Sadie about his history, but it seems like a moot point at this stage of their relationship because his twin is long gone. What would she think anyway? He often wonders about the concept of good twin versus evil twin, and whether there is an element of verity to the theory.

He feels the warm glow of impatience as he thinks about the next steps. He'll have to take this higher up the chain, to the powers that be, to get approval to proceed. But if he does this, then he can prove his theory and get justice for Michael Murphy.

He felt it from the day he walked onto the crime scene. Something about the place of the homicide and about Anjali Murphy's injuries didn't make sense—it didn't add up. All the data and forensics that he and Ridgefield collected that night will be critical. He knows they didn't leave anything behind, collecting every shred of evidence they could from the apartment—bagged and tagged it all. He isn't the only person that feels this way. Sadie thinks so too.

Over the past week, they have often discussed the case, which is important to both of them—in fact, it has brought them together for the second time. After their one-night stand, he never thought it would amount to anything. She said she didn't want a serious relationship and was especially mindful of how it would look to others—a cop and a forensics data scientist fraternizing outside of this case. But if he is honest with himself, which he infallibly tries to be, he doesn't care. Sadie likes him back. And they are good together. They are *better* together.

Back to the case, Brett! He scolds himself. Next step, he needs to confirm that there indeed is a twin, and it isn't a case of Anjali Murphy having a secret second identity. He can use samples from the crime scene and from the hotel room Sadie had searched, and *fresh* DNA from the woman they have in custody—then he can prove who had indeed used the bat. The test would melt the DNA and look for dissimilarities in the genetic make-up. "We're winning, Sades," he says aloud, slam-dunking an imaginary basketball into a netless hoop hanging from the ceiling.

∿

Sadie pins the picture of Riah Arora to the evidence wall, prominently displaying it alongside Anjali Murphy. She twists and ties a red thread on the pins above the images, connecting the two women's photographs. Now that Sadie has added Riah Arora's photo to the board, it makes her question the entire investigation all over again. What if she has gotten it wrong? What is the connection between these two women, other than their appearances?

Broly glides into the room. "Hey partner, MacDonald was trying to get a hold of you, but you're not answering your cell."

Sadie glances at her phone and notices five missed calls from Brett—*shoot*!

"He wants us at the lab. He's got something to show us—pronto!"

THIRTY-SIX

Monday, October 3rd—Early Morning

Riah wakes with a startle and stares into the darkness around her. She closes her eyes, grasping at the images in her mind—jagged fragments of memory. In her sleep, she had been on the precipice of connecting all the pieces together. The reflections that had shimmered like newfound hope in her subconscious were now faint scars, eluding her in the daylight. She was nowhere closer to figuring out what had happened that night in the kitchen, landing Michael in the morgue and her in this cell. What was so sinister that her mind was blocking her from remembering? Had something so unspeakable happened that her mind had locked it out?

She punches the air in frustration, propelling herself into a sitting position. She squints at the grimy clock hanging on the wall—it's three a.m. It's as if she has emerged from one nightmare to wake up in another. How did she get here? Now that indeed is the million-dollar question.

She has only been here since Friday, but it feels like an eternity. Hana said she'd be in holding for forty-eight hours before her arraignment. Now, her forty-eight hours are up and she is due in court today, where she will enter a plea and then hopefully make bail. Hana instructed her that they'd be affirming a *Not Guilty* plea. There was no doubt in Hana's mind that she would get Riah exonerated from this charge—at least none that Hana shared with her.

Hana thought it would be best if Riah came clean about what she remembered and her feelings about not being Anjali Murphy. Riah had convinced Hana to keep the name—Riah Arora—between them for now, appealing to her nostalgia for their childhood friendship. She told Hana that until they figured out the cavernous gaps in her memory, it was best for everyone to believe she was Anjali. She can't even explain it to herself, but the overwhelming gut feeling that she was meant to be Anjali haunts her. It's like her unfiltered memory is within her reach—pumping through the vessels of her brain, lingering on the tip of her tongue—standing by to be remembered, marking time until it can be uttered.

Maybe it will be better to focus on what she does remember—like Hana had suggested to her when they first transferred her here. What *does* she recollect?

Riah recalls childhood moments in India. Crimson sunrises, smoggy cobalt skies, and languishing under canopies of shade. Afternoon teatime and bouncing on her mother's lap. Tepid sugar moon nights and dancing on their rooftop terrace. The taste of the cinnamon and ginger lingering on her tongue. The scent of saccharine *jalēbīs* hanging in the air.

She casts her mind back to the spacious villa in Tuscany and the picturesque hills of peace. It had been home. It had been where she left her heart and where her mother's spirit would always be alive. Not the mother she met the other day—the one that believes she's Anjali—but her birth mother. She conjures up every echo of love for her mother—the way her hair flowed in the wind, how she brushed it a hundred times every morning, right before she sprayed herself with perfume, her own concoction of rose water and lavender oil. In Riah's mind, she will *always* be that little girl admiring her mother in awe.

Then she feels a familiar ache in her chest—remnants of the anguish she had felt when she cremated her mother. She had promised her mother she would do something for her. What was that promise? And why did it evade her so?

The eerie stillness of the cell isn't helping her remember, either. Other than the low electrical hum and the din of the water pipes, the air around is stagnant. It's so unbearably still that it makes her restless. This is not how she had envisioned jail. Why had she ever imagined jail? Had she lived a life where she expected this—to be incarcerated like a caged, helpless animal?

In the distance, a door opens, and then clangs shut—its loneliness reverberating through the long corridor. Silence again. Then comes the echo of heels hitting the floor—click, clack, click, clack—like metal on metal. The footsteps get closer.

"How are they treating you in here?" asks Detective Harper.

What is she doing here? Riah thinks. She isn't sure what to say to the detective, and being behind bars stops her from saying anything.

"Riah Arora," says Detective Harper.

Shit—she knows! The hair on the back of Riah's neck rises, and her skin becomes prickly with goosebumps.

The detective crosses her arms, leaning against the wall of the old county jail, her body language indicating she has all the time in the world. Detective Harper's eyes are fixated on Riah, waiting for her to say something.

Riah rises from the cot and moves in closer. Grasping the metal bars with both hands, she glares back at the detective, stalling for time. Perhaps the detective will say more and reveal the extent of what she knows—which has to be more than Riah's name. And what's in a name, anyway? Even if Detective Harper knows her real name, it doesn't mean she is exonerated for her crimes. Should she ask for her lawyer? Immediately she decides against it—she would save the lawyer card as a last resort.

The detective's patience is superficial—she pushes herself from the wall and draws in nearer to Riah until their faces are dangerously close. Only the metallic barrier separates them, although a world of difference exists between them. What would the detective do if she were standing on this side of the rusty door? Would she be as calm and collected as she looked now? *Smug bitch!* Riah steps away from the door and walks along the cell's perimeter to the far end.

"I'm here to help," says Detective Harper.

"Is that a fact?" she says, crossing her arms and leaning against the cement wall. "Why?"

"You ask a lot of questions for someone in your position," says the detective.

"Because I really doubt that you're here to help me," says Riah with a hint of indifference.

"So, how do you know Riah Arora?" asks the detective, inching toward her.

"Somehow, I feel you already know the answer, detective." She senses that the detective enjoys this part of her job, drawing out the details in a prolonged and agonizing method. Riah can drag this out too. After all, where does she have to go?

"Well, I have my theory, but I'd like to hear it from you." She leans into the cell's bars and holds them with her hands.

The detective's eyes bore through her as if she is trying to pierce her soul. "I don't know," says Riah after a long moment of silence. "I don't remember meeting her."

"But you do know *of* her?" the detective asks, unbuttoning her blazer.

Riah lets the question hang in the atmosphere like a dark, threatening rain cloud.

Detective Harper reaches into the inside pocket, revealing a piece of paper. She unfolds it and presses it against the bars.

Riah's posture stiffens, every muscle becoming tense and rigid in a nano-second. A copy of the second page of her passport and the image from her long-ago, forgotten life stares back at her. The ghost of herself reflecting back through the rubble of her memory. And then the reason why she is in San Francisco, the Edwardian, Margaret, Brandon, meeting Anjali, Sienna, Michael—it all comes down on her like a torrential monsoon.

The detective's eyes stare back at her, two green beacons in the storm.

Riah turns her back on Detective Harper, finally finding her voice. "I'd like to speak to my lawyer, please."

"Argh!" says the detective, clearly disappointed and annoyed. "I'll get her for you. But Anjali, I wish you would have heard me out before lawyering up," she says, barely audible.

"I'm following my lawyer's advice," says Riah, her own voice sounding shaky to her ears.

"Alright, I'll call her and let her know you want her here—but it will take her a while to get here. Will you listen to me in the meantime?" There's a mixture of softness and hope in her voice.

Riah is reluctant with her response. "Okay, but I want to see you make the call first. You can do that for me, right?"

"I can," says Detective Harper, reaching into her back pocket to retrieve her phone. She pulls it out and passes it to Riah. "Do you know her phone number?"

"I do," says Riah as she taps the numbers on the detective's phone, holding her breath as the phone rings on the other end.

On the fifth or sixth ring, Hana answers it. "Hello," she says in a groggy voice.

"Hana," says Riah in a whisper as she turns her back to the detective.

"Riah?" says Hana in surprise.

"Hi Hana, this is Anjali."

"Anjali—where are you calling from?" she asks, sounding instantly alert.

"I'm calling from Detective Harper's phone. She wants to talk to me, but I asked for you to be present," she mutters.

"I'll be there in forty minutes," says Hana.

"Okay," says Riah, relieved Hana isn't mad that she has called so early in the morning.

"Anjali," says Hana before she ends the call, "don't say anything, and stall until I get there."

"Okay, I will," says Riah. She shuts off the phone and hands it back through the metal bars.

Detective Harper takes the phone, placing it in her back pocket. "Let's talk now," she says.

THIRTY-SEVEN

Monday, October 3rd—Early Morning

Hana places her phone on the bedside table and creeps out of bed. Is there enough time to take a quick shower? It's three-fifteen in the morning, and though Riah and Detective Harper want Hana at the county jail right away, there is no way of knowing how long it will take.

It's just like Detective Harper to pull something like this on the morning of Riah's arraignment. Some of Hana's colleagues say that Harper is on the fast track to becoming an FBI agent, so every case she closes is one more peg on her 'homicides solved' wall. Since Detective Harper works in homicide, one would think she'd be concerned about getting justice for the victim's family.

"Hon, is everything okay?" asks Laine, perching on one elbow and rubbing her eyes with the back of her other hand.

"Yeah, boo, all is okay. Anjali called and said the detective wants me to come to the county jail."

"Oh, what do you think they want? Isn't her appointment with the judge this morning?"

"Yes, her arraignment is today. But I'm hoping new information has come to light in the case—and the ADA wants to drop the charges. It's the only reason I can think of why Detective Harper is there."

"Oh, that's good, right?" Laine asks. She pulls her knees to her chest and wraps her arms around them.

"It depends on the information and whether it's positive for Anjali," says Hana, yanking on a pair of black trousers.

"Do you still believe Anjali's innocent?" asks Laine.

Hana can't ignore the hint of worry in her girlfriend's voice. "I do," she says, adjusting her turtleneck sweater in the mirror. Hana pulls her hair into a ponytail and turns around to face Laine. "There are too many holes in this case, so the opposing attorney won't be able to prove Anjali is guilty beyond a reasonable doubt."

"Good. I just want my friend back—she won't do good in jail. Can you bring her anything?"

Hana laughs. "Boo, she's in jail, not the hospital."

"Oh, so I guess that's a no," sulks Laine.

"I know you miss her, and you're worried about her wellbeing," says Hana. "I'm doing my best to get our friend out of this mess."

"I know you are, hon. I know you are."

Hana smiles and kisses Laine on the lips. "I will be swamped for the next few hours and won't have a chance to return home before the courthouse arraignment."

"Can I come to the arraignment?" asks Laine in an uncertain tone.

"You can come to the courthouse, of course, but I'm not sure if the judge will allow anyone else but the lawyers and Anjali in the courtroom—but you can try your luck. You may get a moment to chat with her. But I must warn you, Laine, that the press is all over this, so it might be mayhem there."

"I know—I've been following it all weekend online—I'd like to be there in person to see how she is holding up."

"Alright, I will text you the address," says Hana.

"Thanks for understanding, hon—and I'm so glad you consider her your friend too."

Hana smiles at Laine. Stuffing a couple of file folders in her briefcase and grabbing her raincoat, she kisses Laine goodbye. Hana leaves the three-story townhouse they're renting and jumps into her red MINI Cooper parked in front of their home. On her drive, her mind wanders to the case and Laine. She will have to tell Laine the truth—eventually.

The truth is that she doesn't consider Anjali Murphy a friend. She does, however, consider Riah Arora her friend. In fact, Riah is her oldest and most authentic friend. Sure, she initially became involved in this case because Laine wanted her to help Anjali. But she remains on this case because she knows the woman everyone believes to be Anjali Murphy is actually her old friend Riah.

Hana wants to come clean and disclose the name, Riah Arora. But Riah played the *Yaar card*, just like she did when they were teenagers—it got her every time. But truth be told, she'd do anything for Riah—even risk getting disbarred for withholding information—if it meant she could have these charges dropped. Besides, there's no proof that Anjali Murphy and Riah Arora are not the same person.

❧

Hana walks through the San Francisco County jail doors, greeting the guard sitting behind the glass window with a nod. She tells him she's there to see her client, Anjali Murphy. He asks to see her identification, which she tugs out from her purse. He scans it, slaps it on a clipboard, and pushes the items toward her to sign in. After Hana hands back the clipboard, he tells her Murphy is still being detained on the lower level. She nods and says she knows where it is.

Hana had seen Riah on Friday—right after she had been transferred. Detective Harper had said it was protocol, but Hana believes that by keeping Riah in this crummy detention center, the department is making a point of not being biased in this case. Although Michael was the nephew of the Chief of Police, he wasn't close to his uncle. Michael's father and his brother, Chandler Murphy, had a falling out many years ago and weren't on speaking terms. But being in family law, Michael Murphy wasn't unaware of the pull his uncle had, so he knew it was better to keep his friends close and his enemies closer. At least, this is what Hana has learned through her own research on Michael Murphy.

Hana presses the elevator button to the lower level, taking a deep breath as the elevator descends. The elevator's light flickers, reminding her of being in India, where the electricity was at risk of cutting out at any time—regardless of whether it is day or night. In a way, it also reminds her of how far she has come. This is Hana's first murder case. Her law firm had wanted to add a few more lawyers to this case, but Hana said *no*. This is her case, and the client had only wanted her. Sure, she could have used a few of the firm's junior lawyers to conduct the research and help her prep, but because the press is all over this case, she doesn't want to take any chances that something could be leaked to the press.

The elevator doors open to reveal an empty hallway. The dingy sign on the wall indicates the direction of the holding area. When Hana turns left, there's another guard behind a window in a small room. She shows the badge the upstairs guard gave her, and he buzzes her through the door. Hana finds the interview room where Riah and Detective Harper are waiting for her. She stands outside for a moment, looking in on the two women.

Riah is sitting on one side of the table, head lowered. Her hands are cuffed together and shackled to the table. Detective Harper sits across from Riah, her back to the door. Hana can't see her face, but judging from her posture, she is relaxed. It appears that Riah has been crying. Hana can't help but think of her old friend, Riah, when they were still their teenage selves. It's hard to believe that Riah is behind bars and at risk of being incarcerated while Hana is on this side of the window. If anyone had put bets on the two of them, they without doubt would have put their money on Riah. Back then, no one thought Hana would amount to much. They made fun of her because she dared to dream of bigger and better things than operating her parents' run-down textile stores.

Hana thinks about knocking but decides to barge in. "I wish you would have waited for me before you talked to my client," says Hana, walking into the interview room.

"We've been waiting for you, counselor," says Detective Harper, wearing a smug look on her face as if she knew something Hana didn't.

"Well, I'm here now. Although I would have appreciated a heads up that you would drag me out of bed at three in the morning. And today of all days—the day of Anjali's arraignment."

"I'm sorry about that," says Detective Harper.

Hana takes a seat next to Riah. "Well, what's this all about?" she asks, glaring at the detective.

"It's about Anjali's twin sister—Riah Arora."

Hana presses her lips tight, pulling on her best puzzled and confused face. "I did not know that Anjali had a twin sister," says Hana. She glances at Riah to gauge the extent of what the detective knew.

"Well, she does. And we'd like to talk to her, as a person of interest—"

"What does Riah Arora have to do with the charges against Anjali?"

"I understand you haven't had a chance to consult with your client yet, counselor, so let me bring you up to speed. As soon as I showed your client a picture of her sister—Riah Arora—her memory returned. Just like that!" says Detective Harper, snapping her fingers in unison to her words.

A knot in Hana's stomach tightens as her gaze ping-pongs

between Riah and Detective Harper. The only thought going through her head is—*Oh god, Riah, what have you done!*

"Anjali remembers meeting her long-lost twin sister, and even had her over for dinner. However, she is adamant that Riah Arora left San Francisco on Tuesday, September the twentieth. I'm surprised you didn't know, Counsellor—you and your girlfriend, Laine, had dinner at Anjali's apartment that evening."

"And?" she spits out. Where is the detective going with this? "I don't see how this is relevant—"

"Well, it almost ruined the ADA's case against your client—you know, with the whole beyond-a-reasonable-doubt thing, and her having a twin that could have been there on the night of the altercation. But again, she's convinced that Riah Arora left the country long before Michael came home on Wednesday, September the twenty-first. The same night she confronted him about his cheating."

Hana needs to stop this right now. "I need to consult with my client," she says, rising from her seat. "And in a secure private room."

"Sure, I understand," says Detective Harper. "I suggested the same thing when she confessed to beating her husband with his baseball bat—right before you arrived."

Hana closes her eyes, bracing her head from reeling with all these new revelations. And Riah is going to continue this charade. How long can she let her friend do this? "Thank you, Detective Harper. I appreciate you coming here and helping jog my client's memory."

"You're welcome, counselor. I'm glad I could help," says Detective Harper, wearing her satisfaction in her smile.

THIRTY-EIGHT

Monday, October 3rd—Morning

Riah throws her head in her hands, weeping profusely. Detective Harper has moved them to a secure room without cameras or other recording devices. "Oh, Hana, I'm so, so, so sorry," she says through raspy tears. "I never meant to get you mixed up in this mess."

"*Yaar*, what the fuck was that? You need to explain—and fast!" Hana says, her calm demeanor gone.

Riah hangs her head low. "I killed him. I did it," she says in a whisper.

"Who did you kill? Michael?"

"Yes, my memory came back. I beat him with the baseball bat," she says, louder.

"Why, Riah? Why would you do that?"

"Because I've done it before. I've killed someone."

"What? You mean your *chacha-ji*? *Yaar*, that was a million years ago. What does that have to do with now? With Michael? With your twin sister?"

"Can I start from a million years ago?" Riah asks.

Hana pulls out a chair, and flops down heavily. "Talk," says her friend.

Riah begins from the moment that Detective Harper showed her the passport picture. And then shares how the detective proceeded to show more photos of Riah Arora. The images, explained the detective, were of Riah entering and leaving the Edwardian Hotel. In one snapshot, Riah was wearing a black baseball cap and dark sunglasses, and her long wavy hair was pulled back in a ponytail. She looked like any other tourist, but as she stared at the picture of that lost stranger, the fog seemed to lift, reminding her once again *why* she was in San Francisco—she remembered it *all*. Her memories came back to her like a tsunami after an earthquake. They washed over her and drenched her with the truth.

Riah tells Hana every detail. From arriving at the Edwardian to spying on Anjali at the café. From Anjali following her to the train station to meeting Anjali at the penthouse. From Riah and Brandon crashing the Word Slam to Anjali confronting them. From Anjali having her over for dinner to the two of them deciding to switch places so Anjali could travel on Riah's passport. From discovering that Michael was cheating on Anjali to trashing Sienna's apartment.

She tells Hana about the purple and blue bruises on Anjali's arms—some old, some new. She tells her about Anjali, admitting Michael didn't know that she had found her birth mother and twin sister—the same unspoken fear she had seen on their mother's face once before.

And then, she tells Hana about the deadly fight with Michael. She had blacked out, but somehow, she was standing over his dead body when she came to. It wasn't the first time she had one of these blackout episodes and woke up to a dead man at her feet.

Silence hangs in the air, thick and stagnant.

Hana swallows and then finally speaks. "*Yaar*, you're on the wrong side of time. You can't possibly think all your demons will go away if you plead guilty to a crime you did not commit."

"That's the thing, Hana—I did do it."

"Okay, so when do you want to tell everyone that you are really Riah Arora?"

"Never—"

"*Yaar*!"

"Don't you see, Hana? They think I'm Anjali anyway—this way at least one of us can be free."

"Are you sure about this?" Hana asks, skeptically.

"Yes, it's the right thing to do. Besides, I'm tired of running, Hana—I've been running from this half of my life. Maybe I can finally put all these ghosts to rest."

"Okay, then. I'll let the prosecuting attorney know that you'll be pleading guilty," Hana says, the echo of disappointment in her voice palpable.

⚬⚬

Riah is escorted into the courtroom and seated in the defendant's chair. Her legs are trembling as though she might pass out at any moment. *Be strong*, she tells herself, *you are doing the right thing*. So this is what the inside of a courtroom looks like. She can't say she has ever had the misfortune of seeing one before. It is smaller than she had expected and painted in a pale yellow. She read once that yellow has a calming effect; if it is true, it certainly isn't working in this instance.

Riah peers around the courtroom. Except for herself and Hana, the left side of the room is empty. On the other side sits the prosecuting attorney, the young Nigerian lawyer whom Riah and Hana had met on Friday and earlier this morning. Detective Harper, Detective Broly, and Lieutenant Washington sit behind the district attorney. Behind them are a few other people Riah doesn't know—perhaps they are spectators who came to watch the *show*. Although the courtroom holds a handful of people, it feels like everyone except Hana is against her. Only God knows if Hana will continue to stand by her after this is over. Hana had been disappointed when she learned that she'd be up against this prosecutor, Faye Adebayo.

However, Hana doesn't have to worry about going to trial any-more—after today, it will all be over.

A door to the left of the judge's oak bench opens.

"All rise, and please welcome the honorable Judge Winters pre-siding over today's arraignment," says the court officer.

Everyone rises. The judge walks in and takes a seat behind the bench. Judge Winters is a bald, elderly gentleman. He's precisely what Riah has pictured a judge to look like. At least something has turned out to be what Riah expected. She's relieved; although her arraignment is just beginning, it will be over soon.

"Alright, you may all be seated. I'm calling this court to order on Monday, October the third," says Judge Winters. He nods at Riah, asking her to stand and identify herself.

"Anjali Murphy," says Riah.

"Alright, Mr. Clerk, can you please arraign Mrs. Murphy," he says gruffly.

A male clerk with glasses and a razor-cut hairstyle looms over his desk and speaks. "Anjali Murphy is charged that she, on the twenty-first day of September in the city of San Francisco, did assault her husband, Michael Murphy, causing death in the sec-ond degree contrary to section 267B of the criminal code," he says. "Anjali Murphy, how do you plead to this charge?"

"Guilty," says Riah. She hangs her head low and tries not to fid-get with her hands.

There is a gasp from viewers in the courtroom. The room spins as if she'd spontaneously jumped on a merry-go-round. Hana says something to her, but she can't hear anything over the ringing in her ears. Riah slumps in her chair to catch her breath.

Next to her, Hana mutters under her breath. "*Yaar*, get up—you're not done yet."

Whispers from the other side of the courtroom grow to a steady hum. Judge Winters slams his gavel against the bench several times, and says, "Order in the court! Order in the court. Anjali Murphy, please repeat your plea again, young lady."

She stands up. "Guilty, your honor," says Riah, with more conviction this time.

"Mr. Clerk, please note that the defendant has entered a plea of guilty to the crime she is charged with today."

"Yes, sir," responds the clerk.

The judge slams the gavel against the desk again. "I am ordering the accused be held in custody in the county jail until the sentencing hearing two weeks from today. This court is adjourned for today." He slams his gavel again, signaling the end of the court hearing. He stands and walks out of the courtroom.

Riah rises as two security guards come toward her to take her back to her cell.

Hana gives her a tight hug. "*Yaar*, you're gonna be okay," Hana whispers, reminding her of the hug she had given her on that last night in Delhi, half a lifetime ago. She knows now that she will be okay.

THIRTY-NINE

Monday, October 17th—Afternoon

Sadie removes the photos and scraps of stickies from the evidence wall. The chatter from the newsfeed plays from her phone, bouncing off the empty walls of the interview room. She wouldn't have believed it if someone had told her she'd be closing this case and getting a guilty conviction merely weeks after the murder. Over the past week, she has tried not to let the fact that Anjali willingly confessed to beating Michael in a fit of rage dampen her *win*. One more case solved, one step closer, she reminds herself. She turns her head at the mention of Anjali's name.

> *"Anjali Murphy is being sentenced today after pleading guilty to the manslaughter of her spouse, Michael Murphy, two weeks ago. We are outside the courthouse, just minutes away from hearing Judge Winters' ruling in this case. Based on our sources, the judge has been reviewing all the aggravating and mitigating factors in determination—"*

She turns her phone off. Yes, the aggravating and mitigating factors in this case would be crucial in the judge's sentencing. Aggravating factors like Anjali instigating the chain of events by breaking into Sienna Nash's apartment and vandalizing her bathroom mirror—even if it was with lipstick and likely well deserved—was reckless behavior on Anjali's part. And then the mitigating factors like Anjali taking accountability and accepting the responsibility for all her actions when her memory of that day returned. And with no prior criminal history, and even a statement from the Chief of Police indicating that this was an unfortunate event with grave consequences, but that he was standing by in support of Anjali, would work in her favor during the judge's final decision on sentencing.

Sadie places the final photo in the evidence box—the last one they had pinned to the wall, a picture of Riah Arora. Anjali Murphy's twin sister. Brett had confirmed it with the specialized DNA test he had received approval for and conducted. He had distinguished the strand of each twin's DNA collected from the crime scene and from the twin they had in custody, concluding that they were indeed two different women. She lingers on Riah's photo. Every time she looked at this woman's picture, something still festered in her mind. *What if she had been there that afternoon?*

Even the immigration information Broly obtained corroborated what Anjali had remembered. Riah Arora left on Tuesday morning. She had boarded a flight headed to Florence, Italy, with a short layover in Paris, France. Riah never met Michael. If Michael had met his wife's identical twin sister, Sadie wonders if he would have noticed a difference. *Would Sangeeta have seen the difference?*

"Hey partner, let's go celebrate," says Broly, letting the door slam against the wall. "Winters gave Murphy the minimum sentence—barely a slap on the hand!"

"I bet Mama Bear is happy," she says, placing the lid on the evidence box.

"I bet she is, Harper!"

"She puts on quite a show for the cameras," she says, rolling her eyes at the memory of seeing Sangeeta on the news last week advocating for her daughter.

"Indeed, she does! Reminds me of Monique," he says with a half-suppressed chuckle.

"How *is* Monique these days?"

"Wouldn't know, Harper—she left me for good. Took off to Brazil with some guy named Brando or *something*."

"Oh?" She raises an eyebrow of hope for him yet.

"Come on, I'll tell you the entire sordid tale—I know you like my Monique stories!"

Sadie chuckles. "Sure, I'll catch up with you guys. I just need a few minutes to put this box in the archives."

"Okay, don't be too long—we'll be at Peet's!" he says, leaving the door open.

She's about to follow him but pauses at the faint buzz from her phone. Glancing down, she sees an emoji smiley face text from Brett. She instantly sends him one back.

Brett: *Now we can get away for that vacation!*

Sadie: *I agree, somewhere far!*

Brett: *Where?*

Sadie: *Paris . . .*

Brett sends another smiling emoji—of a girl with a French beret and a paintbrush.

Sadie smiles. *He really does get me.* She flicks off the lights and closes the door.

~

Sangeeta signs the visitor's log and takes the pass from the guard, hanging it around her neck. She glances at her watch, relieved she made it before visiting hours were over today. Riah's confession saved Sangeeta from admitting *any* involvement in the crime. And *her* Anjali was free! But it was all her prayers to Lord Shiva that ensured Riah hadn't gotten a lengthy sentence—*ten months!* The girl had probably survived worse.

Sangeeta enters the visiting area. Riah is awaiting a transfer to another facility to serve her sentence, so Sangeeta is only allowed to see her through the glass window and talk to her on the phone. The visitor side is empty, and Riah is waiting on the other side of the glass.

Sangeeta takes a seat in front of Riah and pauses for a solid look at the girl. Sitting in front of Riah, her heart aches for Anjali. Was it fate that she ended up with Anjali? Would things have been different if she had adopted Riah instead? In a way, now, she will adopt this girl—but she should tell her the truth first.

Riah selects the receiver on her side of the window in a calm, slow-motion gesture.

"Hello, dear," she says into the phone.

"How long did you know?" asks Riah.

"Know what, my dear?" she asks, swallowing the sour bile rising in her throat.

"That I wasn't your precious *Anjali*," Riah says.

She glances around, ensuring no one is listening. "I've always known, my dear."

"You mean when we first met in the hospital?"

"No, I've known from the beginning—ever since you first landed in San Francisco."

"How did you know?" asks Riah.

"I met your mother last year at the villa—I led you here, my dear," she says. "Think about it. Who was the one who gave you the lead to look for your long-lost sister in the United States—in San Francisco?"

"Brandon," says Riah.

"Yes, Brandon."

"And this was your plan all along? To bring me here to take the fall for your daughter?"

"No, that wasn't the plan. You weren't supposed to be there, my dear. If only you had stuck to the plan, left when you were supposed to. Things wouldn't have gotten to this state. If your boyfriend had done what he was supposed to do, we wouldn't be in this mess."

"He's not my boyfriend," says Riah.

"I know he's not. Otherwise, he wouldn't have left you," she says, remorsefully shaking her head.

"Is she okay, at least?" Riah asks, her wary eyes appearing softer.

"Yes—yes, my baby is okay. She's more than okay—she's free." Tears pinprick her eyes.

"Well, I'm glad it worked out," says Riah, leaning forward.

"I owe you, my dear—so much more than I can express right now."

"Yes, you do—*Mom*. I'll see you when I've done the time." Riah flashes a devious smile as she hangs up the telephone receiver and rises from her seat. The guard opens the door, and Riah disappears.

FORTY

One Year Later...

Riah stretches her legs and basks in the serenity of the evening sun. The sight of the sparkling, cobalt-colored water sends shivers along her skin. But she can't think of any other place that she'd rather be—watching the viridescent landscape roll toward the white-capped mountains as the daylight kisses the azure sky goodbye. This is where the belt of possibility stretches for miles and miles long.

She reminds herself not to over-romanticize this duty to her mother. She's at her villa to close this chapter of her life, and then tomorrow she'll return to San Francisco, to her life as Anjali Murphy. But she'd be a liar if she didn't admit that she had dreamt of this moment every night during the past ten months of her incarceration.

Before arriving in Italy, she wasn't sure what to expect. She didn't know whether Anjali would be at the villa *or* if she even made it here at all. Sangeeta had said she never heard from Anjali after their last phone call, shortly after Riah had been sentenced. Sangeeta thought it was best this way—*everyone gets their happy ending, my dear,* she had said during one of their weekly prison visits. Perhaps Sangeeta was right. In a way, everyone she met during the nightmare of a year ago found a happy ending.

Laine has continued to manage *The Artists' Café* and renovated the upper level so that Hana could open her now-flourishing criminal defense practice. And they plan to go to Las Vegas for New Year's Eve and get *officially* hitched.

Sangeeta secretly oversees the operations at *The Artists' Café*. Riah never told anyone that she knew the café was owned by Sangeeta. It was probably a security measure that Sangeeta and Anjali had decided on three years ago. Also, Sangeeta has started dating Louis, the security guard from Anjali's apartment. Sangeeta says she likes his mellow, happy-go-lucky nature—but maybe she just enjoys bossing him around. And according to Sangeeta, Vibha and Rashmi are beyond old-aged, jealous mean-girl clichés.

Although Brandon didn't stick around to see what would happen to Riah, he did send her a postcard from Brazil. It said something cheesy like, *'Wish you were here! B.'* She burnt the glossy card, flushing his ashes down the toilet.

Then, there's the sinuous S—*Sienna*. Riah sometimes wonders where she'd be if she hadn't gotten side-tracked with exacting revenge on Sienna. But she tries to be the bigger person and forces her mind not to go there. Even Sienna got her happy ending—she moved back to New York and gave birth to a baby boy, naming him Michael Nash Murphy.

Finally, the detectives—Harper and Broly. She doesn't really know what happened with them. They probably moved on to the next big case. She hopes never to see either of them again.

And Riah? The real Riah, whatever name she's going by today, still needs to figure out what she should do for the rest of her life. Laine thinks that Riah should write about her stint in prison in the form of a suspense thriller. It's an idea, but what would she name it? *The Long Con* sounds like an appropriate title. If she did write that book, the one thing she'd have to figure out is what happened to the bag of jewels and money, and the keys to the rental car. The police never did find the bag Riah had thrown in the island cupboard right before Michael entered the kitchen. She constantly wonders what happened to it.

Now, it's time. It's time to sprinkle her mother's ashes, so that she, too, can take to the brazen sky and soar into twilight dreams. Reaching into the urn, Riah grabs a fistful of her mother's ashes and sets them free into the atmosphere. She does this repeatedly until she hits granite rock bottom.

Her fingers graze something strange. She tugs and pulls a clear plastic bag out of the urn. Her heart begins to race uncontrollably. She reaches into the bag and extracts a key and a note written on flowered gossamer-like stationery—the same one her mother had used for her last letters to her twin daughters.

> *"Thank you,*
> *For what you did for me, dear sister.*
> *A.*
>
> *P.S. I took a little bit of mum with me."*

Riah examines the key. She turns it over in her hands and realizes it's for an Italian bank's safety deposit box. She will have to take a short detour before her flight tomorrow.

She can't help but whisper her own thank you to the Universe . . .

"Until we meet again, my dear sister."

ACKNOWLEDGMENTS

The Universe has blessed me with so much . . . My sincerest gratitude to these beautiful souls . . .

Thank you, Vanessa Carnevale, for your 2018 Tuscany Writing Retreat and your comments on the first ten pages—the nudge I needed to finally start this novel. And thank you, Gracia, Heather, Jessica, Glenda, and Amanda, for the early-morning writing meditations, the afternoon Aperol Spritz chats, and the late-night laughs. I will always cherish my memories from our retreat.

Thank you, Ava Palmer, Bukky Aina, and Michelle Griffith, for spending your precious time reading the early, unfinished draft of this novel and (still) cheering me on to the finish line.

Thank you to my editors—Mary Chapman, for copyediting the first complete draft of this novel and providing me with essential feedback and suggestions, and Andy Ross, for giving me a critical developmental critique, and guiding me to fix the various plot holes and shape this novel into what it is today. It was an honor to work with both of you.

Thank you to my ever-growing circle of fellow writers—Lucas Horn, J. Knightstone, Bill Harman, JF Garrad, Peter Man, and Purabi Das—your input, advice, and constant encouragement have meant the world to me.

Thank you to my publishing partners—Brooke Warner, Samantha Strom, Lauren Wise, and the entire team at SparkPress who had a part in bringing this book into existence—your advice, direction, and enthusiasm throughout the publishing process have been an invaluable experience.

Thank you to my dearest BFFs, Deepa (aka Shannon) Shah and Rashpal (aka Raj) Belha, for providing me with encouragement and moral support throughout the past thirty-odd years of our friendship. No matter what I write, my favorite works of fiction will be the secret-admirer letters I wrote on your behalf back in Uni.

My most heartfelt thanks to Christine Ries for the countless Saturday mornings (and afternoons) you gave up for me over the last two years of the pandemic. Our read-out-loud Zoom sessions and hearing my characters come alive made the process of editing this novel a less lonely venture. Your voice of reason always got me through my "mini" author meltdowns, and for that, I will be forever indebted to you. You are now promoted to BFF status :)

Finally, to *mērā parivāra* (my family):

Mandeep, my soul-partner—thank you for supporting my childhood dream and sometimes even chasing it down with me. I can always count on you to save backup copies of my work, as only you know my high propensity to "accidentally" hit <delete>.

Sahrina & Sajjan—thank you for being yourselves and my most beautiful works-in-progress.

Shaun, my darling nephew—thank you for constantly making me laugh. I very much believe that my seven-year-old self is dwelling somewhere inside of you, and I hope you never ever lose your gift of storytelling.

To my parents, I know leaving your homeland of India and coming to Canada in the '70s to forge a new life for your children was not easy—thank you for teaching me the value of hard work and resilience. And to my grandmothers (my *Dādī* & my *Nānī*)—I feel your spirits with me every day—thank you for being my guardian angels and never leaving my side.

ABOUT THE AUTHOR

Photo Credit: M.S. Aujla

Jass Aujla was born in Punjab, India and raised in Winnipeg and Toronto, Canada. Her poetry and microfiction have appeared in small press publications worldwide. *Next of Twin* is her debut novel.

Visit her at jassaujla.com

SELECTED TITLES FROM SPARKPRESS

SparkPress is an independent boutique publisher delivering high-quality, entertaining, and engaging content that enhances readers' lives, with a special focus on female-driven work.
www.gosparkpress.com

Murmuration: A Novel, Sid Balman Jr, $16.95, 978-1-68463-091-2. One of the first Muslim women to graduate from West Point, a Jewish US Army captain, and a Somali migrant nicknamed Charlie Christmas risk everything for a refugee boy on a three-decade odyssey that takes them from Africa and Europe to Texas and Minnesota—and redefines what it means to be American in the twenty-first century.

Cold Snap: A Novel, Codi Schneider, $16.95, 978-1-68463-101-8. When a murder shocks her peaceful mountain town, Bijou, a plucky house cat with a Viking spirit, must dive paws-first into solving the mystery before another life is taken—maybe even her own.

Indelible: A Sean McPherson Novel, Book 1, Lauric Buchanan, $16.95, 978-1-68463-071-4. Murder at a writing retreat in the Pacific Northwest, but this one isn't imaginary. Authors only kill with words. Or do they?

Sarah's War, Eugenia Lovett West. $16.95, 978-1-943006-92-2. Sarah, a parson's young daughter and dedicated patriot, is sent to live with a rich Loyalist aunt in Philadelphia, where she is plunged into a world of intrigue and spies, her beauty attracts men, and she learns that love comes in many shapes and sizes.

A Dangerous Woman from Nowhere: A Novel, Kris Radish. $16.95, 978-1-943006-26-7. When her husband is kidnapped by ruthless gold miners, frontier woman Briar Logan is forced to accept the help of an emotionally damaged young man and a famous female horse trainer. On her quest to save her husband, she discovers that adventures of the heart are almost as dangerous as tracking down lawless killers.

Firewall: A Novel, Eugenia Lovett West. $16.95, 978-1-68463-010-3. When Emma Streat's rich, socialite godmother is threatened with blackmail, Emma becomes immersed in the dark world of cybercrime—and mounting dangers take her to exclusive places in Europe and contacts with the elite in financial and art collecting circles. Through passion and heartbreak, Emma must fight to save herself and bring a vicious criminal to justice.